PRAISE FOR *THE TURNING*

"*The Turning* is the most refreshing and inspired page turner in recent years. It captures your heart, mind, and spirit with a real connection to His Grace. *The Turning* is highly commended. Davis Bunn has scaled new heights and brought us with him."

—**Ted Baehr, president of** *Movieguide*

"*The Turning* is a triumph. This novel contains a remarkable mix of high drama, great characters, and a truly inspired examination of what it means to discern the voice of God. This above all else makes the book stand out. Readers will be captivated by Bunn's story, and challenged by this invitation to seek a deeper walk with our Lord. *The Turning* invites us to heed God's call, not with an absence of fear, but rather the mastery of it."

—**Roy Crowne, director emeritus,
Youth for Christ, and CEO, The Hope Project**

"Does God still speak to his followers today? That's the question and the power of this high-stakes prophetic novel ripped straight from tomorrow's headlines. *The Turning* is a mesmerizing look at people who believe they heard the voice of God. The unforgettable cast of characters and the conflicting themes of divine hope against man's darker motives made for one amazing read."

—**Allen Arnold, director of content, Ransom Heart Ministries**

THE TURNING

A NOVEL BY

DAVIS BUNN

MOODY PUBLISHERS
CHICAGO

© 2014 by
DAVIS BUNN

This is a work of fiction. Names, characters, places, and incidents either are the product of the author's imagination or are used fictitiously, and any resemblance to actual persons, living or dead, businesses, companies, events, or locales is entirely coincidental.

Edited by Carol Johnson
Interior and cover design: Erik M. Peterson
Cover photo of street scene copyright © 2012 by Macie J. Noskowski / iStock. All rights reserved.
Author photo: Angel Gray Photography
Page composition: Design Corps

Library of Congress Cataloging-in-Publication Data

Bunn, T. Davis
 The turning / Davis Bunn.
  pages cm
  Summary: "The message was unexpected but instantly recognizable. A voice resonated from a distance and somehow from within. Against all earthly logic, it carried a divine command. And five very different people knew they were summoned to obey. Their actions were demanding, but not particularly grand. Only later would they see a pattern emerge—one that links their tasks together and comes to challenge the cultural direction of the nation. They realize that one small personal response unveiled a new realm of moral responsibility. And this affirmation of everyday hope captures the attention of millions. But power and money are at stake. Malicious elements soon align themselves to counter the trend. To succeed they must also undermine its source. Can we really believe that God speaks to people today? Surely this must be dismissed as superstition or delusion. These well-intentioned but misguided individuals should not be allowed to cast our society back into the Dark Ages. The public debate and media frenzy place an unprecedented spotlight on knowing and doing God's will. The five encounter threats, but try to remain steadfast in their faith. Had God indeed imparted wisdom on selected individuals? Is this sweep of events part of his divine purpose? The movement may herald a profound renewal—one that some are calling The Turning."—Provided by publisher.
  ISBN 978-0-8024-1168-6 (pbk.)
  I. Title.
  PS3552.U4718T87 2014
  813'.54—dc23

                                                                        2013045562

We hope you enjoy this book from River North Fiction by Moody Publishers. Our goal is to provide high-quality, thought provoking books and products that connect truth to your real needs and challenges. For more information on other books and products written and produced from a biblical perspective, go to www.moodypublishers.com or write to:

River North Fiction
Imprint of Moody Publishers
820 N. LaSalle Boulevard
Chicago, IL 60610

1 3 5 7 9 10 8 6 4 2

Printed in the United States of America

This book is dedicated to
Roy and Florence Crowne
who have made the gift of hope
their life's work

DAY
ONE

1

"Who will go for us . . . ?"

NEW YORK CITY

Trent Cooper watched the empty Sunday streets unfold beyond his window. He had never been in the backseat of a limo before. Twice he had ridden up front, playing aide to his boss, Darren, whom he loathed along with everyone else forced to work for the man. Today, however, was different. Today Darren was the one forced to play ride-along. Trent had often studied passing limos, hungering to be one of those people with the power and the expense accounts. The feeling of having arrived, even for a moment, was so exquisite not even Darren's fury could touch him.

His boss must have noticed Trent's satisfied smirk, for he was seething as he said, "Enjoy it while you can, worm. Ninety minutes from now, you'll be just another greasy stain on the sidewalks of Times Square."

"Whatever you say, boss." Trent was usually the guy who just went along. It was protective coloring he had picked up as a kid. Vanish in plain sight, and escape multiple poundings from guys who were bigger and stronger and fascinated by the sight of other people's blood.

"You mocking me? Really?" Darren obviously wanted to pace, which of course was impossible, even in a stretch limo. So he fidgeted. His well-padded frame highlighted every squirm. "You think I'm playing games here, Cooper?"

"No, sir. I know you aren't." Trent glanced over. The guy was a toad in a suit.

"Your future is in my hands. You better be thinking of how you're going to write a resume when your previous employer is just *waiting* to call you a class-A clown."

Trent turned back to the window. There really wasn't anything on that side to hold his attention. To tell the truth, he was a little disappointed in the ride. The stretch Cadillac bounced hard over the smallest dips. The ceiling was low and dark, the rear seat slightly concave. An acre of dark carpet separated them from the backward-facing seats. The divider was in place, making the rear compartment feel like a coffin for two.

"This is your last chance," Darren said. "I want to know what you sent to headquarters. And I want to know now."

The scene beyond the limo's side window was much more interesting. Back home when he was a kid, church would have just been getting out. Trent had always skipped out of those tall doors like he was being released from a weekly prison. People smiled down at him, the poor kid whose family hadn't been able to afford the operations he needed, so the church had taken up collections. They talked in loud voices, like having a cleft palate turned him deaf. His mother kept a vise grip on his hand, smiled back to them and talked with this brittle happiness like they didn't have a care in the world, what with the church family taking such good care of them. Trent had hated them all.

"I've had it with your insubordination, Cooper," his boss said. "I've asked you a question and I *demand* an *answer*."

Trent forced his mind back to the present. He rarely indulged in memory games. As far as he was concerned, the best thing about his past was how it fueled his drive and determination, and granted him the fury required to make it. Even here. In Manhattan. The Capital City of Broken Dreams.

The sunlit streets were just coming alive. Elegant alcoves held sidewalk cafés where laughing people burned through money. Couples dressed in clothes that cost more than his car walked arm in arm toward their next good time. Trent traced a line around the sunlight on his window and mouthed a silent word. *Soon.*

The limo pulled around the corner and parked before the headquarters' side entrance. The door had no sign. Anyone who needed to ask what lay beyond the brass portal did not belong.

Darren leaned over so far his belly flattened against his thighs. "That's it, Cooper. As of this minute, you are *fired.*"

Trent did not wait for the driver to make it around to his side. He opened his door and stepped into the sunlight. Instantly the uniformed guard opened the brass door and wished him a good morning. Trent stepped back and let his boss storm past. He gave himself a moment to breathe in the fresh air, the light, the thrill of finally having won a chance. He whispered to the amazing day ahead, "Showtime."

CLEVELAND

If anyone had asked John Jacobs how he saw himself, he probably would not have replied. John had spent his entire adult life being both strong and silent. But if he were pressed to divulge the truth, he would have said that he was a big man imprisoned inside too small a life.

John knew the church service was over. But he could not bring himself to open his eyes. To do so would require letting go of the most incredibly intense experience he had known in years.

Then he heard his wife call his name. When he looked up, John saw the church's senior usher leaning over the pew, watching him gravely. "I'm fine," he told them both.

Heather demanded, "Why on earth didn't you say something?"

"I was praying," he said. In a very unique manner, true enough.

"You're supposed to be leading Sunday school," Heather said. "It's time to start."

He knew that was beyond him. "Will you do it?"

"John, what's the matter?"

"I'm all right. I just need a little time, is all." He followed her into the classroom, seated himself, and pretended to watch his wife as she announced she'd be teaching and led their group in the opening prayer. Heather had graduated from Bible college and knew the Scriptures better than he ever would. In general she preferred to stand back and let him lead, but many of the insights he brought to the class were drawn from their study time together. Heather had led her college tennis team to the state quarterfinals and still played three or four times a week. She was tanned and lean and carried herself with an athlete's natural grace.

John found himself watching her anew. He saw his wife of twenty-seven years, the mother of their two children, the woman who had helped him bear the intolerable loads of this life, and he loved her so much his heart hurt.

Something must have connected, for she stopped in midsentence and said, "John, will you tell me what it is?"

There might have been another thirty or so people in the room. But the way she spoke those words made the impossible feel natural. The concept of public confession was daunting. But he felt that her request was proper. It was time.

John said, "I have the impression that God spoke to me."

Heather resumed her seat next to him. "Back in church?"

"When the pastor led us in the opening prayer. And it just kept growing." He touched the small book in his pocket that dealt with listening to God. The church had bought several boxes and offered them around. "Heather and I have been studying this in our morning prayer times." John shook his head. He might have been trying to listen. But he wasn't sure he was actually ready for what had just happened.

Heather asked, "How do you know it was the Lord?"

"There've been a few moments in my life I know I'll never forget. Times that I've felt if there was one ounce more joy or love, I'd explode. I just couldn't contain anything more." He spoke with a slow deliberation, normal for John. He rarely sped up his words. "When you said you'd marry me. That was one. Seeing our boys take their first breaths, those were two more. The experience in the sanctuary was that powerful."

A man who had been John's friend since high school asked, "What did God say?"

John sat for a while, then replied, "He asked who would go for him."

Heather asked, "Go where?"

"He didn't say." There had been a unique intensity to the experience. One that left John utterly certain that this silent exchange had not been manufactured by his own brain. "I answered like Isaiah. I said, 'Here am I, send me.' And God said, 'Take the turning, and walk the unlikely road.'"

He took a long breath. Once again the images were so intense he shut his eyes and bowed his head, returning in all but body to the sanctuary and the moment. "I asked how I would know the message was really from God. He said, take the turning, and I would find him waiting there."

"What turning was he talking about, John?"

To that, he shook his head. He knew exactly what God was referring to. But that was something he was not ready to talk about. Not with anyone.

2

"God's hidden wisdom . . ."

NEW YORK CITY

Trent Cooper stood by the vast windows overlooking Times Square, his back to the reception area and his pacing boss. Trent understood the man's terror. They both had good reason to be afraid. The elegant chamber was littered with the carcasses of former executives. The vultures inside the office beyond the double doors were experts at picking flesh from bones.

Trent had never felt calmer.

His every sense was on hyperalert. He stood on the fifth floor, close enough to ground level to observe the people scurry around the square. In Trent's research of the man behind this meeting, one of the articles had criticized the office's location. In New York, higher was better. Penthouses were intended to hold the power brokers. But Trent understood exactly why Barry Mundrose had placed his office right here. Trent did not see hordes of tourists and locals jostling and rushing and pointing and talking. He saw an audience. *His* audience. The people he would both mold and shape into a mass of mouths eager to swallow whatever he next produced. Like a huge flock of baby birds, all their colorful wings flapping as they scrambled and cheeped and craved whatever crumb he decided to deliver.

The reception area held a variety of aromas. Fresh ground coffee, fresh cut flowers, furniture polish, a hint of some exotic spice in the lovely receptionist's perfume. Overlaying was a tight electric burn, the flavor of desert air the instant before lightning flared. Most people could not identify the subtle tang. They fretted and churned without knowing exactly why.

He tasted the air with the tip of his tongue. The charge was as intense as anything he had ever known, and took him straight back to his childhood. He recalled nights huddled in the storm cellar behind their house, his father out on the road somewhere, his mother cradling his head in her arms, probably not even aware of the noises she made, moans linking fragments of pleas to God, hidden and helpless and afraid.

Even there, Trent was never frightened. He loved the sound of the approaching storms, like electric beasts stomping the dry Oklahoma soil, the thunder rolling out warnings of their approach. Until finally, *bam!* the strikes became so close the thunder and the lightning joined into one gigantic explosion, striking faster and faster and faster, his mother wailing her fears, the wind howling, the cellar doors rattling as the giant battered and bellowed. Then it marched away until they were safe to emerge, and there was nothing left of it except the soft rumble of its force beyond the horizon.

That and the flavor of power on his tongue.

The receptionist called from her station by the grand double doors, "Gentlemen, Mr. Mundrose will see you now."

BALTIMORE

Alisha Seames sat at the head table in the church hall. One Sunday each month, the families brought in food and ate together following the service. Actually, it was more like a midday break, because most folks stayed over for a second helping of praise and worship after eating. The main table was on a little rise, like a knee-high stage. Alisha sat with her back to the rear curtain. She loved being up there at the head table. She'd spent extra time on her dress and her hat and her makeup and her shoes. Knowing everybody was looking. Just loving it.

Only not today.

"Alisha, what's the matter, sister? Why aren't you eating?"

She would like to tell Pastor Terry Reeves that she wasn't hungry. But she wasn't going to disgrace herself by telling a lie. She was always hungry. She didn't understand how other people managed to hold to a diet. She could eat a huge meal and twenty minutes later be hungry again. She was always struggling with her weight, and she was always getting bigger.

The pastor was a smooth-skinned, handsome man. Some said he was too young to lead a church the size of theirs. But Alisha knew better. He was not just a great preacher. He was also a leader. She had never been more aware of this fact than right here, right now, when he leaned across his wife to ask again, "Are you all right, sister?"

Alisha knew his wife did not like her. Celeste Reeves thought Alisha was pushy and opinionated. The two women also had a history. Celeste sang in the choir that Alisha led. Celeste had let it be known that she thought she should be in charge there too. Alisha positively lived for that choir, and nobody, not even the pastor's wife, was going to knock her off that perch. When Celeste had realized she couldn't take over the adult choir, she started working with children in one of Baltimore's worst neighborhoods, fashioning them into a choir all her very own. And now the woman wanted to bring them in and join them with Alisha's group, less than a week before the choir's biggest event of the year.

But Alisha couldn't think about that now. Not and stay focused on what needed doing.

Alisha rose to her feet. "Excuse me, I've just got to go . . ."

She didn't finish the sentence because she didn't want to be telling anyone exactly what it was that she just had to go do. Because of her girth, she bumped every chair in turn as she made her way off the narrow stage. She heard the stairs creak as she descended, and she saw people stare at her, and she knew they'd be talking. But this couldn't wait. God had spoken to her, and that was a fact. After a lifetime of praying, it had actually happened, and she dreaded what was coming next. Because as soon as God had said, "Take the unlikely road," Alisha had known just exactly what that turn was. She didn't want to do it. She hated the very idea of what was coming next. But God had said he would meet her there. And that left her with no choice. None at all.

Twenty minutes later Alisha pulled up in front of a house she never thought she'd visit. The Rothmore district of Baltimore was a leafy enclave shining with wealth on this crisp April day. The brownstone townhouse fit the rich surroundings, as did the white Porsche Cayenne parked in the drive. Alisha took a double-fisted grip on her purse and marched up the front walk like she belonged.

The door was answered by Kenneth, of course. It had to be him that appeared, not Alisha's sister. It just had to be like this, the whole nasty business just pressed into her face like God had meant all along to challenge her in the toughest possible fashion. She loathed how Kenneth pretended to be delighted to see her. She detested his accent, like he didn't know better than to stop breathing through his nose when he spoke. "Alisha, what a pleasant surprise. Does Tabby know you're coming?"

She hated that too. How he called his wife like he would a cat. But Alisha didn't snip at him that Tabatha, the name their mother had given her sister, was a fine name. All she said was, "I was in church, and I felt like I needed to stop by."

"Of course. Welcome." He stepped back, waving her inside. Like some highbrow earl or something. Instead of what he truly was, the godless white man who had stolen Alisha's baby sister away. "Please, come in."

The interior was exactly as Alisha had imagined, beautiful and pristine and very expensive looking. A rich white man's idea of a perfect home, full of antiques so delicate Alisha was afraid to sit down anywhere. Kenneth led her into a parlor and said, "Let me just go tell Tabby you're here. I won't be a moment."

As he bounded up the stairs, Alisha seated herself on the sofa. It wheezed softly, like a rich man's sigh. Probably never had a black woman plunk herself down here before. Which she knew was untrue before the thought was even formed. And she wasn't angry at the man. Not really. She was just angry. Like she wanted to yell at God for putting her in this position, but she couldn't, so she just sat there. Being angry at a room.

Past events started running through her brain, tight little bundles of emotions packed around each mental image like grenades. How their mother had gone up to work in Chicago, leaving Alisha and her sister to be raised by their grandmother. How the mother had not come back, not even when their grandmother had become ill, and so Alisha had become mother to the sister who was only four years younger than herself. How Alisha had scrimped and saved and worked so Tabatha could finish high school, and go on to community college, and then win a scholarship to the university where her husband taught sociology. How the first thing Alisha had known about their relationship was when Tabatha had told her about the engagement. What a night that had been. That particular argument had blistered the paint. But it did not hold a candle to the quarrel they'd had the day before the wedding, when Alisha learned there was not to be a preacher, not even a *white* preacher. Instead, they were getting married down in the courthouse. Because neither Tabatha nor her white-bread husband believed in God.

"Alisha? What are you doing here?"

It was just amazing how tiny her sister was. People seeing the two of them together might not have said anything, but Alisha had a lifetime's experience at reading the unspoken verdict in their faces. How Tabatha was beautiful and lithe and narrow-waisted and long-limbed, like a dancer. And Alisha was just plain big.

And there Tabatha stood. Poised and refined. Like she'd been born to live in this elegant, historic row house, with a man who had inherited more money than they knew what to do with, and how they didn't find any need for God. Her little sister. All grown up.

Alisha pushed herself to her feet. "Hello, Tabatha."

"You have to excuse me, I'm a little shocked. I thought you said you'd never set foot in my home."

Kenneth hovered in the front hallway. He cleared his throat, which was probably a white man's way of being nervous. "Will you ladies take coffee?"

Alisha had no idea how to respond. Which Pastor Terry's wife would definitely say was a first. When she didn't speak, her sister said, "We're fine here, Kenneth. Just give us a moment, please."

The woman even talked white.

"I'll just be in the kitchen if you need me."

Tabatha stood there, studying her sister, like she'd never set eyes on the woman before. "Why are you here?" she asked again.

Alisha had not known what she was going to say until that very moment. But the words were there waiting. As she spoke, she wondered if that was what God had meant when he'd said that he would meet her at the turning.

Alisha said, "I've come to apologize."

Tabatha cocked her head. "Why now? I mean, excuse me for asking, sister. But after all this time, don't you think you owed me a phone call before turning up out of the blue?"

"Yes. You're right. And I would have, if I'd thought of it."

"You didn't think to call me."

"No. I'm sorry."

"Two apologies in the space of a minute. After four years of nothing." Tabatha gave a reluctant wave at the sofa. "I suppose you might as well sit back down."

She remained where she was. "I was in church this morning."

"Of course you were. It's Sunday. Where else would you be?" Tabatha walked to the narrow table by the window, opened a silver box, and pulled out a cigarette and lighter.

Alisha watched her sister light up. "I didn't know you smoked."

"Since I was fifteen. We all have our secrets." The smoke deepened her voice, making it sound sultry. "So you were in church."

Alisha nodded slowly. "God spoke to me. And said I needed to do this."

Tabatha eyed her through the smoke. "God takes such a personal interest in your affairs that he tells you to come apologize?"

Normally the acidic cynicism would have been enough to set Alisha alight. In this case, however, she felt nothing. Not even regret. Just a calm so complete she might as well have been seated in her car out front, instead of inside this place where she most certainly did not belong. "That's right. He does."

"Any idea why he waited four years to send down that little note?"

"I suppose . . . Maybe he didn't think I was ready."

"But you're ready now."

Alisha nodded. "You're looking good, Tabatha."

"Money will do that to a person." She stubbed out the cigarette. "I'm happy, Alisha."

"I'm glad."

"I'm not going to stand here and have you use this apology as an excuse to tell me I'm living a godless life."

"I didn't come here to do anything more than apologize."

"Not now, not ever. You hear me? I won't have you sitting on your little church throne and spouting judgment over me or my man. I'm all grown up now, just like you said. I'm living my life. You hear me? *My* life."

Alisha heard that, and she heard how her sister had waited four long years for the chance to say those words. And the knowledge was enough to send a tear hot as lava rolling down her face. "I've missed you. So much."

Tabatha's face went through a remarkable transformation. For a brief instant, the determined poise melted like soft wax, and the woman showed a heart that ached. The eyes liquefied, the lips trembled, the hands danced up and around and down. Then Tabatha took a hard breath, and rebuilt the tight facade that fit this room and this world. "In that case, why don't you join us for lunch. We're having a few people over."

"Thank you, Tabatha. That is so sweet of you. I'm happy to accept."

Alisha just knew it was going to be awful.

3

"Humble yourselves before the Lord . . ."

NEW YORK CITY

Trent entered the boardroom behind his boss. The summons to meet with the CEO of their parent organization on a Sunday had caught his supervisor, Darren, completely by surprise. But not Trent. He had been dreaming of this moment for years.

The closest either he or Darren had ever come to Barry Mundrose was watching him on the stage at the annual corporate gathering. Trent knew it had been a huge risk to send their chairman a confidential copy of his recent report. Darren would have fired him outright the day he learned of what Trent had done, except the news arrived with this summons.

Trent's boss shot him a look of equal parts fury and fear as they passed the lovely receptionist and entered through the double doors. Trent did not care what the man thought. One way or the other, either he got what he wanted inside here, or he was gone.

Trent's boss survived by playing the turtle. At every sign of trouble, Darren retreated inside his corporate shell. Which was why Trent had not shared with him the news that he had gone around him, and three other layers, to the man himself: Barry Mundrose. CEO of Global Communications.

The second chamber held a trio of desks, two for secretaries and a third for temporary staffers brought in to manage a specific project that had captured Mundrose's attention. He liked to be close to the action, and planting an executive here meant he could take the new project's temperature on an hourly basis. Such hands-on direction was the Mundrose trademark. Young staffers who had once sat behind that now-empty desk held any number of senior executive positions, because Mundrose used this place as a training ground, a chance to take the measure of the men and women he intended to lift into the clouds. As Trent passed he shot the desk a hard look, and promised himself for the second time that day, *soon*.

The boardroom held the largest conference table Trent had ever seen, an oval at least thirty feet long. The room held eleven chairs, and nine were arrayed around the far end, occupied by six men and three women. Two empty chairs awaited Trent and his boss at the other end. Lonely. Isolated.

The nine people scrutinized them as the receptionist asked if they wanted anything. Darren responded with a shake of his head. Trent asked for a glass of water.

Barry Mundrose sat in the center position. "Let's see. You're in our advertising division—do I have that right?"

Trent's boss stammered an affirmative.

"All right, gentlemen. You've got five minutes to impress us."

Trent's boss cleared his throat. "I think I'll let my associate speak for us both."

Ever since the summons' arrival, Darren had raged and threatened and demanded that Trent tell him exactly what he had in mind. Trent's reply had remained unchanged. "It's all there in the report. The one you refused to read or even acknowledge."

Trent rose to his feet—no papers, no pad, nothing. These people would have seen every visual image known to the human race. They were professionals at refusing to be wowed by special effects. His only hope was to give them the bare facts, bring them to the same conclusion he had reached.

"The stats I've gathered are all in the report in front of you. The two generations that form our most important audience are also the hardest to reach, and even harder to keep hold of. The attention of Generation Xers and the Millennials wanes so fast, some of our most popular efforts lose traction before the end of their first season."

Trent spoke very carefully, at a pace that some people found irritating, including his boss. He had no choice in the matter. He'd been born with a cleft palate, and the residual effects meant if he tried to accelerate his speech, he slurred his words. And he intended to be as clear and precise as he possibly could.

Trent gave three minutes to a brief summary of the statistical evidence. He mentioned television shows from the Mundrose line-up that had started huge and faded fast. Films that had been megahits, yet whose spin-offs and sequels had flopped. Magazines that had garnered massive initial readerships, then gone bust in the space of two advertising cycles. Trent used two examples from each of the conglomerate's main divisions—film, television, advertising and marketing, music, book publishing, magazines and print, electronic games. He listed the exact revenue figures from memory. He had to be right, because at the table's far end sat the presidents of those seven divisions, along with Mundrose's son and daughter, who served as his joint executive managing directors. Most people who had witnessed Trent's ability to recall anything he had either read or seen assumed he had a photographic memory. They were wrong. At an early age, Trent had studied a book about enhancing memorability and applied the lessons. He was not particularly strong, he had few special talents. So he had done the absolute most with what he had. And that had been enough to get him here.

"*Time* magazine recently described these two generations, the X-ers and the Millennials, as the 'Me-Me-Me generations.' They are the most self-absorbed people ever known. Some have made a talent of superficiality. Others are very attuned to the disadvantaged and forgotten. With both generations, our standard methods of maintaining customer loyalty don't work."

Trent walked over to stand by the window looking out on Times Square. "For us to succeed with this audience, we have to change our entire way of thinking. The Mundrose divisions cannot continue to compete against each other and thrive or even survive. Our audience has become too fragmented. There are too many voices clamoring for their attention. They lose interest too quickly. They have an ingrained cynicism to all forms of commercial promotion."

Trent moved back to the head of the table, drawing them away from the lights and the milling crowds outside, silenced by the triple-paned glass. To his satisfaction, every head turned with him. Even his boss's. "The divisions must be united behind one single project. One concept large enough to demand a *joint* effort of *all* divisions, backed by an entire season's marketing budget."

The two Mundrose children could not have been more different. The son was narrow in every sense, a ferret-faced man with a greyhound's lean body, a tight gaze behind grey titanium glasses, and an accountant's constricted viewpoint. His voice pierced through the room. "You're suggesting we risk an entire quarter's revenue on one project. That's insane. The danger is unacceptable." The man's reaction could not have been better if Trent had scripted it.

The daughter, a flame-haired vixen with a raspy tone, was the child who shared her father's vision and his rapacious appetites. She said, "Not if the project is big enough. Not if the potential for profit balances the risk."

He waited then, holding his breath. Hoping.

Finally Mundrose said, "So give us this trend."

He could have leapt upon the table and raced down its length to hug the man. Would have, if there had been any chance of surviving. Instead, he made do with, "The advertising and marketing divisions conduct an annual survey of these two generations, trying to determine what their interests are, what trends are rising and which are falling."

The Mundrose son snapped, "That is highly confidential information. No one outside the division or this room is supposed to even *know* about those surveys."

The sister glanced across the father to smirk at her brother. Then she turned back to Trent and nodded.

"What I propose is to turn this on its head," Trent said. "If all the Global Communications divisions were to unite, it would create the most powerful cultural force on earth."

Trent's own audacity struck him with such force, it caused his voice to falter. Barry Mundrose was known to take great pleasure in baiting his divisions, forcing them to fight among themselves. When confronted by the opposition, he did not deny, he did not defend. He bragged. He referred to the Global divisional chiefs as his partially trained pit bulls.

Mundrose said, "Go on."

It was all the invitation he was likely to receive. "I suggest that we stop *following* and start creating. *We* decide what the next trend is going to be. *We* shape it. *We* sell it. *We* own it."

His excitement would not allow him to remain still. He started pacing, three tight steps in one direction, three in the other. The acrid electric force was gathered about him, his body a human lightning rod. "Only two issues matter. Can we be first with it—and can we make money from it? The answer to both is an unequivocal yes. But only if we *invent* the concept."

Mundrose's daughter was nodding now, her hair reflecting the light from beyond the windows. "We stop following trends and start designing them."

"Exactly!" Trent strode to the window and punched the thick glass with his fist. "If *all* the marketing forces of *all* our divisions are combined, we have the power to tell the people out there what they are going to believe."

Barry Mundrose ended the meeting with customary abruptness, rising to his feet. "You. Come with me."

Darren was caught in mid-rise. "That's both of us, correct?"

Mundrose did not bother to turn around. "Somebody show that guy the door. Cooper, in here."

Trent resisted the urge to wave his boss a cheery farewell.

ORLANDO

When Jenny Linn was small, her father had pronounced her Chinese name with pride. Jin-Ahn were the Mandarin characters for "golden peace," and her father used to sing the words as he danced her on his knee. But her father had moved on to different names for his only child. These days his most common way of referring to Jenny was "troublemaker."

She pulled up in front of her parents' home in Isleworth, a prosperous and manicured subdivision south of Orlando's downtown. She stared at the house for a time. The force that had resonated through her during the morning's service was still there, but muted now. Which was not altogether a bad thing. Exquisite as it had felt at the time, it had also been equally frightening. As she reached for her purse, she caught sight of the small book her study group had been working through that month. As she rose from her car, she had the distinct impression that the entire month, from reading that first page four weeks earlier, had been leading her to this moment. When she walked up to her front door.

Jenny's mother, petite and silent and very beautiful, stood on the front portico. Jenny's great-grandmother had been the daughter of the emperor's chief advisor, and the first girl child of her lineage whose feet had not been bound, the excruciating process resulting in feet less than four inches long. But the girl's parents had come to faith in Jesus, and eventually pawned their jewelry to pay for passage to America. Jenny had inherited the fine porcelain skin and silky dark hair and sparkling opal eyes of her mother's lineage. The tallest woman in her family, Jenny stood just under five feet three inches high.

She had also inherited her father's iron will. Much to his dismay.

As she climbed the front stairs, Jenny whispered a quick prayer, "Give me the strength to do what you want."

Her mother kissed Jenny's cheek and sang the hello that had formed her early life. "Hello, Sunshine."

Jenny followed her mother into the house. As usual, she felt stifled by the place. The ivory white carpet swallowed every sound. The living room sofa waited to clench her like a suede fist.

Her father wore a dress shirt, white with chalk-blue stripes. Richard Linn liked his shirts starched so they crackled when he put them on. His trousers were from the suit he had worn to church, and his shoes were so polished they glinted.

Jenny crossed the room and kissed his cheek. "Hello, Father."

He murmured his response, as though absorbed in reading the newspaper. He wore silver reading glasses and he held the paper to catch the light through the family room's sliding doors. Jenny knew it was all a ruse. He was upset with her, and he used the *Wall Street Journal* as a means of blocking her out. Such actions were all part of what had become their standard Sunday quarrels. As was her mother's stance in the parlor's entryway, ready to serve as mediator when things got hot.

Her father lowered the paper and announced, "Congress has finally forced the IRS to confess they had targeted conservative groups."

"I heard."

"I suppose a story that big, even your liberal rag couldn't ignore it."

Liberal rag was her father's way of referring to the *New York Times*, the only paper Jenny read. "They put it on the front page," she acknowledged.

He harrumphed his displeasure. "Only after calling it a conspiracy among conservatives for years."

Jenny was surprised by the lack of her usual response. Instead, she found herself thinking back to the incident that had fueled her father's current ire. She had traveled to New York to interview for a job. Afterwards she had gone for a long walk, and discovered herself caught up in a liberal political protest rally. Looking back, she knew she probably should have turned away. But Jenny had never run from a fight. Even when this one had gotten her arrested.

Richard Linn had been furious on several levels. He was an archconservative and a leader of the regional Tea Party. But he was also a product of his Chinese heritage, and his daughter's arrest was for him a public shaming. Jenny had spent four long weeks avoiding this confrontation. As she watched her father carefully fold his paper along the creases and set it on the coffee table, she knew he was preparing himself for another raging argument with his wayward daughter. But there was something else she had never experienced before, an emotional distance that allowed her to observe the moment without her customary indignation. She had not come to argue. And this astonished her almost as much as her certainty that God had spoken to her in church. Leading her to this very moment, when she could calmly meet her father's gaze.

Her father went on. "The IRS audited our local Tea Party chapter five times in five years. And because I was chairman, they did the same to my business. Five times! I've called the congressman's office and volunteered to testify. I'd give them an earful, I can tell you that."

Jenny could feel her mother's strain radiating from the room's far side. Ready to spring into action the moment Richard brought up the real reason for his pent-up anger. To which Jenny would no doubt respond with anger of her own. Provoking her father's next salvo, which was when he would call her disrespectful. That one word was the point at which Jenny usually detonated.

Only not today.

Jenny said, "I have come to apologize."

The request clearly caught Richard flat-footed. Jenny never apologized. She argued. Loudly.

Jenny went on, "I should never have gotten caught up in that march. I had a chance to step away and I did not."

Richard squinted, as though trying to identify who exactly was addressing him. "You hadn't gone to New York to attend that rally?"

"No, Pop. I just let myself get swept up in the excitement."

"Some excitement. Getting yourself arrested." But his steam had evaporated. He seemed to speak words written by another. "You shamed your family."

"I know that. And I'm sorry."

Her mother stepped forward. "Why don't we sit down? Lunch is ready."

As Jenny followed her father into the dining room, her mother patted her on the shoulder. A simple gesture, and a rare one.

Their conversation was stilted, but at least it was cordial. The only risky moment came when her mother brought up the new dentist working with her father. "He's such a charming young man. Isn't he, dear?"

"Good hands," her father said. "Excellent with patients."

"And so handsome. He's mixed blood, of course. So many young people are these days. His mother is Mandarin, isn't that right?"

"Shanghai by way of Boston."

"And his father is from Seoul. He is fluent in both languages."

Normally any hint of pressure from either parent for her to wed was enough to set her off. Today, however, all Jenny said was, "If he works in Pop's office, he's got to share Pop's politics."

"I met him at a Tea Party conference," her father confirmed.

Jenny looked from one to the other. "Do you think I could ever live happily under the same roof with an archconservative? Really?"

They let the matter drop.

As they were clearing away the dishes, Jenny knew she could put it off no longer. "Pop, I was wondering if I could ask your advice."

The two elders froze. In other circumstances, it would have been comic, both parents motionless in shock. Jenny never asked their opinion about anything. She made her decision, and then she told them what she was going to do. Always.

They gradually regained the function of their limbs. Jenny accompanied them into the kitchen and set her plates in the sink. "I've been given my posting in China. It's in Guangzhou. They want me to start in two months."

"You know what I think," her father barked. "If you're moving overseas, go with a mission organization."

"We've been all through that, Pop. It won't work."

"Because you're too stubborn."

"No. Well, yes. I am stubborn. But that's not the reason."

Her calm replies kept her father off balance. "Well, what is it then?"

"I want to become immersed in the local community. Live with the Chinese, learn from them as much as teach them. This does not fit with most mission organizations' traditional strategy."

Again she managed to shock her parents. Her mother said, "You never told us you had even applied to a mission group."

"I didn't want to get your hopes up. They didn't want me, and I had no interest in talking to them further."

"So you're going over with that liberal do-gooder group."

She had to tighten down then, just let the ire rise and then fade away. Her father's back was to her, as it often was when he shot off one of his broadsides against any program the Democrats had initiated. But her mother saw the effort Jenny was making. And she approved with a tiny nod.

It gave Jenny the strength to reply calmly, "They have offered me a job teaching English lit and language at the local university."

"My daughter the professor," her mother murmured.

"It's a two-year posting," she went on. "I thought it was what I wanted. But last week I was offered another job."

That brought her father around. "In China?"

"No, Pop. In New York. That's why I was up there. The publishers have an opening for a junior editor. I have to go up for one more interview, but the woman who will be my boss has assured me the job is mine if I want it."

While still in graduate school, Jenny had begun working for one of the largest publishing houses in America. She had started as a freelance reader, wading through the slush pile of manuscripts that flooded in every day. She had gradually risen up to become an outside line editor, and finally she had been brought up to New York and offered a chance to handle a couple of manuscripts that she had brought in herself. One of them was currently on the *New York Times* nonfiction bestseller list. As Jenny explained this, she realized it was the first time she had ever mentioned the *Times* and not sent her father's blood pressure through the roof.

They were silent for a moment; then her mother asked, "Which job do you want, dear?"

"Both of them. That's the problem."

Her father said, "The New York house certainly won't wait two years for you to start work."

"No. And if I go to New York, I'm afraid I'll get caught up in the profession and the city and never leave."

"It can happen." Her father's gaze was keen, but his voice lacked the normal combative edge. "Sometimes you have to accept that you can't have it all."

"I guess that's right. Thank you." She looked back and forth between them.

He cocked his head. "Have you actually just agreed with me?"

And like that, it was done. The impossible task she had known awaited her, the instant she had heard God's voice. The change she knew the Lord wanted her to make. The unattainable quest. Make peace with the greatest source of conflict in her life. Her father.

Jenny embraced her mother, and then her father. She felt a surge of the same triumphant power rise up inside her as she gripped him. Jenny was amazed at how easy it was to speak the words, "I love you, Pop."

4

"Having a form of godliness, but denying its power . . ."

NEW YORK CITY

Trent followed Barry Mundrose through the adjoining doors leading to his private office. The inner sanctum was larger than the bullpen housing Trent's entire media advertising group. He watched Barry Mundrose cross the Persian carpet and sink into the chair behind his desk. Trent could see no hint of a limp—which was remarkable. Trent's research had uncovered something Barry Mundrose normally kept well hidden. The man had been born with a serious spinal distortion, and had spent his first twelve years encased in a steel-framed corset running from hips to shoulders.

Mundrose waved him into a chair. "Take a seat. What do they call you?"

"Trent, sir." He watched as Barry's daughter, Edlyn, entered the room. She walked behind her father's desk and leaned against the bookshelves. To her left stretched an array of six computer screens, all streaming data from various markets. Trent had the impression she perched there a lot.

Barry Mundrose said, "But Trent's not your first name, is it."

"No, sir. Middle. My first name is Standish."

"Pretty awful thing to hang around a kid's neck, Standish."

Trent saw no need to respond. The important point of this exchange was that Mundrose had found him of sufficient interest to do some research of his own.

"Okay, Trent. Let's talk about what's not there in your report. The concept big enough to justify my going against the grain. You have one, don't you?"

"Yes, sir. I do."

"So why didn't you include it?"

"Because a concept on paper is just words. I want to *show* them."

"You want to knock their socks off."

"Exactly, sir."

"But you'll tell me."

"If you order me to," Trent replied. His gaze on the daughter. Another silent appeal. "But I'd rather have the chance to wow you as well."

"I don't like being blindsided."

Edlyn said, "He's not doing that. He's asking for the chance to prep. Give it to you in Technicolor display."

Mundrose swiveled around. As he cocked his chin, Trent had a glimpse of the man Mundrose had been before seventy-three years ate away at his vigor.

Barry Mundrose had inherited a played-out gold mine in the northern reaches of Alberta, Canada. When the price of gold skyrocketed, Mundrose reopened the mine and pulled out another sixty thousand ounces. He had taken these profits and bought two near-defunct oil companies, whose only assets were a series of almost-dry wells. But shale-oil refining and rising prices had made the fields hugely profitable. Barry Mundrose was now Canada's largest independent oil and gas producer, and its fourth largest gold miner. His son ran those operations from their Calgary offices, while Edlyn handled the other side of the business—the one where Barry Mundrose sank most of his time and money these days. Entertainment and advertising and telecommunications. Only Rupert Murdoch and the Bertelsmann family of Germany ran larger organizations, and Mundrose had vowed to overtake them both.

Trent was determined to help make that happen.

"All right, Trent," Mundrose said. It was decided. "You've got two days."

Edlyn protested, "That's not enough."

"It's fine," Trent assured them. "Thank you, sir."

"You can have the desk."

Trent felt his eyes burn. Which was absurd. "You won't regret this."

"We'll see."

Trent took that as his dismissal, and rose to his feet. Edlyn slid down from the ledge and followed him across the carpeted expanse. He was almost at the door when Mundrose called, "How many surgeries did you have as a kid?"

Trent stared back to the man behind the desk. "Nine, sir. The same as you."

Barry Mundrose's smile shone across the distance. "We all need a reason to fight for what we want, right?"

"Exactly, sir." Trent waited until Edlyn shut the door to say, "Thank you. For everything."

She crossed her arms and waited. Behind him, Trent heard one of the secretaries speaking on the phone, while the receptionist ushered the next set of guests into the conference room. But Edlyn remained intently focused on him. Trent loved how she did that, giving him the green-eyed stare, cold as a leopard. Waiting for him to say the words that had drawn her out this far.

He said it with all the force he could muster. "I owe you."

She did not acknowledge him in any way. Edlyn simply turned and walked back inside her father's office.

Only when the door clicked shut did Trent realize he had been holding his breath.

OUTSIDE CLEVELAND

John Jacobs pulled into the parking lot and turned off his motor. He stared at the gates, and decided this was the hardest thing he had ever done. Which was saying a lot.

The Lake Erie penitentiary had earned its reputation as one of the worst prisons in the United States, and for good reason. Several years ago it had become the first one to be sold to a private company, the Corrections Corporation of America. The CCA promised to do it cheaper and better. But since the takeover, the Lake Erie prison racked up a steady stream of failed audits. Over the next two years, they flunked every inspection, nineteen in all. There were documented reports of prisoner abuse, filthy conditions, broken facilities, dangerous food. And still the state kept packing in more inmates. Overcrowding became a national scandal, with single cells holding as many as three inmates, and double cells containing seven. When confronted in a press conference, the governor responded that yes, he was aware of the complaints and the lawsuits, but he simply did not have money to change things.

John was still staring at the gate when a claxon sounded from within the prison. A few moments later a man-sized door opened in the middle of those massive steel portals. A guard pushed the opening wider, allowing a lone figure to walk through. He wore the bottom half of the suit he had worn at trial, though obviously now several sizes too large. John recognized him instantly. At thirty-three, Danny Jacobs was two years younger than his father—John's brother—had been when he and Danny's mother died in the traffic accident. The boy had shown such promise, a natural athlete with a blistering pitching arm whose fastball at the age of eighteen topped ninety-three miles per hour.

All lost to drugs and fast women and the lure of the life that had brought him here. Six to ten in Ohio's most notorious prison.

Somewhere during the past four years, Danny Jacobs had acquired a slight limp, one that tilted his upper body to the left. John sighed. He had worked around many hard men and had seen what a knife wound could do. His eyes burned at the sight of that poor, wasted boy grown old before his time.

John and his wife had tried hard, serving as his legal guardians, offering him a home to come back to, even after Danny was sent upstate the first time. After the stint in state prison, John had been reluctant to let him into their home again, but Heather had softened his resolve with her pleas. The boy had written to say he had found faith inside. She believed him. She wanted Danny to know he was still loved.

Danny Jacobs had rewarded them by stealing Heather's jewelry, including the three keepsakes she inherited from her grandmother. When Danny had been arrested that second time, John had not even shown up for the trial.

Danny had written him from inside, begging forgiveness. Knowing he had demolished his last connection to family. Knowing he had fallen, and was guilty of everything they claimed and more besides. He had found his way back to the cross, and he was writing as part of his penance. Not expecting an answer. Certainly not deserving one. But writing just the same. Which was how John had learned about Danny's release date. He had certainly not planned to be here. He'd no intention of ever seeing Danny again.

Until that morning in church.

The emotional force that had carried him through those incredible moments was gone now. All John felt now was dread. Even so, the challenge was real. And the conviction. He had to do this.

John rose from the car. "Hello, Danny."

"Uncle John?" The young man was not just lean. He was gaunt. His cheeks were hollow caverns. His red hair had lost its brilliance. His eyes were sunken inside his skull, their former crystal clarity now clouded. The gaze was as weak as the man's walk. "I never thought . . ." Danny stopped to cough. His hands trembled, possibly from emotion, but John didn't think so. He walked around the front of the car and took the cheap satchel. By the time he set it in the trunk, Danny had recovered. But he made no move for the car. Instead, he just stood there, watching his uncle with a haunted gaze.

John asked, "Do you have a place to go?"

"I've been assigned to a halfway house in Toledo." He fumbled a slip of paper from his pocket. But he didn't have the courage to reach out with it.

John stared at this husk of a man and felt the last of his raging embers fade out. "What have they done to you in that place?"

Danny's chin trembled. He cuffed his eyes. But he didn't speak.

"Get in, boy."

As they drove west along the lake, John made a call. He considered it a test, unique and unmistakable. There was no way he could have expected to connect with his buddy on a Sunday afternoon. But his friend answered on the first ring, brushed aside John's apologies. The man had recently become director of the transport center handling truck components headed across the state line to Detroit factories. John laid out the situation with a voice so raw he scarcely recognized himself. Told his friend about Danny's parents and his lost life and his finding faith and losing his way. And the going down a second time.

His friend responded, "They didn't send Danny to Lake Erie."

"Matter of fact, they did."

"Oh, man. The son of a friend at church was almost destroyed by the place."

John glanced over. The man who had once burned bright as a living flame sat there, hunched against the window, staring out at the grey, windswept water. Silent and beaten. "Yeah, that pretty much sums up things at this end."

"You think his faith is real, John?"

"All I can tell you is what he says."

"Where is he assigned?"

"Hang on a sec." He said to Danny, "Read out that halfway house address to me."

Danny picked up the paper from where it sat on the middle console. It hurt John's heart to see the boy's hands shake so.

John repeated the address to his friend, who said, "It's only about four blocks from our main warehouse."

"You know why I'm calling."

To John's astonishment, the man replied as though he had been waiting all Sunday for this very request. "Got a spot open on the shipping floor. The work is basic. But it pays union wages."

"Hold on, will you?" John relayed the offer to Danny. His once-proud nephew stared at him with the longing of true desperation. The lips trembled as bad as the hands. But no word emerged.

John said to the phone, "Danny thanks you. And so do I."

The man gave John directions, said Danny would have to check in with his parole officer, buy some new things, grow accustomed to being a civilian again. Talking with the same flat calm he might use to discuss a truck's timetable. He told John to have Danny report for work in three days at seven in the morning, and hung up.

Forty minutes later, John pulled up in front of the halfway house. He walked Danny inside, waited while he signed in, then motioned him outside again. There would be no hugs. Danny didn't expect it and John had never been one for hugging guys at the best of times. Which this definitely wasn't. John wrote out his cellphone and office numbers. "Don't call the house. Heather doesn't know I'm here."

Danny's voice carried a whole world of sorrow. "Do you ever think I'll be able to tell her I'm sorry?"

"Hard to say. Prove you can hold to the straight life. We'll see."

Danny slowly wiped his mouth, the motion of a man twice his age. "Thank you, Uncle John."

John fished out his wallet, pulled out everything he had except a twenty, and handed over the bills. Danny stared at the money in abject astonishment. John started around the car, pausing only to say, "Danny, look at me. Don't mess up."

The man fumbled over the simple words. "Thank you."

He was still standing there when John reached the interstate entrance and the halfway house vanished from view.

A little over an hour later, John sat in his driveway, wondering the same thing that had held his mind the entire drive home.

Was that it?

If God had intended nothing more than allowing a repentant sinner to find an almost-friendly face waiting for him outside those dark gates, well, that was all right with John Jacobs.

He let himself in quietly, only to have his wife walk in from the kitchen, wiping her hands on a dish towel. "Did you go see Danny?"

John stared at her. "How did you know about that?"

"I read the boy's letters, same as you."

"You weren't supposed to see them, Heather."

"Humph. As if you've ever been able to keep a secret from me." She crossed her arms. "How is he?"

"Well, he's not good."

"I've heard stories about that place."

"From the looks of things, I'd say they're all true."

"Is he going to be all right?"

"He's in a halfway house. I got him a job." John related the phone call, and finished, "I felt like I was laying it on the altar, calling my friend."

"Testing God, you mean."

"I guess. Sort of. Was that bad?"

Heather placed a warm hand upon his cheek. "John, there is not a single solitary thing about what you've done today that is anything other than good."

DAY
TWO

5

". . . trust in him and he will do this . . ."

NEW YORK CITY

Sunday evening Jenny Linn flew north to New York and took a taxi to the Manhattan hotel the publisher had booked for her. Early the next morning, she woke from a dream about a country she might never see. She had found herself standing before a class in a Chinese classroom. She was talking and pointing at something on the board, but she could not make out her own words. Yet she knew they liked her, and they liked what she was teaching them. When Jenny opened her eyes from the dream, she realized she had been crying in her sleep.

The most natural thing in the world was to slip from the bed onto her knees. She did not so much pray as bend over in the agony of self-doubt. Before leaving for New York, she had prayed and prayed, asking God to speak clearly to her again, telling her what she should do. Instead, there had only been silence. So in the end Jenny had requested a one-week postponement on her acceptance of the Guangzhou assignment, and flown to New York for the first editorial meeting with the publisher. Only when she landed at La Guardia, she had discovered a message on her phone saying that the publishing execs had unexpectedly been called away, and they needed to delay the meeting until the following week.

Jenny now bent over her knees, her hands clenched as tightly as her eyelids. Her heart felt terribly heavy, burdened by a sorrow she

47

could not name. Was the dream a sign? Was she doing something terribly wrong, coming here at all? If only she could *know*.

She finally sighed in defeat, rose from the floor, and started preparing for an empty and likely futile day. As she dressed, her cellphone rang. She plucked it from her night table and saw it was her father. "Pop?"

"Good morning, daughter. Am I disturbing you?"

Her father's voice carried the flat hollowness of the car speaker. "No, Pop. Not at all."

"Your mother and I are on the way to the airport. There's a dental conference starting in Denver tonight. We just wanted to see if you had arrived safely."

Her parents' loving concern came through, despite the distance and her father's formal tone. Jenny heard her voice splinter the words, "I'm here."

Her mother said, "Jenny, dear, is something the matter?"

"I just had the most confusing dream. I was teaching in China. And then I woke up in New York."

There was a moment's silence, and then her father asked, "Do you feel like God is telling you something?"

Jenny laughed out loud.

"Did I say something funny?"

She heard the edge to his voice. "No, Pop. I had just been praying for that very thing. For God to tell me what I should do."

She half expected her father to come back with something sharp. Her father disliked any hint of uncertainty. He carried himself with absolute conviction that all the things worth having an opinion about were there in black-and-white. Anyone with half a brain could see what was right. One of Richard Linn's favorite expressions in an argument. He'd even used it against his daughter.

Only not today. To her astonishment, he asked, "Would you like us to pray with you?"

Suddenly she found herself unable to hold back the tears. "That would be really nice."

Her father prayed first, then her mother. By the time they finished, Jenny was weeping openly. She had to take a pair of hard breaths before she could manage, "Thank you, Daddy."

"You haven't called me that in a very long while."

"Just a minute." She set the phone down on the carpet beside her, and used the top sheet to clear her face. As she picked up the phone again, a thought hit her. Unbidden. Unwanted. And yet the harder she resisted, the more certain became the conviction. She put the phone to her ear and said, "I have something I need to tell you. I was engaged to be married."

Jenny's mother drew a very sharp breath, but it was her father who demanded, "When was this?"

"Five months ago. We were engaged for seven weeks. Then he broke it off. He said . . ."

She dropped the phone, her sobs so tight she gripped the carpet in order to draw a breath. She had no idea how long it took before she picked up the phone and went on, "He said we'd taken all this too fast. He didn't love me enough to want to spend a life together. And it was better if we didn't start."

She only realized her mother was crying when she mangled the words, "Better for him, maybe."

"That's exactly what I thought," Jenny agreed.

Her father asked, "I don't understand. You were engaged to be married, and you didn't even tell your own parents?"

"We weren't talking back then, remember, Pop?" The recollection of her rage was enough to help steady her voice. "You were all over me about working for the election of the Democratic senator, remember that? I met my fiancé during the campaign. I wasn't going to give you the pleasure of criticizing his politics too. And when it was over, I wasn't going to let you say that it all fell apart because I had the bad sense to love a *Democrat*. A *liberal*. Because they couldn't be *trusted*."

"I would never have said . . ."

"Come on, Pop."

He sighed. "All right. Yes. You're right."

Jenny smiled through her tears. "Wow. Did I really hear that?"

Her mother said, "Richard, tell Jenny what you said last night."

Her father went gruff and sour. "We've covered enough ground for one day."

"Richard, tell your daughter."

"I said you humbled me, how you spoke. You were the wise one. I felt—"

"Ashamed," her mother filled in. "Your father said he felt ashamed. He wished he had been the one to rise above the arguments. He wished he had been the one to say that he loved you."

Jenny knew it was time. "I need to tell you both what happened last Sunday before I came to the house."

As she spoke, she found herself reliving what had occurred during her Sunday school class, when she had suddenly found herself overwhelmed by the Holy Spirit's presence, and heard the silent voice of God. Telling her to take the impossible turning, and go do what needed doing. And that she would find him waiting for her there.

When her parents did not respond, Jenny asked, "Where are you?"

"Parked outside the airport parking garage," her mother said. "We didn't want to risk losing the phone signal."

Richard's voice sounded gravelly, his words slow to emerge. "Do you think—has this event run its course?"

"I don't know *what* to think. I never expected anything like this to happen. Not to me. I live by my brains, I analyze everything to death. But there it was. The voice of God. Boom. Like lightning from an empty sky."

"Well, I for one think this is just the beginning," Richard said.

"I'm not sure I want to hear that, Daddy."

"I understand. It's very frightening. You fear being called to do the impossible."

"Like going to my parents' house and making peace," Jenny said.

Her mother asked, "Is that a smile I hear?"

"A small one, Mommy. Very small."

"You are worried about losing control of your life." Richard sighed. "That is something you learned from me, I fear. This need of mine to control everything. Including my daughter."

"Good luck with that, Daddy."

He was silent a moment, then asked, "Daughter, would you like us to come up and be with you?"

She was glad she was sitting on the floor, as it saved her from falling down. "Say that again?"

"Your mother and I could skip the dental convention. We could fly up and join you in New York."

"But only if you like," her mother inserted. The pleading was there, but without the customary overlay of tension. "We could offer you support. Pray with you," said her tender, retiring little mother.

There was no reason in the world why those words should make her cry for the fourth time that morning. "I would like that so much. Please come."

John Jacobs should have been having the time of his life. Even his wife said so. There was no reason for the sense of heavy misery he carried with him as the two of them stepped into the hotel elevator.

Monday morning, he had received a frantic call from headquarters. Their Midwest manager was down with an infection serious enough for the hospital to talk quarantine. They had a major new client wanting to talk numbers. John was to go to New York in his manager's place, see this client. The client wanted somebody who could talk turkey. John knew the business as well as anyone. "Take Heather along—you'll probably get some time in between to see the sights," his boss told him.

When they'd arrived in New York, he had learned the appointment had been postponed two days. Headquarters told him to sit tight, they would send someone to cover for him back home. But John had little interest in playing tourist. John felt every one of his fifty-six years, and had ever since the trip to meet Danny. The image of his young-old nephew limping from the prison gates blistered his nights. Heather had prayed with him, then held him through dark hours as he tossed and turned and sighed hard, pushing back against the helplessness that swelled his chest until his heart hurt. So much of his life felt like this, caught in the vise of unwanted events.

The doors opened again, and there before him stood a lovely, dark-haired waif, molded from some Asian race that defined beauty. Her skin held a remarkable glow, like light shining through purest alabaster. Her long dark hair framed a face as perfect as any John had ever seen.

John wondered if she even realized she was crying.

Heather waited until the doors opened and the crowd spilled into the lobby to ask the young woman, "Are you all right?"

The act of blinking caused another tear to escape. "I'm—I'm fine."

"You don't look at all fine. Are you here by yourself?"

"My parents are coming in this afternoon."

"Well, that is then and this is now. Have you had breakfast?"

"I was just going for coffee."

"Would you like to sit with us?" Heather did not wait for the woman to respond. Instead, she did the same kind of thing that had welcomed so many newcomers into their church. She acted as though they had been friends for eternity. "This is my husband, John. Why don't you and I sit down over here while he goes and buys us coffee. How do you take yours?"

"A small latte."

"Coming right up," John told them, listening to his wife pour a verbal ointment on the young woman's sorrow. He did not need to hear the words to know that Heather was doing what she did best. Making things better.

Their Times Square hotel probably had been built in the early eighties, and its former grandeur had turned slightly seedy from the hard use of countless tour groups. The lobby was vast, like an indoor stadium and just as noisy. The tiled floor and distant ceiling and marble-clad walls reflected back every sound in a constant wash of noise. The line in front of the Starbucks stand was long. John didn't mind. He had nothing better to do with his day.

Then he saw her.

The Starbucks stand fronted a three-way split in the lobby, to his left the main bar, right was the sunken area holding the hotel restaurant. Between those two was a long sitting area, with wire-backed chairs and metal tables for the coffee drinkers, and a long, high table where businesspeople stood to work their laptops, and more tables with chairs, and finally a wall of glass overlooking Times Square. Seated at the first table near the windows was a woman he had seen in countless photographs and on television. Ruth Barrett was the widow of Bobby Barrett, one of the great evangelists of the twentieth century. Since her husband's death, she had become well known in her own right, speaking and writing about Christians maintaining a strong prayer life.

The woman looked stricken by some deep, afflicting burden.

"John, dear—" Heather was touching his arm, turning him around. "We're going to move over by the windows. It's so noisy back there I can't hear what Jenny is saying."

"Sure. Fine." He watched the two women pass by Ruth Barrett's table, already back in their conversation, Heather bent low so as to catch the young woman's words. He hesitated a long moment, then decided there was no reason not to do exactly what his wife was doing. Even with someone as famous as this woman. He stepped out of line, approached the table, and said, "Mrs. Barrett, you look as sad as I feel."

He half expected her to offer the sort of practiced dismissal that anyone famous had to use as armor. Instead, she looked at him carefully, then asked, "Are you the reason I am here?"

"Ma'am, I don't—" John caught himself beginning an act of denial. He took a long breath, then released the words, "Truth is, I have no idea. But maybe, yes, ma'am. Just maybe."

She studied him carefully. "Then I suppose we had better have a word and see."

She waited at her lonely table while John ordered their coffees, then helped him carry the cups back toward the far wall. It was much quieter over here, the tables spaced farther apart. All of them were occupied, mostly by people on their own. Heather watched his approach with a puzzled look until she recognized who it was walking beside him. When they arrived, Heather said simply, "Oh, my goodness."

"Mrs. Barrett, this is my wife, Heather Jacobs. I'm John. And this young lady, sorry, I don't . . ."

"Jenny Linn. It's an honor, Mrs. Barrett. My parents think the world of you. As do I."

John asked an olive-skinned gentleman at the next table if he could spare a chair. The table on the man's other side was occupied by a large black woman whose round features were creased with worry or concern or... John hesitated in the act of sitting down. He looked at the tiny woman seated beside Ruth Barrett. Jenny Linn looked as sad as ever. But what held him was how, despite the vast difference in size, Jenny Linn reflected to a remarkable degree the African American woman's expression.

"What is it, John?"

"Just a second." He walked over to the woman's table. "I'm really sorry to be bothering you, ma'am. But I was wondering, are you doing okay?"

She started to snap at him. He could see the flash of ire, the intake of breath, like she was going to level him with a verbal barrage. But then she stopped, and her features seemed to melt. "I feel convicted by every wrong I have ever done."

"Ma'am, can I ask, are you a follower of Jesus?"

To his astonishment, it was not just the woman who responded. The olive-skinned man seated at the next table mirrored the woman's astonishment. She demanded, "Now why on earth are you asking a total stranger a question like that?"

"Because," John replied slowly, carefully, "I wonder if maybe we're all here for the same reason."

"And what reason is that?"

He shook his head. "I have no idea."

The woman revealed a smile that completely transformed her face as she stood. "Ain't that the thing, now."

"I'm John Jacobs. That's my wife, Heather. And Jenny Linn. And the lady—"

"I know who that sister is. I've been watching and listening to her all my life." She was not quite as tall as John, but made up for it in muscular girth. "I am Alisha Seames."

"Would you care to join us?"

"That table already looks crowded."

The olive-skinned man rose to his feet. "Please, I am wondering, would you perhaps have room for one more? We could move the two tables together, don't you see." He spoke with the precise diction of one who translated as he shaped the words. "For I too am drawn here by reasons that I do not understand. And I can only hope that it is my Savior's voice I have been hearing."

6

". . . pierced themselves with many griefs . . ."

NEW YORK CITY

Trent Cooper sat at a narrow table against the stockroom's rear wall. He turned on his cellphone, checking the time again. He hated having to rely on a stranger, particularly at this most important moment of his entire life. But he could not manage what he needed on his own. Success hinged upon the guy doing what he had promised, and delivering on time. Trent checked his watch, which showed the exact same time as his phone.

He had never worked so hard. And he had always worked twice as hard as everyone else. He was painfully aware of the slight indent running from his upper lip to the base of his right nostril. His tongue traced around the soft dimple in the top of his mouth where the doctors had filled the opening that in most people was solid bone. Whenever he was extremely nervous, he could feel the soft tissue vibrate when he spoke. The speech therapist, a young woman with caring eyes, had told him to look beyond such sensations and focus on the people he wanted to reach with his words. She had spent as much time building his confidence as she had working on his speech. Her whole demeanor had changed when she talked about taking control of his destiny, doing the most with what he had, rising above his difficulties, *using* them. She had challenged him in ways that no one else ever had. Certainly not his parents, who accepted their humble station with quiet resignation.

He was brought back to the present by the ringing of his cell-phone. "This is Trent."

"I'm here," the voice said.

Trent released the frenzied tension with a tight sigh. "You're late."

"I'm at the door. And I've got the goods. That's what matters most, right?"

"Five minutes." Trent cut the connection, left the stockroom, and forced himself not to race down the hall. He passed through the reception area and approached the younger of Barry Mundrose's two assistants.

Gayle finished her phone conversation and smiled at him, offering a professional friendliness that meant nothing. The woman was utterly beautiful . . . and cold as glacial ice. "Mr. Cooper, how are you this morning?"

"Scared to death." He was also so excited his heart was racing faster than a hummingbird's wings. "And totally committed."

She nodded gravely. "That is probably a healthy attitude to take."

"I need the money."

"And I have it for you." She turned to the credenza imbedded in the wall behind her desk. The central door revealed an electronic safe. She applied her thumb to the fingerprint reader, then coded in the access. "How much this time?"

"Twenty thousand."

She counted out the bills, put them in a blank envelope, then wrote the amount in her pay book. "Sign, please."

As he did so, he was in close enough to say without being over-heard, "Thank you for not making this harder than it already is."

"Mr. Mundrose has always approved of spending money to make more money. Emphasis on the word *more*."

"Understood."

"And you still won't tell me what you are using this money for."

"If you insist, I will. But secrecy is vital. So I've made a careful accounting of every cent, and as soon as this presentation is done, I'll give you the full breakdown."

"Very well, Mr. Cooper. But sooner or later, you will have to learn the lesson of trust. That is, if you survive long enough."

He breathed the day's first easy breath. "Thank you. Again."

But she was not done. "You already have spent four hundred and thirty-seven thousand dollars. That is not the most expensive outlay of anyone who has been granted such an opportunity. But it's close."

He finished the thought for her. "Either this works, or there won't be enough of me left to make a greasy stain."

She gave him her brightest smile. "So nice to know we understand each other."

Trent picked up the manila packet and took the elevator to the ground floor. The entrance to Barry Mundrose's suite of offices was around the corner from the building's main doors. The security guard standing duty in the small foyer knew him now, and hefted the box Trent had left with him that morning. The guard's flat gaze said it all. Trent was just another desperate young executive. They came, they went. Very few stayed around long enough for the guard to even learn their names.

Trent's contact stood in front of the building's main entrance, doing a tight little two-step in time to music in his head. Overhead the sky was slate grey, so the guy's sunglasses were out of place. But Trent didn't need to see the guy's pupils to know he was in low-altitude orbit.

In another era, the guy would have been called a trendsetter. They came in all shapes and sizes. Most of them were hopeless cynics who had no talent for actual creativity. So they clawed down the artists who threatened their space, and lifted up those who in turn lifted them. They were a disparaging, pessimistic bunch, whose humor dripped with venom. They loved nothing more than the quick line that destroyed a dream, a life. But Trent was not here because he liked the guy.

Beyond them, Times Square was filling up. The people were mostly young, and they chattered with an animated electricity that Trent could feel in his gut. Most of these new arrivals were dressed as vampires, werewolves, ghouls, and a bizarre mix of all three. It said a great deal about Times Square that few people even gave these newcomers a second glance. Trent wanted to gawk and smile and go race over and talk with them. Because their presence meant the first part of his plan was in place. But only the first part. And just then he had to play the hard guy in order to make this trendie understand that his job was not done. Not by a long shot.

The trendie was dressed like a depraved yuppie vampire—skin-tight black jeans and pointy-toed loafers and a starched dress shirt, with a black cloak connected by what appeared to be a solid gold chain, and bloodstains dripping from the corner of his mouth. "Well. You certainly took your time getting here," the guy said, sounding like he had his nose pinched.

"You took the words right out of my mouth." Trent passed over the box. "Forty top-of-the-line digital mini-recorders, as promised."

"There's no way they will give these back."

"All I want are the memory chips," Trent assured him. "And some really solid footage."

"They understand, and they'll deliver."

"They better, for your sake." He passed over the envelope. "Twenty thousand."

Disdain fought with greed on the trendie's wasted young features. He accepted the cash with two bony fingers. "Really, here on the street, how *gauche*." His tone dripped with cynicism.

"There's another twenty for you this afternoon."

The trendie stopped in the process of opening the envelope. "Say again."

"I know you expected me to argue over the cost. Or at least insist on paying only part until after you delivered. But the cost is not as important as the results. I need you to do what you said, and I need you to *be on time*. You will have three minutes' notice. No more. Get it right, and your payout is doubled. Tell me you understand."

Something in Trent's expression stifled both the disparaging quip and the nasal inflection. "I read you loud and clear."

"Do this right, and you can count on me for a regular assignment."

Trent turned and went back around the corner. He meant what he had said. He desperately needed someone who could help set audience trends, and who would be loyal to Trent personally. Barry Mundrose had a personal cadre of his own trendies, but Trent could not afford the risk of one of them running to their boss with word of what he had planned. He had not even used Barry's in-house headhunter to find his own trendie. Trent had paid an outside agency five thousand dollars to track the guy down. Then he had given him just twelve hours to deliver.

But it was all worth it. If he succeeded.

His entire project depended upon delivering a complete and utter *shock* to the corporate system.

Trent reentered the side doors, nodded to the security guard, punched the button, and stepped into the elevator. He checked his watch, and instantly was flooded with an adrenaline rush. He was not afraid anymore. His heart hammered so fast he heard the blood sing in his ears. There simply wasn't room for fear.

He checked his watch another time. The hands looked frozen.

Thirty minutes and counting.

7

"You led the people whom you redeemed . . ."

NEW YORK CITY

The man's name was Yussuf Alwan, from Damascus. "In Syria, before the civil war, I was a doctor. A surgeon. When the fighting reached my city, I escaped with my family to Beirut. My brother, he runs a business there. My wife and two daughters, they are safe, thanks be to God. I train at the NYU hospital for my certification. When this is done, my family, they will join me."

Ruth Barrett was smaller in person than John would have expected. But beneath the grandmotherly smile and kindly gaze, he suspected was a core of tungsten steel. She asked Yussuf, "And you are a believer?"

"Since time beyond time, yes, madame. The legend of my family is that we were in Damascus when the apostle Paul himself came and recovered his sight and spoke the words of salvation." Yussuf was balding and portly, probably in his forties, and he once might have been quite handsome. But the strain of a homeland torn apart by war was evident in his features and his gaze. "For many in Syria, faith is a tradition, you understand? It is heritage."

"Not a living faith?" Ruth responded.

"Yes, is so. But my family, we were part of the home-church movement. You have heard of this, perhaps? Missionaries come from the west. They speak of renewal. Of fellowship with all people. Sunni, Shia, Alawite, all united under the banner of Jesus." He stared out the window, at the crowds milling about Times Square. "And now I am here in this place."

Since he had brought these folks together, now John had resumed the role he felt most comfortable with, which was as a silent observer. A man as big as he was could not easily disappear in plain sight. But he tried.

Or rather, he would have. But his wife had other ideas. Heather kept shooting him looks, and when that didn't work, she finally said, "John, dear, what are you waiting for?"

Which meant he really had no choice but to clear his throat, and lay it out. The voice in the sanctuary. The trip to the Lake Erie jail, wondering if that was all there was to it. Then the call to come to New York. And the weight he had felt on his mind and heart ever since arriving here.

When he was done, Jenny Linn shifted in her chair and related her own tale. She described the incredible peace she had made with her father, the trip, the conversation with her parents that morning. Then Alisha related her own experience, the voice in church, the visit with her sister. How her work selling radio advertising brought her up here to the company's home office every other month. But how her morning's meetings had all been canceled. Which was why she was sitting here.

Then Ruth Barrett described the sense of God having been there in her little study that past Sunday morning, waiting for her to arrive, impatient for her to *listen*. So she had done as she felt called, and come to New York to visit the daughter who had walked away from her faith, and now lived out of wedlock with a young man Ruth refused to even name. And who was not the father of either of her daughter's children.

Then Yussuf spoke again, relating how the previous Sabbath marked the end of a surgical rotation in trauma care, how the gunshot wounds had brought back all the violence and hardship of his homeland, how he had gone to church seeking only to escape, and instead had found God waiting for him. When he finished, it was Heather who asked, "Did you feel called by God to do something?"

Yussuf's head jerked in a tight spasm. "No. No call."

"I don't mean to pry." Heather hesitated, then went on, "But the others here felt God telling them to make some unwanted turning."

"No, is not a turning." Yussuf refused to meet her gaze.

Heather leaned back, watching her husband.

John asked, "Why are you here in this hotel, Yussuf?"

The Arab did not reply.

"Did you come here because you felt called to do—?"

"Is impossible, this thing, what God wants." His forehead was beaded with perspiration. "No man can see what I have seen, and now do this."

John waited, and when no one else spoke, he said, "What if I went with you?"

"You do not know what you are saying."

"I know God's power has been upon us all," John said. "What if the reason we're all here is to offer you his strength in human form?"

His dark eyes scattered tension around the table. "You do not know me."

Alisha replied, "We all know Jesus."

Ruth said, "Tell us how we can help."

The letter was tattered evidence of war's calamity. The single sheet, stained and yellowed, shook in Yussuf's hand like a tragic leaf. The others gathered about him downstairs as he waited by the entrance to the banqueting department. The kitchens were off the small, windowless conference rooms that served as spillovers from the larger chambers upstairs. The padded doors were shut, the corridor empty.

"This is a terrible thing," Yussuf said.

Ruth Barrett said, "You are right, of course. It is impossible. We can't be doing this."

Yussuf glanced over. "You are making joke?"

"No, my brother. I am agreeing with you. Your fears and your anger are not just real, they are justified. But you know you have to do this."

The placid features drew together in real pain. "But why?"

"Because God is using these acts. I did not understand it until I listened to each of us. We are gathered here with our deeds as living testimony to the power of God. Only he can bring hope to such impossible circumstances." She spoke with the calm of a woman whose entire life had been centered upon worshiping that same one of whom she now spoke with such assurance. "Now let us join hands and pray one more time."

The story had been told in the jumbled style of a man who had sought to blind himself from the memory. Yussuf had been working in his clinic, which served as a day surgery for the northern districts of Damascus, Syria's capital. They were seeing more and more gunshot wounds as the civil war continued to escalate and draw ever closer to their city. Treatment centers like his had become increasingly sectarian. The hospitals in the Sunni districts only treated Sunni, and so forth. Yussuf's clinic stood upon the main highway dividing the Alawite section from the Christian. He treated everyone.

That day, a gunman had burst into the clinic, hunting an opponent who was also Yussuf's patient. He had shot the injured man, then turned his gun upon the three members of Yussuf's staff who tried to stop him. One of them had been Yussuf's sister.

This letter he now held had traveled to Damascus, then overland to Beirut, where his wife had wept over the words and sent it on to him in New York. How the gunman had escaped to New York, where he worked in the kitchen of the hotel on Times Square. He had found Jesus, and he had written the doctor to ask his forgiveness.

Which Yussuf could not give. "My sister's children, they grow up without a mother." He wept openly now. "My daughter, she was named for her. My sister was not even meant to be working that day. She came because I was shorthanded. I murdered her. My own flesh and blood."

Ruth and John and Heather and Jenny and Alisha, they all stood about him. Their hands rested upon him and upon the shoulders of each other. Bound together in concern for a man who had been a stranger until only minutes ago. John said, "Ask Jesus what you should do."

"I cannot," he wept. "I cannot do this thing."

Then the padded doors leading to the kitchen swung open. Not one man emerged, but three. All were Arabs. Two wore silver crosses about their necks, and supported the man in the middle, who wept harder than Yussuf. When the man in the center saw the surgeon, he collapsed, falling to his knees and gripping the doctor by the legs.

Hard as it was, painful as it felt even to him, John had the distinct impression that it was also one of the most beautiful moments of his entire life. Watching the doctor reach out his hands, lift the man from the carpet, and embrace him.

Afterwards Yussuf accepted their invitation and returned to the table by the windows. Yussuf knew he probably should acknowledge the gift they had granted him, but just then he felt utterly undone by the experience by the kitchen.

The others looked exactly like he felt, their features slack and their limbs nearly motionless. They reminded Yussuf of patients who had crowded his waiting room following the first few attacks.

After the Syrian civil war had brewed for a time, people grew a thicker skin, a frightening tolerance, especially the children. Yussuf had found it incredible how fast children adapted to new circumstances, even civil war. It was why he had left behind his beloved homeland, abandoning his people in their hour of need. He had felt he had no choice, after hearing his youngest daughter giggle over her dolls while they hid in the bomb shelter one night. People could adapt to anything. But the first assaults were still emotionally traumatizing. That was what he saw among those sharing the two small tables. People trying to make sense out of the impossible emotions and events.

What made the strongest impact was seeing the invisible hand of God made real. The power of love, the gift of hope they had all witnessed, was as strong as a physical onslaught. They sat and watched silently as the waiter from downstairs, the same Syrian Alawite who had murdered Yussuf's sister, laid out a feast. His name was Mahmut, and he continued to shed tears as he and the two Arab pastors unloaded the trolley. They left glasses and water pitchers and a coffee service on the second trolley, there for anyone who wished to help themselves. Mahmut was following an Alawite tradition, old as the Syrian hills, whereby a penitent offered a feast to those he had wronged. It was part of the formal act of apology, seeking to lighten the hand that held the rod or the blade.

Yussuf backed from the tables without turning away. Had he turned his back on the gift of food, Mahmut would rightly have seen this as rejection. So Yussuf moved away just far enough for his words to be masked by the lobby's tumult, and brought out his phone.

The number he dialed was answered on the first ring. The voice demanded, "Did you do it?"

"With the help of friends."

"What? You let others be there and told me to stay away? How is this possible?"

"I only met them here. You are my friend, my prayer partner—"

"I do not understand."

"No. Which is why you need to come and witness this for yourself. How soon can you arrive?"

"Soon. I am in a café across the square."

Yussuf spun about, then remembered himself and turned back to face the table while he said into his phone, "Can this be true?"

"I wanted to be near in case you needed my help."

"We are at the back of the lobby, in the alcove overlooking the square."

"Five minutes, perhaps a bit longer. The square is jammed, and the police are out in force."

Yussuf cut the connection just as Mahmut finished laying out the meal. Mahmut stood by the tables, back to the windows, hands clasped in front of him, his head bowed. His tear-streaked face drew stares from across the lobby. Twice the pastors had to step away and stop some manager from intervening.

"I thank you," Yussuf finally said.

"How may I be of further service?" came from Mahmut.

"There is nothing I require, brother."

"There must be something."

The words were a formality, spoken in Arabic, which made them even more powerful as far as Yussuf was concerned. "I would appreciate your prayers."

The Alawite sect contained a rigid caste structure, one that trapped its members from the moment they took their first breath. To have a Christian whom he had wronged request a spiritual boon was, well, unthinkable. Mahmut stared at him, but it was unlikely he saw anything through his tears. "You would let me do this thing?"

"I would treat it as an honor. Pray for me, for my friends here, for our mission."

"What mission is this, may one ask?"

"I do not know." Yussuf could see that Mahmut did not believe him. So he continued, "We have been drawn together by God's hand. We did not know one another until just before I met you. If they had not found me here, I would not have had the strength to come downstairs."

"Then I am in their debt as well."

Yussuf said in English, "Mahmut thanks you for the role you played, the strength you granted me."

Ruth Barrett asked, "Are you and your friends able to join us?"

The two pastors lay open palms upon their hearts and backed away. Mahmut said, "I must return to my duties. Please excuse me."

"Wait." Yussuf took a pad and pen, and wrote down his cell-phone and email address. "Contact me. I will tell you what this mission proves to be."

Mahmut stared at the paper as though it was his manumission. "I am your humble servant."

When they embraced a final time, Yussuf found himself becoming unbelievably calm. His heart beat at the slow pace of a funeral drum. So many burdens rested upon his people. So many wounds no human hand could heal. "Thank you for writing to me, Mahmut," he said. "Go in peace."

8

"In our union . . ."

NEW YORK CITY

Trent shifted to the sofa in the corner of Barry's outer office. In the space of twenty-five minutes, three different teams passed by the secretaries' desks. There were nineteen in all, eight women and eleven men. Most were in their late twenties and early thirties. They carried computers and tablets and easels and rolled plastic displays and flat artist valises crammed with exhibits. None of them were inside for more than eight minutes.

He sat there, motionless. Waiting. There was nothing more he could do. He was one inch from being nothing more than the last guy to try and fail.

Or succeed. Maybe.

When the third team was ushered out, Gayle came over and said, "You're up, Mr. Cooper."

He rose on unsteady legs and walked to the closed double doors. But as Gayle started to open the door, he said, "You're clear on the task and the timing?" He was entering the conference room the same way he had the first time, empty-handed, without notes or tablet. Gayle's eyebrows raised, but the only thing she said was, "I would have hoped that by now you would know I am both a pro, and trustworthy, Mr. Cooper."

"Call both numbers immediately. Tell the first person, three minutes. The second, five minutes."

"Duly noted." Before she shut the door, she murmured, "Good luck."

The simple gesture should not have meant as much as it did. Trent walked unescorted to the head of the table. Today, the conference room was jammed. Each of the division chiefs was joined by two aides—standard format, Trent now knew. They called such larger meetings the action board. They were not there merely to decide. Whenever an idea was approved, it was also set in motion. Budgets granted, targets set. Future careers set in place.

Or destroyed.

He had less than ten minutes to prove himself.

"All right, Cooper." Barry Mundrose was again flanked by his daughter and, this time, the head of his film division. The son was back in Canada. Trent had no idea whether that was a good thing or not. "You've got the floor."

Trent began, "The fastest growing profit center within the entertainment industry is dystopia. This is the term collectively used for a phenomenon that includes a myriad of directions. But it all is based upon one core concept. The Generation Xers and the Millennials fundamentally disagree with the assumption that tomorrow is a better day. They reject the notion that the future holds greater promise. Today's youth reject these concepts. They are scorned as myths belonging to a different era."

The younger executives who crowded the space between the table and the walls were trained in the same blank expressions as the directors who lined the table's opposite end. But there were no smirks, no whispered asides. They sat and they listened. Trent took that as a good sign. He heard the clock ticking in his head, and hurried on.

"Dystopia, the opposite of utopia, is a word drawn from this grim forecast. Our two target generations see the future as bleak. There aren't enough jobs. The world is dying. The environment won't be saved. There aren't answers to all the problems. Wars are growing worse, peace is a myth, politicians are liars. This trend is playing out in entertainment. The current zombie and vampire series are perfect examples of dystopian trends.

"But our goal today is not to identify what has worked in the past. Our aim is to establish a *new* trend. One that *we* own. We create it, we build upon it, and most important of all, we profit from it."

A growing din outside the window rose in volume to filter through the triple panes of heat-hardened glass. The diaphanous blinds were down, blocking out the grey daylight and the flickering advertising screens around Times Square. Trent pulled an electronic control from his pocket and drew back the curtains. "What we want is a theme that echoes what these generations already feel but have not yet put into words. It must grow organically from their impressions of the world. It must give voice to their hidden secrets."

Barry Mundrose shifted impatiently. "We've got that. So tell us what this new theme is."

"I'll do better than that," Trent replied. "I will *show* you."

As if on cue, the square below erupted. The clamor lifted the entire executive board from their seats. They gaped at the mob spilling off the sidewalks and pouring into the streets.

Today's crowd was huge. Twenty thousand, thirty, forty—the numbers no longer mattered. They were every color, every race. Most wore some concoction of mask and mascara, creating a bizarre array of ghouls and vampires and werewolves and ogres and aliens. Their actions were so frantic and illogical they looked insane, borderline violent. The police whistles were joined by a massive mash-up from drums and wind instruments of every conceivable variety.

The crowd waved thousands of identical signs and banners. The sea of waving placards all carried the same three words:

Hope Is Dead.

And at that instant, the electric signs surrounding Time Square all went blank.

The sight was shocking. The brilliant displays were so constant, most scarcely saw them at all. Until now, that is, when they were absolutely black.

And then in unison they all flashed up the same three silver words, emblazoned upon screens of midnight blue.

Hope Is Dead.

The crowd went completely and utterly berserk. They broke free of the guard rails, flying into the traffic, clambering upon the roofs of cars and trucks, dancing with a dark glee that was just one step away from rage.

The police and the cars and the other pedestrians froze in shock, totally engulfed within a scene of bedlam. By now the whole conference room was fastened against the panes, as frozen as the spectators below.

Four hundred thousand dollars had bought Trent ten minutes and a promise that it would happen upon his command.

Trent pulled his gaze from the scene he had created and glanced at the others around and behind him. All of them, including their boss, were locked on the thousands and thousands of ghouls linked in jubilant frenzy.

Then another gaze pulled away. The daughter of Barry Mundrose backed up slightly, so she could look down the length of the boardroom. Edlyn's green eyes were as hard as emeralds, but Trent thought he saw a hint of something else there. An electric current that shot down the room, and set his body vibrating. Then she turned back to the window.

Beyond the glass, the crowd began shouting the words and dancing in time, until the entire square was filled with the ragged chant roared from thirty thousand throats.

Hope Is Dead.

9

"Come near to God . . ."

NEW YORK CITY

Alisha sat by the hotel lobby window and cradled the phone in her lap. She wasn't dreading this call. Not really. It was all so far beyond what she wanted and how she thought, such things as pride really didn't matter anymore. Well, it did. She was still human, after all. But what she had just witnessed downstairs was so big, her heart was so full, she just had to put all that pride aside. Even when it hurt. Because it did. This was *her* choir. And it was a lot more besides. Alisha could see her reflection in the phone's darkened screen. She studied her round features and strong determined gaze. And she also saw the hurt. The choir was her way of making things right with the world. And doing it her way.

As she punched the numbers, the phone seemed alive in her hands. When the pastor's wife answered, Alisha said, "Hello, Celeste. Do you have a minute?"

"Of course I do." Her tone hardened a notch. Alisha heard it because she had been hearing it ever since the woman had arrived at church with her husband. "Where are you at, Alisha?"

"Still in New York."

"People have been asking about you, what with the event this weekend. How much longer does this meeting last?"

"Another day and a half." Alisha rose from her chair and faced out the window. Down below scurried people from all over the world. Rushing around, caught up in making their plans happen. She wished God had taken the time to actually speak to her. Just lay it out in black-and-white. But the divine silence didn't change anything. "I just saw a miracle."

"You what?"

"A real one. The hand of God and everything. And it showed me clear as day—" She took a big breath, like the one she had needed before ringing her sister's front bell. And in that moment, she knew what she was doing was right. Being difficult didn't change a thing. "Those children of yours are going to sing."

There was a long pause, then Celeste said, "Who is this I'm talking with?"

"I mean it, Celeste." As soon as she said it, she felt the lifting of a weight she hadn't even realized she carried. And with it also came the realization. "You need to bring the regular choir together with those kids. Tonight."

"Now I must be dreaming."

"You know I'm right. I've never even met your children. But how long have you sung with our people?"

"Since two days after Terry and I arrived in Baltimore."

"There you go. So you get the choir together and you train them with the children. If anybody asks, you tell them I said this was how it has to be."

"What about the Kennedy Center gala?"

"What about it?"

"You mean . . . you want me . . ."

"Girl, how can I lead fifty kids I don't know and who don't know me?"

"But you'll be back in two days. There's still time for you to rehearse them yourself."

"Maybe I'll be back," Alisha corrected.

"Sister, what is going on up there?"

"I told you. A miracle."

"Wait, now. I've got to sit down. All right. You mean it, what you're saying?"

"You think I'd talk like this if I didn't?"

"Terry's been going on for two weeks now, saying God was going to make all this right. And I've done nothing but show him the sharp end of my tongue. Now I've got to go in there and tell him he was right all along."

Alisha saw her smile flash in the window's reflection. "It's hard, isn't it?"

"Girl, it's just awful."

"I have to go."

"Alisha, wait. You'll still be singing with us, won't you?"

"That's in God's hands."

Alisha returned to the table and waited for the others to start in on all that fine food left by the Syrian and those Arab pastors. But nobody made any move. She started to say something, when the famous lady seated next to her said, "Let's bless this food and this moment."

Amen, Alisha wanted to say. But something kept her silent. Which was as strange as how she didn't feel all that hungry. She hadn't eaten breakfast, nothing but a coffee, not even a roll. First time since the church had fasted before the last revival she'd skipped her morning meal. She was hungry, and she wasn't. She wanted to talk, and she wanted to stay silent. She was conflicted, plain and simple. And she was burdened.

She took a plate from Ruth Barrett's own hand, and let the lady spoon her out some of this and that. She'd eaten most of those things before. Mediterranean food, like what they ate in the Holy Land. She'd always wanted to go there, and had tried the food a number of times. The flavors were different and beautiful. Only today, as she put the first bite in her mouth, she didn't taste a thing.

She couldn't remember the last time she'd had such fine food set in front of her, and she couldn't eat. Alisha set her plate down on the trolley behind her chair.

Ruth asked, "You're not hungry, dear?"

"No, and I don't understand it either."

She handed Alisha her own plate. "Put mine over there with yours, please."

"Maybe it's everything we've been through here."

"Perhaps. But I feel . . ."

Alisha nodded. She felt it too. Something she could not put her finger on. But it was there just the same. "Burdened."

"I should be celebrating," Ruth said. "I've just witnessed a miracle."

Alisha looked at her. The woman was beautiful in a way that wasn't touched by years. "I can't believe I'm sitting here, talking with you like I was somebody."

"Dear, I'm just another sinner, who's learned where other sinners can find bread."

Alisha was going to respond but was interrupted by another astonishment. Yussuf, the Syrian doctor, had remained standing after the waiter and his pastor friends left. He waved and beckoned, then embraced a slender, smiling man. And the day became just a bit more astonishing, for the slender young man was wearing a yarmulke.

Yussuf turned to the tables and announced, "This is my friend and prayer partner, Dr. Aaron Silva."

The bearded young man had a lively, cheerful voice. "What have I missed, and why did I miss it?"

Whatever had impacted the others and left them without appetite, it certainly did not affect the newcomer. He settled into the chair next to Alisha and reached for a plate. "This looks splendid. Who should I thank for the feast?"

"Mahmut," Yussuf replied, seating himself on the table's other side.

"Who is Mahmut?"

"The man I came to see."

"Mahmut? He did this?"

"It is a tradition among the Alawites," Yussuf explained. "An act of contrition."

"So. There is indeed a goodness to be found everywhere." Aaron picked up a stuffed grape leaf. "This is delicious."

Yussuf said to the group, "Aaron is an intern at the same hospital as me."

Ruth asked in a voice that was remarkably gentle, "You are a follower of Jesus?"

"I am indeed." Aaron cocked his head. "Do I know you from somewhere?"

"This is Ruth Barrett," Yussuf said.

"Astonishing. And you just met here?" Aaron wiped his fingers on a napkin, then stretched his hand out in front of Alisha. "An honor, Mrs. Barrett."

"Call me Ruth, please."

Alisha resisted the urge to back further away from the exchange. She glanced from the diminutive older woman on her left to the bony young man on her other side, and thought, *They got to stick me between the skinniest two.*

Aaron glanced around the table. "Why is no one else eating?"

Heather said, "I was just thinking the very same thing."

But no one else made a move toward the food. Alisha studied the faces around the table, and thought of an expression from her childhood. *Rainbow nation.* Back then, it was meant to represent a change from the white-dominated halls of power. Making room for African-Americans and other races in every profession. But this was something else entirely. Alisha nodded slowly. *The rainbow nation of God's children.*

Ruth asked, "What is it?"

She started to reply, but was halted by a sudden sensation, similar to the experience she had known in the Sabbath worship. A compression of the very air surrounding her. And yet different, because right here and now, she felt none of the joy. Instead, the burden of sorrow only grew heavier.

"Alisha?"

Alisha studied the faces around their tables. Folks who had been total strangers before this day were bound to her now. John and Ruth and Jenny and Yussuf. They all showed the very same strain as she felt. She said, "We're sad for a reason."

"I woke up feeling wretched, and it's just grown worse ever since," John Jacobs agreed. He was a man who clearly preferred to hang back. Alisha had known men like that all her life. The ones who often married the noisiest women. She had hoped she might one day find a man like that for herself.

His wife asked, "Are you ill?"

"No, it's not like that. What Alisha said makes all the sense in the world."

Jenny said, "I've been crying all morning. I never cry."

Ruth said, "My heart feels like it weighs a ton."

Alisha nodded agreement. "One ounce heavier and mine would fall out of my chest and go right through the floor."

Yussuf said, "I thought it was just me. And everything that just happened."

"It's not just you," Alisha said. "And it's not because of Mahmut."

They were all watching her now. John Jacobs asked, "What's going on?"

Usually the only place where Alisha liked being the center of attention was at church. Never in front of strangers. But none of that mattered here. She said, "We're feeling God's heart."

Jenny Linn sighed, like she had been released from some chain. "You're right."

"That's exactly it." John looked at her like he was sharing his darkest secret. "It's been staring me in the face, and I didn't see it."

"All morning I have been looking for reasons to be sad," Ruth said. "What a selfish and self-centered person I've turned out to be."

"We've all been blind," Jenny said.

"God is sharing his heart with us," Alisha said. The words came out unbidden. But she knew she was right, and she knew she had to speak out. "He's doing it for a reason."

Ruth reached over and took her hand. "What is his purpose?"

Alisha looked down at the slender white fingers intertwined with her own. If Celeste could see her now. Sitting here in a New York hotel lobby, holding hands with Ruth Barrett. "I expect we'll find out soon enough."

John could see the others were now more comfortable with the wait. They did not understand the purpose, but he felt they all shared a sense that the divine hand had brought them together for . . . something. John studied Alisha, the woman seated across the table from him. The change in his vision was staggering. Before, she had been a big woman, very big, and very reserved. He could tell she was not comfortable here, the only African American in the group. But that was before. Now, she was . . .

He breathed the words. Not speaking them. But wanted to shape them just the same. She was their sister.

Suddenly John felt hungry. He picked up a plate and began spooning food onto it. The others started doing the same, even

Jenny Linn, who looked like she didn't eat anything at all. Ruth asked Alisha for her plate back, then leaned forward and said to the guy in the skullcap, "How did you and Yussuf become friends?"

It was Yussuf who answered. "I had just arrived in America. I was introduced to a church by two nurses at the teaching hospital. They told me of another doctor who was also attending. As soon as I heard of this one, I felt God's hand on me, and said I would like to meet him."

Alisha watched as Aaron loaded his plate up for the third time. Or perhaps it was the fourth. She said, "You always eat this much?"

"Aaron is a medical marvel," Yussuf replied. "The man can eat a whole cow at one sitting, and not gain an ounce."

"I've done my best not to ever hate another human being," Alisha murmured, eyebrow cocked.

"When my friend breathes his last," Yussuf went on, "we are going to open him up and discover a small nuclear reactor."

Ruth asked, "How did you come to know Jesus?"

"I was not looking for him, I can tell you that." Aaron set down his fork with genuine reluctance. He made a fastidious process of wiping his fingers and then his mouth and beard. As though the tale required a singular purpose. "I had a patient. Severe melanoma, spread all through her body. She accepted the news with a peace that shattered me. I had entered medicine because I was a fighter. This woman shamed me with her bravery. So I decided to read the Christian Bible. See what it was about this myth that could blind a woman to the enemy we call death."

Yussuf was smiling. "Tell her how far you got."

"Three chapters into Mark." Aaron smiled back. It was clearly an old joke between them.

"His first gospel," Yussuf said.

"Six pages," Aaron agreed. "The very first night."

"Clearly Jesus felt my friend needed help understanding what he was reading."

"He was there in the room," Aaron said. "Me. The scientific mind. Born with a microscope in my hand."

"Talking with an invisible friend," Yussuf said.

"Out loud, no less," Aaron said. "On my knees."

"Tell them what happened when you read the book of Acts," Yussuf said.

"When I read what happened to Paul on the Damascus Road, I told Jesus, 'Thank you for not turning me blind.' I was working thirty-six-hour shifts at the hospital just then. Blindness would have been difficult to explain."

Ruth was the only one who did not smile. "How did your family take the news?"

Aaron used bony fingers to comb his scraggly beard. "Not at all well."

"They shunned him," Yussuf said, his gaze impossibly deep. "They said the prayer, what is it called?"

"Kaddish," Aaron said, still stroking his beard.

"The prayer for the dead," Yussuf said. "For a son. Because he knows Jesus, they do this thing."

Ruth reached across Alisha to grasp Aaron's shoulder. "I will pray for them to have a change of heart."

John found his chest pinch at the sight of Alisha also reaching over and setting her own hand on the man's shoulder. "Let's all do that right now," Alisha agreed.

They joined hands, balancing plates on their knees, touching people who a few hours earlier had been total strangers, bound together now by a need to share another's burden. When they were finished, it seemed to John that everyone was reluctant to let go.

Then Jenny, looking perplexed, rose from her chair and said, "Something is happening."

One by one they were all drawn over to the windows. The glass ran almost floor-to-ceiling, great slabs so thick the traffic noise was reduced to a soft murmur. But something out there was making such a din John could hear it clearly, shouts and whistles and what sounded like a foghorn. He touched the window and felt it vibrate against his fingers. Times Square was one huge, heaving mob.

Ruth said, "What are they wearing?"

"Costumes," Jenny said, her face pressed against the glass. "Vampires and the like are very popular these days."

"Looks like a club or something," John said. Indeed, it seemed as though virtually all the people he could see wore the outrageous get-ups. And they waved hundreds of signs. Thousands. But they were so jammed together and they moved their banners with such frantic motions, he could not read the words. Then suddenly—

Alisha had moved up beside him. She said, "This is it."

John nodded. He felt the same way.

"I do not understand," Yussuf said.

"Hope is dead," Jenny said.

Ruth asked, "What did you say?"

"It's what the signs all say. I know this, it's a mass of people connected by cellphone and iPads. They secretly plan these huge gatherings, and when they all show up at the arranged time, somebody has a dump truck full of banners."

The mob possessed a manic quality as they danced and writhed and screamed. The scene reminded John of his one time in New Orleans during Mardi Gras. He had been there for a convention, and friends had insisted they go check out the action. John had felt exactly as he did now. Utterly excluded, like a face of humanity had been revealed in which he wanted no part. Back then, he had run down an empty street, flagged a taxi, and gone back to his hotel. Today, however, he finally understood why God felt so sad.

"'Hope is dead'?" Ruth asked. "Why are they doing this?"

Alisha said, "Those poor people. Can't they—?"

And all the electronic billboards surrounding Times Square went blank.

The sudden absence of lights was so shocking, it silenced even the mob. The police also stopped their whistles and looked around, fear evident on many faces, as though waiting for some bomb to go off.

Looking back, John often thought that was exactly what happened next.

At once, all the neon signs flashed back on, this time showing the same electric blue background, the huge silver letters shouting at them from every direction, every angle.

Hope Is Dead.

The crowd went wild.

DAY
FIVE

10

"... minds set on what that nature desires ..."

Trent Cooper had slept a grand total of nine hours over the past four nights. And he did not care. Sleep was for creeps. Sleep was for the audience. Sleep was for people who weren't traveling in a Bentley. To Teterboro Airport. Where he was going to climb aboard a private jet and fly to Hollywood. Who needed sleep?

"What are you smiling at?"

Trent glanced at Edlyn Mundrose, flying with him to LA. Or perhaps it was the other way around. He really didn't care. "Everything."

She pulled another file from the briefcase open between them. "You need to buy some new clothes."

"No time." He really didn't mind her coldness. Or her cryptic way of measuring each word like gold. "Less money."

"Gayle."

"Yes, Ms. Mundrose."

"Give him the envelope."

The lovely secretary from Barry Mundrose's office was riding in the front passenger seat. She turned around far enough to hand Trent a manila folder. "Sign, please."

He accepted the file, opened it, and found himself looking at a check for one year's salary. He read, "Eighty-two thousand, four hundred and seven dollars."

Edlyn said, "We are closing out your current contract, Mr. Cooper. The page attached to the check is your termination agreement."

When he had first been offered the job, Trent had been astonished at the precise salary offer. It could not be divided into monthly amounts that made sense, then or now. Not that Trent had complained. "I don't understand."

Barry Mundrose's daughter did not even bother to look up. "You are no longer an employee of the advertising division. Where you go, *if* you go *anywhere*, now depends upon you delivering."

He stared at a check that represented his entire annual salary, and more money than he had ever held in his life. "So this check . . ."

"Call it a golden parachute. Or maybe a signing bonus. It all depends." She gave him two seconds of those glacial eyes. "You copy?"

He signed the document, pocketed the check, and handed the file back to Gayle. "Absolutely."

"Good." She plucked out another folder. "So make time and buy some new threads."

He looked down at himself. He had dressed for the trip in his best jeans, black, and what he'd considered a nice enough jacket, tan. Freshly laundered dress shirt, pale blue striped. Polished loafers, even if they were a couple of years old. He had never given his clothes much attention. The whole dress-for-success attitude was so dated. Only now, as the Bentley pulled up by the gates leading to the private aviation terminal, he felt like a hobo knocking on a stranger's back door.

Gayle must have noticed his unease, because as Edlyn stepped out and strode impatiently away from the vehicle, Barry Mundrose's secretary said, "I think you look very nice."

He could have hugged her. "Thanks."

"Don't let Ms. Mundrose get to you."

"All bark and no bite, is that what you're saying?"

"Oh, no, not at all." She was very grave. "Edlyn's bite is highly poisonous."

The Bentley's driver hefted two Louis Vuitton cases from the trunk and followed Edlyn Mundrose inside. Trent was secretly relieved to see Gayle pull out a valise of her own. It meant she would be traveling with them. Even if she was there to serve Edlyn and not him, he liked the idea of having an ally on this first journey. Trent was fully aware that Gayle, if need be, would stand back and watch the corporate carnivores take him down. She had probably watched it happen any number of times. But she was the nicest person he had met inside the company's HQ, and it felt good to have her along. Great, in fact.

Of course, the fact that she was stunningly beautiful did not hurt at all.

They followed Barry Mundrose's daughter through the lobby and out the rear portal, where a pilot saluted Edlyn and took her cases from the driver. He smiled a brief welcome at Trent and Gayle, but his attention remained firmly upon Edlyn as they crossed the tarmac and climbed the stairway.

The Gulfstream was the most ostentatious demonstration of power that Trent could have imagined. It contained a kitchen, a fully equipped bar, a conference room, twelve reclining seats, three bunks, a bedroom, and a bathroom whose shower was walled with alabaster tiles. All the bathroom taps were gold plated.

They had settled into their seats and had taken off when a phone rang. Gayle answered with the ease of a woman well versed in private flight. She handed Trent the phone and said, "Stone Denning for you."

Stone Denning was one of the most powerful directors in Hollywood. He was a notorious figure who loved a good fight almost as much as he did a wild party. He had boxed in university and liked to invite his stars to go a few rounds. When on location he always staked out a nearby ring and traveled with several pairs of gloves. The lollipops who ran the entertainment shows loved him. Stone Denning was always good for a story.

"This is Trent Cooper."

"That means exactly what to me. Nothing."

Trent ran through several responses, and settled on, "Thank you for the call, Mr. Denning."

"Turn that jet around. I won't have another corporate weasel come waste my time."

"Not even a weasel who's bringing you ten million dollars in extra advertising?"

Silence. "Who are you, anyway?"

"I'm the guy who's traveling to LA to deliver a check."

"Nothing from Mundrose comes without strings."

"You're right there. I have the money and the proposition."

"Give it to me now."

"Can't do that, Mr. Denning. I need half an hour of face time."

"How many other weasels are with you?"

"Just one." On a hunch, he passed Edlyn the phone. "He wants a word."

Barry Mundrose's daughter did not even look up from the file in her lap. She just took the phone and said, "What." Edlyn listened for ten seconds, then broke in with, "Do what he tells you, Stone."

Trent took back the phone. "When and where, Mr. Denning?"

The director had grown sullen. "Bel Air Hotel bar. Six o'clock."

Trent did not confirm because the director had already hung up. He handed the phone back to Gayle, then turned to Edlyn and asked, "Ms. Mundrose, would you like to hear me repeat my mantra?"

She might have smiled. It was hard to tell, a quick flicker directed at the papers covering the table before her. "Sure. Why not."

"I owe you."

This time, Trent was certain she smiled.

11

". . . my whole being waits . . ."

WESTCHESTER COUNTY

Barrett Ministries was headquartered in the rolling hills of West chester County, about ninety minutes from New York City. The land had been bought back in the sixties, when most of the region had been horse country. Over the years, however, Westchester County's meadows had sprouted a new crop of mansions, and pickups had gradually been replaced by New York limos.

The feed stores were mostly gone, and what once had been farming villages now housed boutiques catering to the wealthy newcomers. The Barrett enclave remained a small exception to the rule, however. Their hundred and eighty acres filled a shallow valley with peace. The main structures contained a hotel, a conference center, a chapel built to hold seven hundred, an outside arena that could hold two thousand, and a sprawling network of offices and seminar rooms and broadcasting studios for both television and radio.

While they were still recovering from the Times Square spectacle, Ruth invited the entire group to travel back with her. She had not made a big deal of it, saying in her quietly emphatic way that they needed to gather and pray for guidance.

So John used his meeting as a test. His company was the nation's largest shipper of fresh produce, and John was assistant manager for the Midwest depot, a high-stress occupation if there ever was one. The company's fleet of four hundred and nineteen trucks, two-thirds of which were refrigerated, had to be accounted for on an hourly basis. Delays meant rotten produce and lost profits. Transport companies operated on hair-thin margins. Every fluctuation in gas prices, every storm, every problem with a driver or an engine, was cause for worry. Their company succeeded because they were reliable.

That morning, John entered the offices of the world's largest importer of foreign-grown produce and laid out all these facts, while his heart and mind remained filled with the emotions and images of a previous day. Twice he had to stop and clear his throat, as the recalled sensations threatened to overwhelm him. The managers heard him out, then being New Yorkers they tried to whittle him down. Normally John would have sweated bullets over such negotiations. But today he just couldn't be bothered. He told them the terms were the terms, rose to his feet, and thanked them for their time.

In the evening, his company's senior VP phoned with the news that the group had accepted the deal, and wanted him to personally supervise their operations. John asked for an extra week's vacation. The vice president pointed out that John's own manager was barely recovered, and a deputy from Baltimore was handling the depot. John thanked the man for the opportunity, asked him to reconsider about the vacation, and hung up. Then he simply waited. Either it happened or it didn't. Five minutes later, the VP called back and agreed.

John probably should have been amazed at how everyone was gathered downstairs in the lobby the next morning. Yussuf was there with Aaron, the two men having taken annual leave from the hospital. Alisha described how her company required all leave to be scheduled months in advance, but a friend had needed to shift her plans, and so here she was. Jenny Linn introduced her parents, and related how she had accepted the job offer from a New York publisher, and had ten days before she needed to report for work. They were still coming to terms with how natural it all seemed as the van drove them into Westchester County.

Even so, they were a subdued bunch that gathered on Ruth Barrett's front porch. The broad veranda overlooked a grassy vale of springtime green. Blooming dogwoods and cherry trees marked the long drive that meandered alongside the stream. A glade of oaks and maple lined the hill that hid the ministry complex. Traffic thundered softly from beyond the hills to John's right. Here there was sunlight and birdsong and a crisp breeze.

It was Jenny Linn who said what he was thinking. "We should do something."

"We are," Ruth said. A cane rested on the floor beside her padded rocker with its embroidered cushions. Something in the set of her mouth left John convinced she did not wish to discuss whatever ailment was afflicting her. "We are waiting on God."

But he wanted it known that he agreed with Jenny's sentiment. John pointed to the world beyond the valley. "Out there is a group aiming on robbing the world of hope. Stealing it away, like thieves in the night."

"And what precisely do you intend on doing?"

"Whatever it is we've been brought together to do," Jenny said.

"Which is exactly what we are doing." Ruth reached to the side table holding a pitcher of lemonade and untouched glasses. She took up a much-used Bible, opened it to Acts, and read words from the first chapter.

John nodded in time to the telling, about the final meeting between the disciples and Jesus. About Jesus telling them to wait there in Jerusalem. John could scarcely hold back until she was done to say, "I know all that. And I'm telling you, we need to go out there and *do* something."

"Ever since I got here," Alisha agreed, "I'm feeling uncomfortable in my own skin."

"Like electrodes were planted in my flesh," Yussuf agreed.

"Only days ago we were merely a few believers who listened to God and he brought us together." Ruth's chair made a gentle rhythm on the varnished floor as she rocked. "Three days ago, we were burdened by God's sorrow. Now we all share a need to go and *do*. I take this as a good sign. But it is not enough."

"We need to plan," John said.

She smiled at him, like she might at a well-intentioned but wayward child. "No, friend. We need to *wait*."

"I don't know if I can," John said.

"What if God is waiting for us to get out there and speak?" Alisha asked.

"I shouldn't be sitting here," Jenny agreed. "There's something he wants me to *do*."

Richard Linn opened his mouth, but then shut it and remained silent.

Ruth said, "Please tell us what you were thinking, I'm sorry, I don't remember your name."

"Richard. I, well . . ." He shot his daughter a worried look.

"Tell us, Daddy."

"I've spent too many hours doing just that. Telling, rather than listening."

Jenny smiled for the first time that day. Her mother sniffed softly as Jenny took hold of her father's hand. "Go ahead."

"It seems to me that unless you know where God wants you to go and what he wants you to say, you're just running on a wheel of your own making."

"Like Fred," Jenny said.

"I'm sorry, who?"

"My hamster when I was little."

Alisha harrumphed a laugh. "Girl, you haven't stopped being little yet."

Jenny seemed to like that. "Little-er, then."

Richard said, "My daughter would watch that little beast for hours."

"I liked to watch him run. His legs moved so fast they were a blur."

"And he still didn't go anywhere," Ruth said. She pointed to the Book in her lap. "The disciples were told to go to Jerusalem and wait. They gathered and they prayed. How hard it must have been for them to sit there, taking no action, while outside the world wanted them all dead."

Aaron startled them by speaking for the first time that day. "There should be twelve of you."

Alisha looked at him. "I been thinking the exact same thing."

"It's bothered me ever since we watched the Times Square mob," Aaron went on. "Twelve were called. But only you five showed up. Out there are seven more that God chose, but who didn't act."

"And now we're not being allowed to do just that," John groused. "Act."

Heather shook her head. "Climb down off your wheel, John. Ruth is right."

"I know she is. But it doesn't make it easy."

"Welcome to the upper room, friends." Ruth reached out both hands. "Now let's join in prayer and ask God to show us the way."

LOS ANGELES

When the jet landed at John Wayne airport in Burbank, two limos were pulled up on the tarmac. As the jet rolled over and the engines whined down, the drivers emerged and straightened their jackets. The pilot lowered the stairs and saluted his departing passengers.

Trent followed Edlyn Mundrose down the steps and watched as she slipped into the first limo. The driver collected her bags from the pilot, climbed in behind the wheel, and took off, leaving Gayle to travel with him. Edlyn never once looked their way.

The limo was an anonymous black Lincoln. Nice enough, but after a Bentley to the airport and a private Gulfstream ride across the continent, he would have at least expected to be met by a Caddy.

Gayle fielded three phone calls as they threaded their way along the LA concrete spaghetti. She spoke quietly with her hand cradling the receiver, and Trent felt no need to listen in. His own phone rang as they exited the I-405. The detective service he had hired confirmed that his requested files would be ready in an hour. As he closed his phone, Gayle said, "I suggest we shift our reservations to the Bel Air, since that's where Mr. Denning said we should meet. It will make a statement."

"Only if Stone Denning bothers to check."

"His people will make it their business to know."

Trent nodded as if it all made sense. Welcome to Hollywood.

He thought of other young men and women who had come before him, granted an instant in the corporate spotlight. The limos, the thousand-dollar hotel rooms, the access to the throne room. He wondered at the difference between those who had made it and those who were not even memories. He knew that most people granted this chance failed. He hoped he had what it took. He knew some of them mistakenly assumed that a glimpse of the high life meant they could claim it as their own. They padded their expense accounts with all the tight pleasures of that kind of living. He knew they flamed hard and went down harder. He also knew there was no chance of that happening to him. He had few friends, and none of them so close as to turn needy if and when success struck. He allowed himself pleasures on a carefully distilled basis. He had fought too hard to get here. He wanted it too much.

But that still did not guarantee anything.

They turned onto Wilshire Boulevard, and Trent spent a few moments gaping at the tall palm trees and the polished buildings and the cinematic billboards. A pair of LA honeys waited by the Rodeo Drive traffic light, skintight jeans and the oversized sunglasses and the fancy shopping bags all part of the Hollywood dream. Their heads swiveled as they watched his limo pass. Trent smiled briefly at the thought that *they* were watching *him*. Then he turned away, consumed by his hunger to climb the ladder, rung after precious rung.

He would do anything to make it happen. Whatever it took.

Their destination was a chrome-and-glass structure on Wilshire Boulevard across from the Ferrari dealership. Trent watched an F500 emerge from the lot, roar through the next light, and smoke two black strips down a full block and a half. When he and Gayle climbed from the limo, the air tasted of burned rubber.

The sign by the building's front door announced simply: Mundrose. They were greeted by a cheerful staffer. Trent assumed she had been alerted by one of Gayle's phone calls. The woman led them straight to the executive elevator. The building had only five floors, and still the directors had their own lift.

They were shown to seats in the penthouse reception area. The atmosphere sparked with the tense energy of making things happen, California-style. Trent waited for the staffer to depart, then asked, "Is there anything you can tell me about what I should expect?"

Gayle was elegantly beautiful in a discreet pearl grey dress and matching pumps. "You have researched Colin Tomlin?"

Tomlin was the head of the LA advertising group and the man they were scheduled to meet. "Of course."

She nodded, as though his response confirmed something she needed to know. She would not waste her time with someone who did not bother to prepare. "Barry acquired this management agency four years ago. He added to this an advertising firm connected to every major network and studio. Then he acquired a marketing and promotion group. He paid over the odds for all three."

"But their combined value is now much more," Trent guessed.

"Correct. The former head of the agency is now president of the LA group. He makes more than the division chief, who was at the meeting in New York." She eyed him coolly. "Do you understand what I am saying?"

"The guy on the other side of those doors thinks he should have been at the meeting."

"Tomlin considers himself the head of his own division. He thinks the director in New York should be answering to him. Selling his group to Barry Mundrose made Colin Tomlin a very rich man. But he wants more. He wants access to the inner sanctum."

"So to get a call from New York telling him to meet with me . . ."

Gayle nodded to the secretary who was headed their way. "He is not your friend. If he can knife his boss by stabbing you, he will do so."

Colin Tomlin neither rose nor offered his hand as together they crossed the broad expanse of his office. Trent suspected the man had positioned his desk so as to make the visitor feel both uncertain and under inspection, as though approaching a throne. Trent's research had described an incredibly vain man, born to money and title in England, product of Eton and Cambridge. Tomlin had begun his career acting in British television, but when it faltered he reinvented himself as a representative of other actors. This took him to Hollywood, where he showed a remarkable talent for using his urbane British polish to hide the unseen blade.

Tomlin was strikingly handsome for a man in his late sixties. Impeccably groomed in a striped shirt with white collar and cuffs, gold Cartier cuff links and matching watch, woven silk tie, Palm Springs tan. He watched them with cold lizard eyes as they seated themselves.

Trent knew the man expected some form of the corporate duel. As in, Tomlin's boss had ordered this. So do what the head office demanded. And Trent knew before Gayle had spoken that it would get him nowhere with this man.

So Trent's first words were, "Tell me what you want."

Tomlin had the upper-class Brit's ability to dress every word with scorn. "Pardon me?"

"I don't owe your division manager anything. When I made my pitch to the board, he didn't utter a word. What he said behind my back is anyone's guess, and quite frankly, I don't care."

The man even blinked slowly. "This signifies precisely what to me?"

"The most vital component of this entire plan is advertising. Success of my project is dependent upon getting it right. My future is in your hands."

Tomlin steepled his fingers. "Go on."

"I don't even know enough to tell you what I need. I have some ideas. But they are unrefined. Incomplete. Just like me."

Tomlin's languid gaze took in Trent's dress. "You took the words straight from my lips."

He took no offense. Why should he? Edlyn's remarks had been far worse. Instead, he found himself liking the man. No doubt a dangerous sentiment, but true nonetheless. "I have Barry Mundrose's ear. For how long, I couldn't say. But today, that's how it is. So I'm asking. What would it take for you to become my ally?"

Colin Tomlin took his time. Trent could almost see the mental gears grinding. Trying to see whether it was even worth making the effort to change his mind about this one. Then the LA director's gaze swiveled to Gayle. He started to speak. Then thought better of it. Instead, he turned his chair around to face the window and the pale LA sky. "There is one item."

"Name it."

"The entertainment industry's fastest growing component is electronic gaming. Which also happens to be our advertising division's weakest segment. I have identified an ideal target. They are open to being acquired. The price they are asking is acceptable."

Trent finished for him, "Your New York director turned you down."

"He really is becoming rather tiresome. He says there are two perfectly valid reasons for refusing my proposal. First, the company is based in Austin, not LA. Austin is where they should be, as it's home to a growing proportion of the e-games industry. And second, they have a division that produces games of their own. Quite good ones, actually. But that takes us out of the advertising and promotion business into production. And Mundrose already has an e-games company. The fact that they have not produced a hit in almost four years has somehow managed to escape the man's attention."

Trent rose from his chair and started pacing. He had always thought better on his feet. He spun several ideas through tight mental trajectories, until he found one that might just work. Maybe.

Trent had no idea how long it was before he returned to his seat. Colin Tomlin was still studying the blank LA canvas beyond his window when Trent asked, "What if I said I needed an e-game production company that could drop everything they were working on and focus their entire corporate attention on my project?"

Tomlin glanced at him. "Is that actually the case?"

"Two hours from now, I meet with Stone Denning," Trent replied. "If he accepts my proposal, then everything moves into high gear."

"Including a new electronic game."

"Right. We'd need a preliminary concept for an advertising blitz that I can take over and show him."

Tomlin mulled that over. "You require visuals for a new ad campaign in two hours?"

"Yes. Is that even possible?"

"Do you have an idea of what you want?"

"Rough at best," Trent said. "I'm more than open for your input. I'm desperate."

"Not a bad attitude to take, really." Colin Tomlin turned back to his window. "And the actual product?"

"Ready to release with Denning's new film project."

"Which is when, precisely?"

Gayle replied, "Labor Day."

"A new electronic game based around a film in production, from scratch to completion in less than four months." Tomlin did not smile. But the edges of his eyes tightened. "I would rather expect that to require a full team's best efforts."

"The advertising blitz should start day after tomorrow, and build all summer long," Trent said. "The group in charge would need to coordinate everything toward a full nuclear explosion the first week in September."

"Including a marketing campaign for this new e-game."

"E-game, print, radio, television, film, the works. All tied to the same theme."

"That would tax us rather a lot," Tomlin said. "Of course, New York will insist upon being in charge."

"What if you ran everything from here?" Trent replied.

Tomlin's lizard gaze slid back to Trent. "My so-called superior would never agree to such a thing."

Trent said to Gayle, "Make the call."

Start to finish, the entire process took less than fifteen minutes. Gayle placed the call to Barry Mundrose's second secretary. She spoke softly, hung up. While they waited, Tomlin went back to observing the empty sky. Trent paced. There was no way his body could hold all the tension. He had to force it out through motion. Gayle took her phone over to the sofa in the corner and talked quietly, then passed the phone to him.

Trent told Barry everything. The need, the urgency, Colin's initial hostility. He then related his solution. And the objections that had been raised by Tomlin's superior. And would surely be raised again. And the risk Trent faced in bringing down this NY director's wrath. But how he saw no alternative than to make a powerful enemy.

When he was done, Mundrose said, "Ask Gayle if the Austin proposal reached my desk."

When he passed on the query, Gayle replied, "Not that I am aware."

Mundrose accepted the news in silence. Trent kept pacing.

Ninety seconds later, Mundrose said, "I'll take care of the people at this end. Give me Tomlin."

The Brit accepted the phone, said, "Here, sir." Tomlin listened intently for three minutes, then said simply, "I will get started on this immediately."

He cut the connection and spent a few moments fiddling with the knot of his tie. "It seems that I underestimated the potential of this meeting."

Trent returned to drop into his seat. "Barry said yes?"

"He did indeed." This time, it was the edges of his mouth that crimped along with his eyes. "Shall we begin anew?"

"Fine by me."

The LA group manager rose and walked around his desk. "How do you do. I'm Colin Tomlin. And it is indeed a pleasure to make your acquaintance."

Trent felt his heart take off on wings he did not even know he had. "Likewise, Mr. Tomlin."

"Please, I insist you call me Colin." He waved toward his door. "Shall we begin?"

12

"A God in heaven . . ."

WESTCHESTER COUNTY

After the prayer time, Jenny Linn took a walk with her father. She found an exquisite pleasure in reaching over and taking his hand. As though the years of arguments had never existed. Richard looked at her fingers intertwined with his own and said, "You used to walk with me like this all the time."

"I remember."

"If your mother tried to hold your hand, you would holler like a banshee. Even at three years old, you had a will of iron."

"Your genes at work."

They left the road and walked down to the stream. The grass was littered with petals from the cherry trees. There was not a breath of wind. Richard said, "This is nice."

"Thank you for coming, Daddy."

"Thank you for making room for us." A few steps, then, "I feel your work here is very important."

"So do I."

"Can I ask you something?"

"Anything." It was ridiculous for that single word to cause her eyes to burn. But for years any question from her father seemed to probe for weakness. Her normal response had been to ready herself for the next attack. But here in the meadow, such memories belonged to a different world. A different life.

Even so, his question was immensely surprising. "Do you think that your mother and I could join with you in studying this book about listening to God?"

"Of course, Daddy." She stopped and turned to him. "Why are you asking me?"

"Because neither of us wants you to feel that we are horning in. This is your role. God has called you. Not us."

"Daddy . . ." Jenny looked out over the surrounding green. In the far distance, John Jacobs walked alone, his shoulders bowed by a burden she could feel from where she stood. "I can't think of one single thing I would like more to share with you."

LOS ANGELES

That evening Trent Cooper sat at a table in the Bel Air Hotel bar and read two files sent over by the detective agency. He had printed out both documents in the business office. The young woman in charge clearly noticed the content, because she transformed the carpet between her desk and the printer into a catwalk. She didn't say anything directly to Trent. The Bel Air hotel did not permit overt flirting between staff and guests. But her look and her walk and the way she touched her lips with her tongue said it clearly enough. Definitely available.

Trent did not let his smile break out until he was safe outside again. Clearly the young woman didn't see anything wrong with his jeans or his rumpled jacket.

Each page was stamped with the agency's logo, and below that was written, *proprietary information.* Trent had no idea what the words meant, other than the suggestion that the data was worth the ten thousand dollars he had paid the agency for a rush job. The information was complete enough, a full workup on the career and personal life of one Stone Denning. The A-list director had experienced an astonishing rise, a truly Hollywood tale of riches and fame.

Stone Denning had started as a mail clerk at CAA, one of the largest agencies in film and television. He had written a pilot script on the side, then used a buddy who was one rung further up the ladder to place the script with Fox. The script had spawned one of the most successful dramas in the network's history. Stone Denning had coproduced the series with his buddy, who had taken over as show-runner when Stone had moved into film.

Stone's first full-length feature was a buddy-cop drama that drew a huge and global audience. In the seven years since, Stone Denning rose to become one of the hottest figures in Hollywood. Currently he worked on the second of a five-film deal with Mundrose reportedly worth a hundred million dollars.

Trent set the professional overview aside and turned to the personal data, which contained a dozen photographs, most of which were highly unflattering. Despite his power and growing income, Stone Denning was constantly flirting with bankruptcy. He regularly dove into new business ventures, many of which could have been successful if he only had taken the time to manage them well. But he had a filmmaker's attention span, which rarely lasted more than the six months it took to shoot a new project. All but two of the ventures had gone bankrupt, saddling Stone with massive debt.

Stone's family life suffered from the same insatiable quest for the next big thing. At thirty-nine he was already divorced four times, involved in an additional three paternity suits. His ex-wives and former flames and legal costs ate up 70 percent of his disposable income. He spent the rest on a stable of sports cars, a Malibu beachfront mansion, a raging lust for high-stakes poker, and a nightlife that exhausted Trent just reading about it. The summary at the end of the analysis read, *Insatiable appetites, a series of bad judgment calls, and looming debts make Stone Denning open to persuasion. His hunger for the gambler's high also suggests he will listen most keenly to what he sees as a high-stakes bet.*

The more he read, the more certain he became that Stone Denning was his man.

"Am I interrupting?"

Trent shut the file and rose to his feet. What he saw left him stunned. "Wow."

Gayle wore a sheath of silk that was somehow both black and silver. Her stockings were a pale gold, reflecting the bar's firelight, making her appear to dance even when she stood still. "Might one assume that is a note of approval?"

"Assume away. Absolutely." He knew he wasn't making sense. But the impact was staggering. The woman had always been lovely. Now she was nothing short of stunning. A Los Angeles star-making beauty. "You ought to be up there on the silver screen."

"Tried. The camera doesn't like me." She allowed him to hold her chair. "I modeled my way through university. Hated the life."

It was the most she had ever said about herself. "Where did you study?"

"Vasser." She pointed at the file. "Doesn't it say?"

"This isn't about you. It's a rundown on Stone Denning."

"Oh, may I see?"

He passed it over. "What will you drink?"

"What are you having?"

"Mineral water."

She made a small moue. "I think I'd prefer a Gibson."

"So would I. But it'll need to wait until after this meeting."

"As I am only playing the observer, I don't feel any such compunction." She opened the file. "Make it a double."

He met the waiter midway across the floor, delivered the order, then returned to the table by the corner windows and sat studying the room. The Bel Air hotel bar was a masterful rendition of a rich man's study. Dark wood and Persian carpets and silk drapes and chandeliers and leather furniture. Along with an overworked AC, the roaring fire was kept in check by a glass shield carved with the hotel's emblem. Trent resisted the urge to turn and watch her read. At best, Gayle was a temporary ally. At worst, she was a spy who would not hesitate to imbed the knife as deep as it would go. Trent kept his gaze on the fire and honed his strategy for the meeting to come.

Gayle closed the file and returned it to him. "This confirms my every suspicion."

"You've met Denning?"

"Twice, briefly. When he was over for meetings with Mr. Mundrose."

"What do you think of him?"

"The file sums it up rather well. *Insatiable* is a word meant to describe Stone Denning. He has no off switch. Have you seen any of his films?"

"All of them. Most of them several times. I love his work. Which I suppose is a sign of my lowbrow tastes."

She shrugged. "Stone Denning makes money. Some say he has his finger on the pulse of America's younger generations. I personally think he simply is the right man for the job."

"You don't like him."

She eyed him coolly over the rim of her glass. "It's not my job to like people, Mr. Cooper."

"Call me Trent, please."

She sipped her drink, set it down, and did not reply.

"What do you want from this?" When she did not answer, he pressed, "I'm not talking about the purpose behind your being here. In LA. With me. I mean . . ."

"I know what you mean." She met his gaze. Her eyes were a remarkable shade of pale brown. Almost gold in the firelight. The cool gaze of a lioness. "Ask me that question in another setting."

Meaning, once he had shown he was going to be around long enough for her to want to reply. There was no reason why her answer should tear a rent in his gut. She was the beautiful assistant to one of the most powerful men in the entertainment universe. "No problem."

"Good." She offered him a tiny smile. "Trent."

Stone Denning ordered the hotel's most expensive whiskey with brusque assuredness, a sixty-year-old single malt. He waited until the waiter deposited his glass to demand, "All right. You've got exactly three minutes to tell me why I shouldn't just walk out that door."

"We have a new strategy for the marketing campaign," Trent replied. "We need your help."

Two hundred dollars of amber liquid caught the light as Stone raised the heavy crystal. "What's in it for me?"

"I told you on the phone. Ten million dollars."

"For the film's marketing." He shrugged. "Chump change. The ad budget for this film is fifty mil and climbing."

"No, Mr. Denning. For you, personally."

"The way you said it from the plane, I thought—"

"What I said is correct. There's an additional ten million in advertising. But there is also another ten for you."

The director was dressed in LA chic, stovepipe slacks and dress shirt beneath a cashmere vest, the shirttails dangling around his chair. The gold watch was big enough to have fit over both wrists, and jangled noisily as he drank. But he was listening now. Intently. Stone Denning glanced at Gayle and said, "I know you, don't I?"

"We met when you visited Mr. Mundrose, Mr. Denning."

"Sure. You're the lady in Barry's front room."

Gayle gave him a professional smile. "It is kind of you to have noticed, Mr. Denning."

"There's a lot to notice." His boyish grin was slightly marred by the two scars that ran from his neck to his earlobe, the product of a glove that frayed in a particularly intensive boxing battle. "In my head I called you Legs."

Her expression chilled slightly. "Mr. Mundrose sends his compliments, sir, and asks you to give Mr. Cooper's concept your utmost attention."

"For ten mil, I can pay attention. For a while." His gaze lingered a moment longer, then swiveled back to Trent. "So give."

In response, Trent opened his laptop, plugged in a pair of earplugs, handed them over and said, "This will take exactly four minutes and seventeen seconds."

"Precision. I like it. But it's too long for a decent trailer." He started to fit in the plugs, then asked, "These earphones are clean?"

"They're new." Trent hit "play."

The three network evening news programs had given the Times Square mob extensive coverage, calling it the largest such gathering in recent memory. The owners of the signs around Times Square all sang the same tune, which was, their electronic boards had all been hacked. They had to give some excuse, since they were all under exclusive contract. Which was why it had cost Trent so much to put on the show.

Stone watched with a singular intensity. When the last clip ended, he took out the plugs and asked, "This was your idea?"

Gayle was the one who replied. "Mr. Cooper actually manufactured the entire event. The board was agog."

"I bet. 'Hope Is Dead.' Classy. Packs a punch." Denning rubbed the stubble on his chin. "They had some incredible frontline footage. How did they get it?"

"I planted roving camera teams all over the square."

"You own the raw tape?"

"Every inch. There's some random amateur stuff out there. But this was my own arrangement. The pros didn't have time to show up. Can I show you one thing more?"

He could tell Stone Denning wanted to dismiss him. But the lure of national news coverage on all stations was too great. "Go for it."

"I've just come from a meeting with Colin Tomlin. His team has roughed out a basic concept for our lead advert." Trent hit "play" and leaned back.

Colin Tomlin had personally overseen the making of this mock trailer, remaining on hand for the entire two hours. His top art director and videographer and their teams were on hyperdrive with their boss in attendance. The result was a staggeringly powerful montage. All three news shows were patched in, along with intensely professional images from the mob itself. Connecting it all was a theme Trent had come up with on the flight. It still was rough work, but for a preliminary concept it carried remarkable force, or so he thought. Straight up to the climactic moment, when the electronic screens of Times Square all went blank, then flamed on with the same three words. *Hope Is Dead.* The words then melded into the poster for Stone Denning's new film. The words were whispered by the female voice-over one final time. *Hope Is Dead.*

Stone leaned back in his seat. Trent saw the argument forming in Stone Denning's eyes. The dark gaze went brooding, then tightened, crinkling the entire face. An expression made to battle the world. Trent felt his gut go cold. The director was going to turn him down. Which meant moving to plan B. Only Trent did not have one.

But all Denning said was, "For me to take this on, it's got to be my idea."

Trent felt a relief so strong his voice went reedy. "No problem."

The man was so ready to fight for this, he could not stop. "I've got to work this up as my plan, my theme, my idea. People need to think I convinced you."

"I can see that," Trent said. "Ten years from now, when Hope Is Dead has become the decade's theme, people will think of you."

Stone Denning cocked his head. "You don't mind giving up the rights to your idea?"

"Why should I? I was never going to be on point. That's your job. That's why Barry is willing to pay you ten million dollars. To be the face. It makes all the sense in the world for you to be the one who originated it."

"That's right. It does."

Trent took that as his invitation, and laid it all out. The need for all the Mundrose divisions to unite and build a corporate brand that lasted a full season.

Stone saw where this was headed. "You want me to build this into all my projects."

"You have a pilot in production for a new television series. You also have a film that just wrapped. We want both to become components of this new package."

"The film has wrapped. The cast is gone. We're editing."

"They are available for another few days shooting."

"All of them?"

"All the stars. If you started tomorrow."

Stone crossed his arms. "You checked."

"Thoroughly."

"Who pays?"

"Their time would be covered by your production budget." Trent then offered the kicker. "Your television pilot will also be approved."

"Nobody's seen it yet."

"The offer is firm, Mr. Denning," Gayle confirmed.

"Full season run," Trent finished.

He looked from one to the other. "You guys make quite a team."

Trent kept his gaze on the director. "We want you to select whichever of the two you think would best support an electronic game. We want our new e-game division to start work tonight. We will roll out the game in time for the launch of your project."

Stone Denning laughed out loud. "Four months? You're nuts."

"The first week of September will mark the release of the film and the pilot and the game," Trent repeated. "The full series can follow in the new year. All three will carry the banner *Stone Denning Presents*. The tagline for everything is the same. Hope Is Dead."

"What's the rush?"

"Barry Mundrose didn't say." He shot an uncertain glance at Gayle. "But I can guess."

"Tell me."

"I think he feels we've got a winner. I think he wants to move before anyone else can steal it from us."

Stone Denning studied the remaining amber liquid in his glass, then tossed off the drink and rose to his feet. "I don't think either of us will be sleeping much between now and Labor Day."

Trent could scarcely believe he had heard correctly. "You're in?"

"My agent will scream. But 15 percent of ten mil should shut him up." He offered Trent his hand. "You're steering this boat?"

"I—"

"This is Mr. Cooper's project for the duration," Gayle replied.

Stone Denning crossed to the door, glanced back, nodded once, and was gone.

Trent was grateful the chair was there to catch him.

Gayle studied him for a moment, her gaze carefully assessing. "Just breathe. In and out. It passes."

He said weakly, "I need to get back to the ad agency. But first I think I'll have that drink."

"I'll see to it." She rose to her feet, patted his shoulder, and said, "Welcome to the majors, Trent."

DAY
SIX

13

". . . whoever stands firm . . ."

WESTCHESTER COUNTY

John slept poorly and woke feeling as though he was not welcome in his own skin. He showered and dressed and joined the others for breakfast. But he remained a man apart.

The morning sky was china-blue, the air crisp. Two young women from the campus set out meals in the vast kitchen-dining area. They were silent and efficient, and departed as John filled his plate with eggs and corn muffins and fruit. Watching the two depart in the Barrett Ministries van heightened his sense of not belonging. These people had spent their entire lives rising up within the ministry, while he had spent his days working hard and getting nowhere. John ate his breakfast and brooded over the possibility that perhaps God had made a mistake.

After breakfast, Ruth asked Aaron if he would lead them in a devotional. Aaron slipped the silken yarmulke from his pocket and fitted it over his head, then opened his Bible. "Ever since Yussuf first told me of his experience, I have found myself reflecting on the prophet Isaiah. His life, his personal ambitions, his literary abilities, everything was transformed in the most unexpected of manners. Of course, the death of his king Uzziah was not a surprise, as Israel's leader had been ill for quite some time. So they buried one ruler and prepared to anoint another. As we know from our own times of transition, the people and their priests were no doubt worried over what was to come. Israel was beset by problems, and faced the very real threat of war with the Northern Kingdom. Isaiah was a young man at the time. We can assume this from the number of kings he served. We know he was intelligent and gifted. I personally see him as someone who is also quite ambitious. He has every reason to toe the line, especially in such a period of uncertainty and change.

"Instead, what happens?" Aaron paused and looked at each face in the little group. "Everyone around Isaiah was taking part in one of the most vital and intimate components of the temple ceremony. As the incense was lit and the smoke filled the temple's innermost chamber, it seemed to him as though the very walls of the temple dissolved. One moment he stood in the holy chamber, the next he was confronted with *true* holiness. He stood before the heavenly throne, and about it moved fiery figures in an act of constant worship. They called out the words that are known nowadays as the *Kaddosh*, repeating over and over the one word that most describes the Lord of all. *Holy*. And there upon the throne resided the one true and eternal God. Isaiah was drawn to his divine magnificence, and he was blinded by it. He was filled with awestruck joy, yet he also knew a soul-shattering dread. For he was, by his own trembling declaration, unclean. He could not be where he was. He did not deserve such a gift. He was the most unworthy of men."

John watched the morning light gradually strengthen, casting the room in a glow of sunlit amber. The kitchen-dining chamber, a full forty feet across, was divided by the long serving counter. The tables and the kitchen surfaces were all fashioned from the same wood. John suspected it was maple. Where the sunlight touched, the wood shone like polished gold.

Aaron continued, "The fruits of the Spirit require us to grow beyond our comfort zone. Like Isaiah, we are the most unworthy of believers. And yet God has called us. Each and every one of the family of Jesus. We are *all* invited to move beyond the failures and limitations that confine us."

John grew increasingly convinced that he should not be there. With these people. Listening to words about the fruits of the Spirit. He managed truckers for a living. He was about to rise and stalk from the room when Ruth turned to him and said, "I feel you should be our spokesman."

John felt as though this gentle woman had reached across the table and punched him in the soul. "You don't know what you are saying."

Ruth met his protest with a calm, "It's not important what I say. It's important that we heed God, if indeed this is what he wants."

"It should be you."

She nodded slowly. "Logically, perhaps. Mine is certainly the better-known face."

"That's not it. You're—"

"A reluctant servant who has failed far more often than I've succeeded," she replied. "I know."

"No, that's not . . ." John felt he was fighting for breath. "I can't. I just can't."

But Ruth did not budge. "Pray on it. That's all I ask. And if you feel God's hand upon this, remember that he realizes you are the right one precisely because you must rely on his strength."

John walked around the fields separating the streambed from the hills. He kicked at rocks and he argued with the weeds. Heather had wanted to come with him, and now he was glad that he had said he wanted to be alone. There was no reason to taint her day as well.

Ruth's suggestion that John was to play some role out front had drawn his unsettled feeling into sharp focus. The very concept was just about enough to send him crashing. He kicked at another stone, and wished the earth would just open up and swallow him whole.

He had spent his life in the background. Where he belonged. John lifted his gaze to the sky, and heaved a silent plea, begging in a panic far beyond words for the Lord to ask somebody else. But the day remained still, the wind absent. The air was tight, but he knew the compression was of his own making. He dropped his head, defeated by the silence.

He turned back and looked at the house. Far in the distance, traffic hummed and hustled along unseen highways. This place was held in a sanctity all its own.

He saw himself crossing the distance. Climbing the stairs. Walking down the porch to where Ruth Barrett sat in her padded rocker, waiting patiently for the Lord to call on her again. His wife would be there too. A woman strong enough in her faith that she did not need God's voice to know what should be done. John saw himself standing over the two ladies and Yussuf and Aaron and Jenny's mother. And confessing the awful truth that had kept him chained his entire adult life.

He studied the people seated back there on the porch and knew all of them or any of them would be better at the job of spokesperson. None of them carried anything like this burden. And they needed to hear this before . . .

Then it happened.

John was gripped by the sensation that the air around him gathered together. The atmosphere grew so dense it was like breathing underwater. Everything he saw seemed to hold an illumination from within. Every blade of grass was a unique and glorious creation. A butterfly fluttered past, and he could have wept from the glory of sunlight and wings. John remained as anchored as he ever had been to the present moment, to the field and the surroundings. And yet he felt himself drawn far beyond himself, up into a realm that embraced earthly life with abounding and endless love.

The whole world drew one long breath. And then the silent voice spoke, a thunder so powerful it shook him like a human gong.

Now.

14

". . . create in me . . ."

LOS ANGELES

Trent stood in the Mundrose LA offices, surrounded by the power of technology. The windowless chamber contained both the editing and transmission stations. The opposite wall held a massive flat-screen, fully fifteen feet wide and nine feet high. The resolution was unbelievable. He watched basketball players like giants go thundering past. The ref's whistle blasted from two dozen speakers. Beside him, Gayle winced at the piercing detonation, or perhaps it was the sight of the two men slamming into the bleachers. Trent just grinned. He had not stopped smiling for hours.

Colin Tomlin returned to stand beside him. "The deal is concluded."

Trent forced himself to turn from the screen. "Congratulations."

Colin studied the younger man. "Rather a heady mix, wouldn't you agree?"

"Unbelievable." Trent turned back to the screen. "Here it comes."

Colin actually smiled. "How many times have you seen it?"

Gayle replied for him. "Dozens."

"I like how it's been planted in the critical moments," Trent said.

"We control the entire game's advertising," Colin said. "It's part of the package. It should be. Barry paid half a billion dollars for the rights."

They stopped and watched as the advertisement ran once more. The effect on this screen was incredible. Trent felt the excitement ripple through his entire being. His first taste of wielding entertainment power was the most exhilarating thing he had ever experienced. Seeing it up here on the screen made it all real. Not just plans any more. His future.

The ghouls and vampires and zombies who dominated Times Square shouted in rising crescendo the words that seemed framed by blue flame, shining down from every direction. *Hope Is Dead.*

When the game resumed, Colin asked, "How much longer are you staying in LA?"

"I'll know soon enough," Trent replied.

Gayle explained, "My associate tells me Barry wants to speak with Trent about what is happening here."

"The online activity should spice his evening," Colin said. When Trent's phone chimed, he added, "Give him my thanks regarding the acquisition, would you?"

"You want to tell him yourself?"

"He asked for you, old chum."

Trent answered his phone. "Mr. Mundrose?"

"Give me the stats."

"We've registered six million hits and climbing."

"So the public is swallowing our package." Barry Mundrose actually chuckled. "It's like hooking a fish big as the globe itself."

"It's awesome," Trent agreed. "Colin says to tell you the deal is done, and he sends you his thanks."

"So it's Colin now, is it. Is Gayle there?"

"Here beside me."

"Give her the phone. And Trent."

"Sir?"

"Well done."

He handed the phone to Gayle, stared at the screen, and wondered if it could ever get better than this.

WESTCHESTER COUNTY

John had no chance to share his experience with the others. As he returned to the porch, one of the kitchen assistants rushed out with the news that calls were coming in regarding an advertisement being repeatedly played during a playoff game. They followed her inside and waited as she logged onto YouTube, then told them that over five million people had already done the same thing.

John's mind remained filled with images from the advertisement long after they returned to the porch. The impact was so powerful he almost missed hearing Ruth Barrett say that they were called to respond. And John Jacobs was the man to do it.

To his astonishment and dismay, all the others agreed that John should be the front man. None of his protests made any difference. He felt himself drawn closer and closer to the point where he would be forced to reveal the secret he had carried for over thirty years.

Jenny interrupted his thoughts. "Why don't you let me write out your words for you?"

"What an excellent idea," Heather said. "Don't you think so, John?"

"I haven't agreed to do this," John protested.

"I've just agreed for you," Heather announced, with that steely glint in her eyes.

"Just speak from the heart," Jenny Linn told him. "Whatever you feel is important. I'll help give it structure. But as far as possible, I'll keep this in your own words."

"She's a great writer," her father said. "Has been since she was a child."

The blush darkened her golden skin. She told John, "Don't try to edit yourself. Just let it flow out. Whatever comes to mind. I'm ready," she added, paper and pen in hand.

But her words only seemed to tighten John Jacobs further, until he was seated with his arms wrapped around his chest and his face creased from forehead to collar. "I can't see beyond my own failings."

Ruth smiled sadly. "My husband used to say the same thing when he was struggling with a sermon."

"He didn't have my failings to deal with."

"No," Ruth replied. "He had his own."

Heather stroked his shoulder, gentle motions that he did not really feel. "I want you to listen to what Alisha had to say while you were out in the meadow. And I want you to see if God uses this to make your way clear. Will you do that?"

"I'll try."

At a nod from Heather, Alisha began, "Like I told the others, I was singing even before I could talk. I thought it was my destiny. But when I got my chance in the spotlight, I failed. They took me into the recording studio, they gave me the mike, and they let me hear it after. I was good. But I wasn't good *enough*. I lacked the sort of control that a professional has got to have.

"So I stayed in the choir, and I pretended it was enough. After a time, they let me lead the choir. And I did with them what I couldn't do with myself. I *controlled* the sound. And we got better and better. And for the last eight years, we've been singing in the national church celebrations at the Kennedy Center."

John said, "I don't understand how this—"

"Wait, John," Heather urged. "Let her finish."

"My pastor's wife, she's been off working with a school group for a year. Before, Celeste was pushing and fighting for my job in front of the choir. I told myself she started with the kids because she couldn't beat me in the church. But after a time, I could see how happy that lady was. How those kids lit up her life. And then she came in and she said she wanted to join the two together. Her kids and my choir."

John found himself nodding in time to Alisha's words. "So she has been planning this for a long time." He picked up the story. "And you suspected she was trying to sideline you. She was using the children to push you off the podium."

"And that's why I said the children couldn't sing." Alisha's broad features were meant to hold joy, not the pain that pinched her now. "Isn't that just the meanest thing you ever heard?"

"No," John said. "It's not."

Alisha didn't respond and went on, "After Yussuf and the shooter met back in New York, I called the lady and said she could bring the kids. I told Celeste she has to lead the choir at the Kennedy Center concert. Because there isn't the time for me to get to know these children."

John asked, "When is the big performance?"

"Tomorrow. And I need to be there. Those folks are my *family*. But I *can't*. Not alone. I'll stand and I'll look at Celeste there in my place, leading those kids who will *not* have control. And I'm afraid I'll lose what I've found here."

"Of course we'll go with you," Ruth said, but her gaze remained fixed upon John. "It's the same thing all over again, John. That's what you need to hear. No one is saying you don't have reasons to refuse. But God is asking each of us to stretch beyond what we think we can do. That's what it means to be called."

John wanted to say that he couldn't. The request was too great. The risks too vast. But Heather continued to stroke his arm, a soft urging to remain silent, to accept.

Ruth picked up her cane and used a two-handed grip to push herself from the rocker. When Alisha reached over, she waved the help away. "John, all I'm asking is that you do it this one time.

See if the Lord is with you. If not, then we'll make other arrangements." She opened the screen door, then turned back to offer him a beatific smile. "If he is, though, who are you to argue with the Lord?"

"I suppose . . ."

"That's fine, then." The screen door slapped shut with soft finality. "Now you get started putting it down on paper with Jenny. I need to make a call."

15

". . . we might become heirs . . ."

AUSTIN, TEXAS

Reverend Craig Davenport sat in his home office. The wood-paneled study was his inner sanctum, the one place where he could come and shut out the constant demands of running such a large church.

But this afternoon his retreat had been invaded. In more ways than one. And on the very day the entire church knew he kept for himself. No phone calls. No interruptions. Nothing save a funeral or a wedding would draw him out. Yet this was one request he could not refuse.

Jason Swain was a vital member of his team. Young and super-intelligent and a rock. His mother was from Bulgaria and his father from Canada. He had inherited his mother's dark features and his father's quiet demeanor. He oversaw the sanctuary electronics, but on a voluntary basis. The church had a paid staff that ran the electronic board and the recording studio and the television cameras. Jason was a full-time employee of one of Austin's electronic gaming companies. The church had repeatedly tried to hire him away. But Jason loved his work. He continued to serve as one of the church's hardest working volunteers.

This was the first time Jason had ever asked anything of Craig. He had told the church's weekend secretary that he simply had to meet with the pastor. Today. Now.

The pastor stared in horror at the screen, and had to agree. This was something that could not wait.

When the advertisement had run its ninety-second course, Craig said, "Give it to me again."

Jason did not exactly wring his hands. He was small and strong and his normally placid demeanor had been replaced with a tension that had him perched on the edge of his seat, like a human spring wound so tight he might shoot through the ceiling at any moment. "Word came down last night. The Mundrose Group is buying our company. They have ordered my chief to halt work on every current project. The entire team is ordered to start work on a new game. One based around the latest film from Stone Denning."

Jason had already been through all this with his pastor. But the advertisement Craig had just seen charged the words with a very real dread. "And the film is about an invasion."

"From outer space, right. Earth faces an alien invasion of zombies and ghouls and werewolves and trolls, you name it. All our nightmares are explained by foretelling this. They travel from world to world, consuming everything and moving on."

"Sick." But there was hardly any surprise there. Craig had spoken for years about families needing to control what entertainment they ingested. Especially the children.

"Right. The difference is, it's just the start. There's a film and our new game and a television show and books and music, on and on. Our advertising group is going to work on nothing but this project. They aim to shape the cultural watchword. Instead of *following* a trend, they are going to *make* it." He pointed to the blank laptop screen. "This ad is the lead-in."

"Show me again."

Jason hit the keys, then moved back out of range. Craig sat and watched in silence.

The advertisement started at a gravesite in the rain. But the soundtrack was of a huge celebration, tens of thousands of voices screaming and chanting and singing, the words completely unintelligible. Umbrellas hid the black-clad onlookers from view at first, as the camera slowly panned around to reveal a vast array of vampires and ghouls. All of whom were grinning. Standing on the grave's other side were the stars of Denning's new film and his upcoming television drama. Beside them were the biggest music stars in the Mundrose firmament. And in the grave was a coffin engraved with the simple word, *hope*. They switched to the Times Square mob, and the screen flashed with a kaleidoscope of quick-fire images—ghouls dancing on car roofs, the police watching helplessly, an invasion force of the undead. Gradually the words they yelled and chanted and sang came into focus, as the image panned back, showing all of Times Square completely filled with insanity, as every screen circling the compound shone with the same three words. *Hope Is Dead.*

When the screen went blank, Jason said quietly, "I don't know what to do. I love my work. I love my *job*. Designing the next cutting-edge game is the only thing I've ever wanted. And this company is totally cutting edge. I don't want to leave my friends, my church . . . But how can I stay and be a part of this? What am I supposed to do?"

Craig knew this young man's quandary demanded his full attention. But just then all he could think of was his own sense of futility. "You say this is already out on the Internet?"

"That's what they do with a new concept. They show it on television, and at the same time they put it on the web. Then they measure the audience response. They played this ad three times on the top sports show this afternoon. It's already gone viral. Nine million hits already."

Craig's Fridays were spent working on sermons. He polished the lesson to be given that week, and started sketching out the next. Or the one after. And he wrote. That was the output side of his Fridays, leaving Saturdays for some wife and family time. But Craig tried to spend a couple of hours each day simply absorbed in the Word. And what he had felt all that day was the frustration every pastor knew. That his message was not getting out to the greater world, the culture that was moving ever faster and further from God's truth.

The blank screen mocked him with his feeling of futility. The knock on the door startled them both. Craig's wife poked her head inside and said, "Honey?"

"I'm busy."

"I thought you should know." She stepped inside. "Ruth Barrett is on the phone."

"What does she want?"

"To speak with you. She says it's urgent."

Jason's expression was miserable. "I should be going."

"No, son. Stay right where you are." He hit the speaker button. His wife stepped inside and shut the door, leaning on it. "Ruth?"

"Hello, Craig."

"How are you doing, sister?"

"To be honest, I don't know how to answer that."

Craig's chair rocked as he nodded with his entire body. "I know exactly what you mean."

"Craig, have you seen the new advertisement that the Mundrose Group released today?"

The pastor stared across his desk at the dumbfounded young man. "Matter of fact, I have."

"The dear young ladies who help around here were alerted by a text message from friends. They just played it for us."

"I'm appalled by what I've just seen," Craig said. "Who is 'us'?"

"That's why I'm calling." Ruth stopped. "This may sound a bit odd."

"You mean, odder than watching a mob make a mockery of God's eternal gift of hope?"

"Craig, for the past week I've had the distinct impression that God has been speaking with me. And not just me. I've been brought together with a group of people who've all received the same message. We now feel the reason we were drawn here was so we could respond to this attack."

Craig sorted through several different reactions. He had not seen Ruth Barrett since he had spoken at her husband's funeral. He had served on Bobby's staff as a young man fresh out of seminary, and counted Ruth as one of his dearest friends. The analytical side of his brain said that the elderly woman could very well be awash in grief and loss. But she did not sound addled. Ruth Barrett sounded as she always did. Steady and calm and focused. So he said, "Attacked is exactly how I feel."

"As we watched this, I was struck by the urge to call and ask if you would help us."

"What do you need?"

"We are fashioning a response. One in this group I'm involved with will serve as our spokesman. His name is John Jacobs. He's never been in front of a camera before. He is scared to death. But he is the only one among us who has any doubts about it."

Craig loved having a reason to grin. "Doesn't that just sound like God at work."

"I'm calling to ask if you would please look over our response. And if you feel like God is at work here, help us get out the word."

"Gladly."

"Thank you. And one thing more. Pray for us, if you would. And allow me to contact you again once we know something more."

"I'll be waiting for your call, Ruth."

"Thank you, Craig."

He cut the connection, leaned back in his chair, and said, "Well, now."

His wife asked, "That's why you two are meeting?"

"Jason just showed me the ad."

"Do I want to see it?"

Craig looked at his wife. "It's just awful."

"Maybe later, then."

Jason no longer looked so distressed. "I can't believe what just happened."

Craig nodded and said to the young man, "I don't have an answer for you. Except to pray for some clear direction from the Lord."

Jason rose to his feet, shut his laptop and stowed it in his backpack, and revealed a truly magnificent smile. "For the moment, that is more than enough."

"You're going to stay in your job?"

"For the moment," he repeated, pointing at the phone. "In case they need an insider."

16

". . . a still small voice . . ."

WESTCHESTER COUNTY

An hour later, Jenny read out what she claimed were John's own words, fashioned into a statement. John saw the delight on all the other faces, but he himself was still trying to come to grips with the fact that they expected him to talk in front of the camera. His reluctance and his doubts apparently meant nothing to them. In fact, they only seemed to strengthen their confidence in him.

Ruth returned to the porch, listened in approval to John's first attempt at reading Jenny's pages, then said, "You and Heather, come with me, please."

She led them through the kitchen and dining area, leaning heavily upon her cane. One of the kitchen workers must have noticed a disturbing change, for she called over, "Are you having a spell, Miss Ruth?"

"I'm fine."

But the young woman watched her with mounting concern. "Should I get your medicine?"

"No, thank you." Ruth crossed the main foyer and entered a hall leading into the east wing of the one-story house. She led them into Bobby Barrett's study, and John stopped in the doorway.

Behind him, his wife said, "I remember this room."

The desk and the big academic Bible on the carved reading stand, the bookshelves with their leather-bound volumes, it was all like he had seen on the weekly broadcasts growing up. Before he had gone and thrown his life away.

Ruth's voice called to him from a side alcove. "Come on in here, please."

John followed Ruth into a walk-in closet holding about a dozen suits. Beside them were a pair of shelves with starched shirts still in their laundry packets. Silk ties. Three pairs of polished shoes.

"I gave everything to the homeless shelter but these." Her hand stroked the sleeve of a grey pin-striped suit. "I suppose some of the people around here presume I'm holding on to these like they are part of some shrine. Which is ridiculous. But I did so love watching Bobby prepare."

"Ruth . . ."

"Bobby only wore these when he was preaching. He said it was part of putting on his game face." She turned around, her eyes overly bright. "You and he are almost exactly the same size."

"I can't," he said. "Those are his preaching clothes—"

"They were." She drew him forward. "I think you'd look good in navy."

Heather said, "Try it on, John."

"But—"

"You didn't bring a suit. You need one." Heather sorted through the shirts. "This one will look nice on you."

Ruth selected a matching tie. When she saw that John had not moved, she said, "Bobby would want this, John. I'm certain of it."

"My name is John Jacobs, and I am speaking to you from the headquarters of Barrett Ministries."

They had brought him over in a van. Their entire group came, and all of them had some compliment over how he looked, how the clothes suited him and the moment. Alisha kept working her laptop, reading off names of churches to Ruth, who noted them in a small, hardbound notebook. John had no idea what importance it held, but he suspected it was somehow tied to what he was about to do. Aaron and Yussuf and Richard tossed ideas back and forth with Jenny Linn, apparently working on concepts for future broadcasts. John had difficulty hearing anything over the thundering of his heart.

"Today one of the world's largest entertainment conglomerates has declared on national television that hope is dead. I am here to say that their message is wrong."

The broadcast team was prepped and ready. They were young and dynamic and very professional. The producer knew John was a total beginner, and worked to make him as comfortable as possible. The television prompter was stationed a few inches from the camera eye, so John could read while appearing to look straight at the audience. A dot of red fingernail polish was painted in the prompter screen's right corner. The producer suggested John hold his gaze on this one point, otherwise his eyes would appear shifty. The producer was a young man in his late twenties, who slipped the headphones around his neck and read through the speech with John four times, coaching him on when to breathe and when to punch a word. The young man's name was Kevin Burnes, and John suspected he would be quite handsome if he cut his hair and tucked in his shirttail. Kevin held to a perpetual smile, with a gentle voice that steadied John.

But the real help came from another direction.

"The world has been granted a gift of eternal hope. The Bible states this, and I am here to tell you that the gift is real. Jesus died to make this available to each and every one of us who seek him. He is there, and he is calling to us. His hands are outstretched, waiting for us to realize what it means to live with hope."

In the moment when the makeup lady finished dabbing powder on his nose and forehead, John felt overwhelmed by an adrenaline-drenched panic. The lights came on, bright as electronic suns. People scurried in the shadows beyond the lights' reach. And then it happened.

"The Mundrose broadcast makes a mockery of God's eternal promise. They do this for profit. God offers hope for the sake of our souls. A choice has been set before you. I am here today to ask you to act."

At that moment, John found his fear subsiding. What was more, he sensed people praying for him. He did not hear their voices. He did not need to. But he knew they were gathered with hands clasped, praying for him to do this.

John sat in a mock version of Bobby Barrett's study. In the pastor's own suit. Waiting while they tested his voice for level and gain. So he could speak to the world. And do this because in the silent intensity, he knew he was following God's design for this time. He *knew* this with utter certainty. And suddenly his fears held no significance whatsoever.

"At the bottom of your screen is a website where you will find a list of sponsors that stand to profit from Mundrose Entertainment and their message of despair. You will also find a list of alternate products. I am asking you to consider switching brands. Send these people a message in the only language they understand, money. The fate of souls, now and those still to come, hangs in the balance."

DAY
EIGHT

17

"The desires of your heart . . ."

LOS ANGELES

When Trent woke up, he had no idea where he was. Sunlight fell through a window to his left, spilling across a floor of hand-cast Mexican tiles. Gradually the previous day's events flowed into his brain. The flight on the private jet, the meeting with the world-famous director, the confrontation with the Hollywood publicist, the advertisement, the web-based response. Trent had remained in the broadcast studio for hours, watching the response grow to his concept. *His concept.* Gayle had finally given in to exhaustion and left sometime after one. Trent could not possibly have slept, not after the publicist announced their ad had become the most watched video on YouTube. The limo had finally driven him back to the hotel under a rose-hued dawn.

The Bel Air Hotel bungalow was not luxurious in any standard sense. The antiques were rough-hewn, the floor tiles cast by hand. The bedroom's chandelier was simple brass. The four-poster bed would have looked at home on an upscale ranch. Trent emerged from the bathroom and realized that probably had been the designer's intention, to create the homey feel of an elegant hacienda inside a Hollywood hotel.

Then he heard the knock on the door. Trent slipped into trousers and crossed the parlor. "Yes?"

"It's Gayle."

He opened the door to find her holding a silver tray containing a coffee thermos and single cup. Trent greeted her, then hurried back into the bedroom for a shirt. When he emerged, she was holding out a steaming cup. "Thanks."

"You have a call with Edlyn in—" Gayle checked her watch. "Now, actually."

His phone rang. He took time for a couple of hasty sips, then answered, "Good morning, Edlyn."

"Is your computer running?"

Gayle must have known what was coming, because she was already at his desk, booting up. "Five seconds."

"Go to the website for Barrett Ministries."

"I know that name." He passed on the name to Gayle, then remembered, "Isn't he dead?"

"Yeah, a couple of years ago. Okay, click on the tab labeled *Hope Now.*"

A face Trent did not recognize popped into view. The man's name meant nothing. "Who is John Jacobs?"

"No idea."

The man looked like a plumber, was what Trent thought—big and relatively fit but certainly not made for the camera. He spoke in a flat Midwestern voice, poor inflection, and Trent caught his eyes shift once as he followed the teleprompter. This John Jacobs was criticizing their advertisement. He talked about Jesus. He announced the website, listing all the Mundrose sponsors. Then he stopped cold. No fade out, nothing. The screen flashed the same website. Start to finish, one hundred and twenty-five seconds. A ridiculous length.

Edlyn said, "Click on the web address."

He did so, and watched an astonishing array of names come into focus. There were two lists, actually. One was headed, *Mundrose sponsors*, and the other, *Alternate suppliers of similar products.*

Trent rubbed his face, wishing he was more awake. "Should I be worried?"

"Are you kidding? This is fantastic."

"I don't follow."

"Apparently this guy's little diatribe was shown on the screens of several thousand churches this morning. Pastors all over the nation started their sermons with clips from our advert, gave their little talks, then finished with this John Jacobs here, whoever he is. A pastor in Austin, Craig Davenport, started this rolling. Or so I've been told."

"Sorry, I don't follow. You say this is good news?"

"Our publicity department is breaking out the champagne. They could not have designed a better response. Remember *Pretty Woman*? Some church group tried to set up a boycott. The film grossed over half a billion dollars. By some accounts, the boycott added a hundred mil to the total."

"They're doing our job for us," Trent realized.

"There's no such thing as bad publicity," Edlyn confirmed. "We want you to stay out there a couple more days, build on this with a second ad."

"I can do that." His mind gradually accelerated. He felt fragments of a new idea begin to swirl in his mind.

"Because this is your first top-level assignment, we want Gayle to remain there as your support."

Trent struggled to fashion a response that would not reveal how delighted he was with this bit of news. All he could come up with was, "Understood."

But Edlyn must have taken his hesitation as concern, for she said, "We're not spying, Trent. Well, we are, but in a positive sense. Now give me Gayle."

He basked in the glow while Gayle spoke briefly into his phone. The clock on the side table said it was three in the afternoon. She hung up and said, "It sounds as though I'll be around for a bit longer."

"Have dinner with me." The words were out before he had a chance to come up with reasons not to speak. "Two colleagues, a free night, nothing more. Please."

She was dressed in what he supposed was LA casual-chic, pastel shorts and a cotton top shaped like a man's dress shirt but with short sleeves. But her smile, for the first time ever, seemed genuine. "I know just the place."

WESTCHESTER TO WASHINGTON DC

The filming had left John so exhausted he barely managed the walk back to the stone cottage, where he undressed and collapsed into bed. He woke up after midnight to find Heather sleeping peacefully beside him. Ravenous, he quietly crossed the starlit courtyard, entered the main kitchen, and ate two bowls of cereal. He sat on the porch for a time, welcoming the night-clad solitude. He remained unsettled by how everyone seemed so comfortable with him being the spokesman. As he stared at the stars draped overhead, he recalled sitting in front of the camera, only this time he felt as though all his faults and all his mistakes were there on public display. Finally he returned to the cottage, slipped into bed beside his wife, and gave in to slumber.

Somewhere around dawn, he had a dream.

In it, John glimpsed his own world, but from a different perspective. For that brief moment, he observed through the eyes of a different John Jacobs.

In the dream, John sat in a diner where he often breakfasted with old friends. Only now he was a whole man. In this dream version of his life, John had never stained his life with rash violence or prison

148

or regret or guilt. Instead, he laughed easily, and he shared thoughts with the confidence of a man who had risen to his full potential.

And then the dream took a remarkable shift.

John left the diner and found himself inside the Barrett Ministries television studio. He was once more dressed in the borrowed suit of a departed evangelist. He spoke the same words that scrolled down the teleprompter. Just as he had done the previous evening. Only in the dream, John *belonged*. He was *made* for this role.

When John woke up, he discovered that Heather had slipped away, letting him rest. John rose and showered and dressed, then joined the others for prayer and breakfast and a sunrise service in the main chapel. He knew he had every right to be left riddled with fresh grief from the dream. After all, the life he had once thought was his to claim had disappeared the instant he had opened his eyes. And yet John was filled with a distinct whisper of promise. Without saying exactly why, the dream had left him with a marked assurance that by coming here and accepting the challenges that had been placed before him, he was growing. He was being made whole. He was a man whose days held a greater purpose and hope.

After church they went straight to the county municipal airport, where a pair of rented King Air turboprops waited to get them to the Kennedy Center. They needed two planes because the television crew traveled with them. John watched Heather set a suit bag on top of the camera equipment. He was about to go over and ask his wife what was going on, when Yussuf and Aaron walked up. Yussuf said, "Please excuse me, Brother John. I need to have a word with you."

John found it remarkable how the man's formality carried such a sense of friendly warmth. "Should we wait until we're airborne?"

"A perfectly valid question," Aaron agreed. "Since the pilots are waving at us. Again."

Yussuf said, "I already said you should get on board."

"And yet I am here. Asking a question which you have not yet answered." Aaron gave a massive shrug of his bony shoulders. "What a delightful trip we're having."

Yussuf said to John, "I wanted to tell you, in the prayer time this morning, I felt God's hand upon me."

Aaron gave him mock indignation. "There is a reason why I am only hearing about this now?"

John liked the spark between the two men, the easy banter, the genuine friendship. "What did God say?"

"That you are to make yourself ready for God to use you," Yussuf replied. "I was seated and trying to pray, but in truth I was thinking about your time before the cameras. When the lights came on, you became a man of authority. I understood then why God had chosen you."

Aaron was no longer smiling. "I thought the same thing."

"Because your authority came not from you. And I admired you for your courage."

"I didn't want to do it," John replied.

Aaron shrugged a second time. "How many of the prophets were people who sought the honor and the burden? God called, you answered. That is the important issue here."

Yussuf went on, "God spoke to me in that moment. He said you were to make ready to speak for him again."

John glanced over to where the pilot waited impatiently. "Did he say what I should talk about?"

"Six words," Yussuf replied. "'Be ready when hope is revealed.'"

As John climbed into the plane's cramped cabin, Alisha waved to him. "Sit across the aisle from me, will you?"

"Sure thing." He followed the woman's example and folded up the center armrest so he could use both of the small seats. He pointed Heather into the row in front of him, then waited while the plane revved its twin engines and took off. As they reached cruising altitude, he studied the woman seated across the narrow aisle. Alisha's features were creased with a very real pain. He leaned in close and asked, "You want to talk about it?"

"I do and I don't."

John nodded his understanding. "Well, when you make up your mind, I'm here."

She reached over and took hold of his hand. Heather saw the gesture and turned so she could smile at him. Another ten minutes passed before Alisha said, "I'm afraid of what I'm gonna find when we land."

The prop's noise granted them a remarkable degree of privacy. "I don't understand."

"My whole life, I've been the one keeping things right. When my grandmother got sick and my momma didn't come home, I was the one making a home for my little sister. It came natural to me. Like God gave me this gift to organize things. Where somebody else might have seen only the lack, I made do. I found ways to keep it all together."

John felt tiny tremors run through the hand holding hers, a communication far beyond the words themselves. He said, "Even when your heart was broken."

Her response was at a much deeper level than her expression. Her entire body was gripped momentarily by the stress of maintaining control. Her hand clenched his painfully tight, then slackened with the rest of her. Her eyes were shiny now, her voice deeper. "I put all I had into shaping my church choir."

John nodded slowly. He caught the power she put into that word. *My* choir.

"We been at the Kennedy Center eight times. Tonight makes nine."

"All because of you," John said.

"Two hundred choirs try out. Eleven get tapped. Only three have been invited back every year."

The communion through her grip filled in the unspoken. "And tonight you're not in charge. You gave that up to be with us."

"It didn't start off that way." She looked at him for the first time, and tried hard to smile. "If God had said that up front, you'd be holding somebody else's hand right now."

"I doubt that very much."

She turned back to the front. "So tonight the pastor's wife is gonna be leading my choir and fifty kids I didn't want up there on the stage. And I'm gonna have to smile my way through it. And hope they do good enough so we get invited back another year. 'Cause when this whole thing here is done, the choir is just about all I've got left."

"What about your sister?"

"I don't want to talk about her."

The snappish way she responded would normally have been enough for John to drop the subject. But not today. Not when he suddenly felt a rushing sense of divine intent. "You need to invite her, Alisha."

She turned back to him. "What are you going on about?"

"Tonight. You need to ask her to come."

"Brother, you don't have a single solitary idea what you're saying."

He nodded, both to the words and to the pleasure he felt in how she had just addressed him. "You're right. But I know what I know."

She stared at him. "Tabatha won't come."

"That's not the point."

"We're not talking about what I want to talk about."

"Alisha, you need to do this."

"Here I thought this day couldn't get any harder, I'm getting advice on my family from a white man who's never even met my sister."

"Will you call her?"

"Will you leave me be if I do?"

He leaned in close. "You're a good woman, Alisha. It's an honor to call you my friend."

152

18

"Establish the works of our hands . . ."

LOS ANGELES

Trent's Sunday was spent in solitary confinement, locked in his room strategizing. When Gayle learned he needed some time to formulate a response to the Barrett Ministries video, she announced that she had not had a day off in three months and could be found at the pool. The detectives had placed him on their list of top clients. Trent learned this little item when he phoned their headquarters on a Sunday morning and started to beg the on-duty officer for a connection to someone with clout, only to be informed that the manager on call had been alerted the instant he phoned in. He ordered a salad for lunch, and ate it seated in a minuscule courtyard reflecting on life at LA speed. However fast he moved, he still had another race to win, another quest to claim as his own. He had never been happier.

The preliminary workup on John Jacobs was delivered at midafternoon. Trent thanked the manager, slotted the information into his concept, and went in search of Gayle.

There was no response at her door, so he phoned her cell. She answered on the first ring. "I must have dozed off. Am I late?"

"Not at all. I need some advice."

"I'm still poolside. Should I come up?"

"Stay where you are. I'll be right there."

Even the hotel pool was designed to offer privacy, with shrubs and colorful sunshades to segment the deck. Gayle was stretched out on a divan in a discreet corner. Her one-piece costume was a tawny gold that heightened the luster of her skin. She sat up at his approach and wrapped the towel around her legs.

Trent forced himself to focus on her face as he drew over a chair. "I'm sorry to trouble you."

"This work is why I was sent to LA. What do you need?"

Trent outlined what he had in mind. As he talked, she resumed her professional mode, slipping the oversized sunglasses onto her hair. "Edlyn needs to hear this."

"Should it wait until tomorrow?"

"Absolutely not." She had Edlyn's private line on speed-dial. When Edlyn Mundrose came on, Gayle pitched her voice so he could hear. "Trent has come up with a concept I found rather remarkable. I told him you would want to hear this without delay." She passed him the phone and went on, "Tell her just like you did me."

He could feel his heart squeeze, as though suddenly too big for his chest. He did what he had been taught by the therapist all those years ago, when nerves were enough to render him speechless. Just another throwaway kid whose defect made it all too easy to vanish in the shadows. He spoke slowly, shaping each word carefully, not moving on until the last one had been carved from the air and set precisely in place. "John Jacobs has a prison record."

"Did you use our in-house people to research him?"

"No, I thought we should be more discreet."

"Good. Go on."

"Jacobs had just turned nineteen. He was an underaged drinker using a fake ID, and got into a bar fight. He almost killed his opponent. He served six months for aggravated assault."

"This just keeps getting better."

"I thought rather than go at him directly, we might want to play on the church angle. Have some pastor do it for us. Bring up the man's past, and then talk about who he is now. Jacobs worked a number of dead-end jobs, then went to work for a trucking company. He's assistant manager of their Midwest depot."

Edlyn was silent for a long moment. "The man is not a pastor?"

"He has no seminary training. None."

"This is gold. We have a former church leader we've used in the past. I'll work out a deal."

Trent could scarcely believe her level of tense enthusiasm. "Great."

"Colin can feed this to our tame reporters. Tell him I said, go for maximum damage."

"Understood."

"This is good work, Trent."

He was still shaping a simple thank-you when he realized the phone had gone dead. He handed the phone back to Gayle and managed, "You were right to contact her today."

"Thank you for noticing." She rose from the divan, opened the towel, and reshaped it so that it formed a sarong just below her arms. The view of her long legs was astonishing. "I'd best go dress for our dinner. Meet you in an hour?"

They dined on the rooftop of the newest luxury hotel in Beverly Hills. The hacienda-style palace was located two blocks off Rodeo Drive and fronted a minipark, which at sunset was filled with strollers and lovers and happy dogs. They sipped champagne and leaned over the balcony and watched the day's soft light play over the scene below. Trent turned from the noisy throng to the elegant setting. Glass-clad torches rose by each of the restaurant tables. To his left, beyond a Plexiglas wall, two couples frolicked in the rooftop pool. Overhead the sky was tinted in rainbow hues.

Gayle was dressed in a sheath of porcelain-blue silk. Trent wore a suit he had bought that afternoon at the Valentino shop on Rodeo, demanding to be shown only what he could buy and wear immediately. In response, the store manager herself had ordered the in-house tailor to come in on a Sunday. The manager had then shown Trent an array of suits and matching shirts and ties. It was the first time in his entire life he had ever shopped without looking at the prices. His heart had almost stopped at the final bill. A suit, a jacket and matching slacks, three shirts and two ties and a pair of loafers put him back five thousand dollars and change.

Now that he stood beside Gayle, dressed in the finest clothes he had ever touched, he considered it an investment in a future he just might be able to claim as his very own.

The maître d' announced their meal was ready, then ushered them back to their table. Once they were served and the food tasted, Gayle lifted her glass and said, "I'd like to make a selfish toast."

"Fire away."

She tinged her glass against his. "To the future I always promised myself."

"Funny," Trent said. "I was thinking the exact same thing."

"Were you?"

"Yes. About me, though."

She went silent. Trent did not mind in the slightest. He felt a heady sense of disconnect. There was nothing holding him down this night. Not his past, nor the hunger that had gnawed at him through so many dark hours, not even the fear that he might never get a chance. He was free. All he needed to do was look across the table at the beautiful, silent woman to know this was true.

When their plates were removed and coffee served, Gayle said, "I apologize for tonight. I haven't been very good company."

"I have never had such a nice time," Trent replied.

"You don't mind the silence?"

"Why should I? It's the first quiet moment I've had in a week."

"You're very gallant."

"That's a new one. But thank you."

"You are." She swept a hand over the table, taking in the setting and the meal and the evening. "I promised myself this. I feared it might never come."

"I know what you mean."

She studied him over the rim of her cup. "Yes, you do, don't you?"

"Will you tell me something about yourself?"

"Why, haven't you had your detectives work up a file on me?"

"I started to," he confessed. "Then I decided I would be better off knowing only what you wanted me to know."

"Gallant, just as I said." She nodded her thanks as the waiter refilled her cup. When he moved off, she said, "My father teaches at a state college in West Virginia. My mother is a nurse practitioner. My sister is a dental hygienist. Her husband is a horticulturist. Once each winter they all pile into my parents' camper and vacation in Florida. Kids too. All three generations. They don't understand why I won't come along." She sipped her coffee. "I don't want to talk about them anymore."

"All right. Fine."

But she turned to the fire and continued, "Already in junior high school I knew I had to escape. My classmates called me a snob. But I knew I had what it took to be different, to be—"

He said it for her. "Better. More."

"I had to cut myself off. I *had* to. I studied and I planned and I worked three part-time jobs. In the summer I studied acting and voice and drama at my father's college. I won the scholarship."

"You modeled."

"I hated the work, but the money was good. When I graduated I landed a management trainee job, but working my way up the corporate ladder never appealed to me."

"I understand. All too well."

"I met Barry and Edlyn together at a charity event. Barry knew instantly I was after something more. He pays me as much as his assistant managers. I love my work. Everything except the way Barry's visitors treat me like potential prey." Her gaze tightened. "Do you have any idea how many offers I have received?"

"Hundreds."

"More. Some days they fall like rain. But I don't want to be someone's prize ornament. Nor am I interested in being a rich man's paramour, no matter how large the gifts. Do you understand what I am saying?"

Something about the words, or the way she spoke, caused his heart to race. He was amazed that his voice remained steady. "You want a partner."

She watched him, her cat's eyes glowing in the firelight.

"You want to claim a future and work for it. Enjoy it because the prize is earned. Together."

The moment crystallized, a time apart from the night and the elegant rooftop restaurant. It was only the unspoken bond that Trent felt growing between them. Then the waiter approached their table, and broke the spell by asking if they wanted anything more.

Trent paid the bill, fearing the moment was lost to the night. But as they rose from the table, Gayle slipped her arm through his and moved in so close he felt they were joined from shoulder to thigh. When they were alone in the elevator, she said, "It's so good to know we understand one another. So very, very good."

But neither the sentiment nor the happiness lasted beyond the first ten minutes of their limo ride back to the hotel. The car had just swung onto the highway when Gayle's phone rang. Trent wanted to protest when she drew it from her purse, saying how even top aides needed Sunday evening off. Then he was glad he remained silent when Gayle said, "It's Edlyn."

"Does she normally phone on a Sunday night?"

"No." She keyed the phone and said, "Yes, Edlyn?" She handed it to Trent.

"I'm here."

"Two of our major sponsors have been rattled to the point that they're talking about withdrawing their airtime commitments."

"Can they do that?"

"It's not a question Barry wants to raise. Is that clear?"

"Totally."

"We're moving ahead with your planned attack. And I want something more."

"Any ideas?"

"That's your department. Have it ready by nine tomorrow. Make it bloody."

19

". . . wiser than human wisdom . . ."

WASHINGTON DC

John and the group arrived at the Kennedy Center at four-thirty, two hours before the curtain time. Ruth and Heather suggested he change into the suit. The male dressing rooms were crammed with men and boys of all ages, fitting into rented tuxes and testing their voices. He emerged backstage to find Alisha waiting by the dressing room entrance, attired in a floor-length silk frock of crimson and gold. "Wow. You look great."

Her cheeks crimped into deep dimples, though the effort brought no easing of the strain in her gaze. "I did what you asked. My sister said she'd think about it. Which means she won't come."

"But you called her. That's what matters."

She might have nodded, before gesturing to an approaching couple. "I want you to meet Celeste and her husband, Pastor Terry Reeves. This is John Jacobs."

"We watched you speak to the world about what matters." Pastor Terry was a man whose smile showered warmth on all concerned. "It was inspiring and challenging."

His wife did her best to smile agreement despite her evident tension. Then she went back to scanning the crowd. "Ruth Barrett is part of this?"

"She and Heather already went out to their seats," Alisha replied, then asked John, "Will you stay back here?"

"Long as you need me," John said.

The pastor smiled warm approval, then said to his wife, "'Bout time you got your folks in line, right?"

Alisha watched them walk away, her face still tight. John reached for her hand and stood holding it, just letting the woman know she was not alone.

The Kennedy Center held a number of different venues. The largest was the Concert Hall, reserved for events like tonight's. Crowds spilled down the enormous outer chambers, decorated with flags and vintage bunting from all fifty states. Tickets had been sold out for weeks. All proceeds went toward some charity John had never heard of. The eleven choirs appearing this evening were kept in some sort of frenetic order by a phalanx of grey-jacketed ushers. They all stretched midway down the rear entrance hall, a carpeted expanse as vast as many main concert chambers. Alisha's choir was scheduled to sing second and occupied the angle where the main staircase connected with the hall. The children were from seven to mid-teens. Dressed in unaccustomed finery, many of them were awed into stillness by their surroundings. Alisha surveyed them with a flat, empty gaze. "Look at those children."

"What about them?"

"They're scared to death. Celeste needs to do something. She needs to do it *now*."

He thought the kids looked fine. But what did he know? "So go tell her."

"Those are *her* children. I don't have any right—"

"Alisha? There you are!" A slender woman with a dancer's frame stepped swiftly through the throng, followed by a tall white man in a jacket and no tie. The jacket had leather elbow patches. John had always disliked that look and normally felt uncomfortable around men who wore them. He stepped back a pace and watched as the two women embraced.

Alisha's face was a remarkable combination of shock and delight. "What are you doing here, Tabatha?"

"Girl, you're the one who left the tickets at the office."

"I know, but . . ." She turned to the hovering guy. "Hello, Kenneth."

His voice was as stiffly formal as his smile. "Alisha, how nice of you to invite us."

"Can I introduce a friend of mine? This is John Jacobs."

The younger woman gave him a swift up and down. John could see the questions in her gaze, as in, were he and Alisha an item? John said, "Good to meet you, both. Alisha, you really need to speak with Celeste."

"I told you, tonight this is not my choir."

"You're the one with experience," John persisted. He had no idea why he felt so certain about inserting himself into this. Only knowing he had to speak. "Do you see her anywhere?"

"She's over there talking to the program director."

John looked over the heads of the gathered choirs to the woman speaking with a man whose headset was lowered around his neck. Celeste's eyes looked tight with fear. Her husband stood beside her, surveying the choir with a worried look. "Do this for the children," he urged softly.

Alisha looked at him. "Hold on. These are the children I didn't want here."

"Then go for the choir. *Your* choir."

She bit her lip. "Will you come?"

"Of course I will."

Her sister asked, "Alisha, what is going on?"

"You go find your seats. We'll talk later. Come on, John. If we're doing it, we got to do it now."

John let her forge a way through the crowd. Alisha stopped on the carpeted floor below the stairs where the pastor's wife stood, and said, "Celeste, can I ask you something?"

The woman might have been frightened, but John also had the impression that the lady was cross by habit. "I'm busy, Alisha."

"I know that. And I'm sorry to bother you. But I need to ask you something."

Reluctantly the pastor's wife stepped away from the official. "What?"

"Do those children look scared to you?"

"Well, of course they do."

"I'm just wondering, do you think maybe they should have a chance to warm up?"

"What, here?"

"See, the thing is, they're gonna walk out there on the stage, and they're gonna see four thousand people watching them. And they got to hit that first note right."

Celeste wrung her hands, a tight little gesture, then forced her arms down to her sides. "I'm well aware of that. But we can't practice now."

"Why not?"

"Girl, you see how crowded this place is."

"What's more important, you bothering these folks, or these children missing their cue?" Alisha gave that a beat, then went on, "You're doing two songs, then leave and come back for the end when we all do the 'Hallelujah' together, isn't that right? So have them sing the chorus."

Her husband murmured, "She's right, Celeste."

Alisha held out her hand. "Come on, let's do this together."

John watched the two women proceed back through the crowd. The pastor stepped down beside him, nodded to the two, and said, "What you're seeing there is a true miracle in the making."

Celeste knelt before the children and gathered them forward with a sweep of her arms. In front of her young charges, her face underwent a remarkable transformation. Gone was the tight dissatisfaction, and in its place was a shimmering joy, a light that touched John as she stood and pulled a small tuning whistle from her pocket. She blew softly, then swept her hands through an exaggerated downbeat. And the children launched into song.

As Alisha had predicted, their start was ragged. But by the third note, the kids were in it together, and in tempo. Alisha and Celeste shared a smile as the antechamber gradually went silent.

And then, to the surprise of all, a great male voice boomed out in the distance. He was swiftly joined by another, and a third, and abruptly the entire antechamber was filled with hundreds of voices, all singing at that remarkable level just one notch below a shout.

"Hallelujah!" filled the back hallway, and John saw the children break out in magnificent grins, for they knew they were leading this crowd. They were not simply part of this mass of big people. They were *making it happen.*

John stood in the wings throughout the entire performance. When all the choirs had sung, they joined together onstage for the final event. The choirs spilled off the staggered bleachers and filled the periphery, right to the edge where the stage ended and the orchestra pit began. They had clearly practiced where they were to stand, but even so the littlest children looked on the verge of being lost to the throng. Then one of the baritones reached down and hefted the smallest of the children onto his right shoulder.

The kid's smile was so huge it lit up the entire chamber. Suddenly the littlest ones were up on shoulders everywhere, one even clambering up onto a stool that the stage manager slipped out from his place behind the curtains. They were the stars this night, and their joy swept out over the choirs, the orchestra, the audience.

John had heard Handel's "Hallelujah Chorus" all his life. But never had it sounded as fine as it did just then. When the number was finished, the listeners, on their feet, did not merely applaud. They shouted the joy back, hands raised in gratitude.

When it was all over, the lights had dimmed, and the audience departed, John was ready. He did not make anything happen. He simply made himself available.

The Barrett Ministry camera crew was led by Kevin Burnes, the producer. He directed the team with a soft voice and swift hand motions, ignoring everything but the next shot. They were joined by two local stations and the Gospel Music Channel, who had filmed the performance for a nationwide broadcast. John let some woman pat his face with powder and some young man station him over where the children clustered around Celeste and Alisha. John knelt on one knee on the backstage floor and spent almost an hour asking the children the same three questions. What was it like? How did it make you feel? What will you take away from this night? The children's responses tugged at him. With little prodding, they told him how they had left behind very real hardship and families that didn't work and struggles and dark hours. How for a brief time tonight they had seen what it meant to hope, to reach beyond, to live for the big dream.

When it was over, he did not rise. Nor did he ask the children to stop their happy chatter. Or try and write down the words. He simply let it come. Where from, he had no idea. But he knew the words needed to be said. Crouching on the raw plank floor, surrounded by happy faces, John said to the camera, "This is what we as the family of believers are called to do. Bring light to the dark hour. Show there is living hope. Tell others it is right to reach beyond where they are, and live for the big dream."

He rose to his feet, the camera lens following him upward, and went on, "The people out there who tell you hope is dead are not just lying. They are trying to make money from despair. They say it is just a trend, merely the direction society is already going. But we know differently. These people are failing in their responsibility to society. They should be showing a better way. They should be *challenging* the status quo. Not profiting from making things worse.

"It's time for us in the family of Jesus to stand up and be heard. We need to tell them, no more. We need to speak in the only language they hear or understand. Money. You know the drill. Go to the website at the bottom of your screen. All the companies that back this negativity, refrain from buying their products.

"It's time the world realizes what we stand for. Hope is alive and well. Hope lives in Jesus. For all time and beyond."

DAY
NINE

20

". . . by the truth . . ."

LOS ANGELES

Three-thirty the next morning, Trent rose from his rumpled bed, ordered coffee, and paced. He turned on his laptop and studied the video John Jacobs had shot in the Barrett Ministries studio. By this point he had the quietly irate message almost memorized. He viewed it now in order to take aim. Today was the day he took this man down.

The enemy was out there, and needed to be crushed.

At a knock, Trent turned off his computer and greeted the room service waiter. He drank his first cup standing by the window, looking out over the hotel grounds. He felt a subtle gnawing at his core. Much as he tried to tamp it down, the video struck a chord from his own past. John Jacobs could have been a member of his parents' church. The feeling of being drawn back into everything he had been so determined to leave behind made Trent tight with fury.

Gayle arrived at seven-thirty. They took the limo to the office in silence. Trent idly observed the sleepy streets through the side window, gathering himself for the day ahead. When Gayle's phone rang, she handed it over. Edlyn wanted a word.

"Where are you?"

"Five minutes from Wilshire. Less."

"Have Colin show you the new Barrett video, then call me."

Trent felt a surging heat rise from his gut. He handed the phone back and said, "Apparently the ministry has come out with yet another video."

"Is it serious?"

"Bad enough to rattle Edlyn's cage."

Colin and most of his team were upstairs when they arrived. From the grim expressions, Trent assumed they had already seen it several times. He asked, "What have they done now?"

"See for yourself," Colin spat out. He rolled a finger at the technician, who hit the button.

John Jacob's burly features did not gain anything by being portrayed on the massive screen. Trent watched in silence, his rage mounting by the second. The video was utterly unprofessional. Even the timing was wrong. It ran a full three minutes and fifteen seconds, more the length of a cinematic short than anything that could be fit into an advertisement slot. Trent's marketing expertise told him an audience's interest waned after ninety seconds, even when faced with the most appealing of film leads. Three minutes and fifteen seconds of a message-driven video was absurd. It broke all the rules. It was made to fail.

The video started with what had actually been the end of the choral performance, a kid standing on a stool and another seated on the right shoulder of a massive baritone. Both of the kids, African American, were dressed like little dolls in rented tuxedos. Their smiles defied the flattening effect that digital cameras tended to have on emotions. Their unmasked joy was a fist that punched straight at Trent's soul.

The "Hallelujah Chorus" continued to play throughout, but was muted so the people speaking could be heard. The music formed a chorale to the scene that unfolded backstage after the performance. John Jacobs down on the bare plank floor on a knee, a burly depot manager surrounded by several dozen children. They in turn were flanked by a huge number of choristers. John asked the same questions over and over. How did they feel? As if kids' sentiments mattered to anyone.

With very little prompting, the children responded along the same lines. Through this experience and the people they had met, they were learning to see a future that held hope. How they were determined to hold on to this lesson. How great to see what it meant to make goals and work hard and hold fast to tomorrow.

Occasionally the camera switched back to a view of the kids singing, flashing on their faces in time to their words spoken backstage. The music welled high and strong as the camera moved back to take in the entire stage, then it cut back to John Jacobs and his final few sentences. The music rose again, the last bars of the chorus, the kids lifting their voices and their hands. And then the audience rising, quick tight views of a dozen faces, a hundred, all of them mirroring the same joy as the kids. The same hope.

When the screen went blank, Trent asked, "When did they shoot this?"

"Apparently last night at the Kennedy Center," Colin replied. His British polish only barely managed to keep a lid on his fury. "The Gospel Channel is running this at the top of each hour. Their ratings have taken a significant rise."

Gradually his mind moved beyond the anger and the fear over this unexpected assault. From his position at the rear of the large studio, he could observe the LA crew. The room seemed to hesitate, uncertain how to respond to what they had all just witnessed. He asked, "What's the traffic on the sites carrying their video?"

A young technician by the side wall had the figures ready. "Four million hits since this went online. Don't know what it is on YouTube."

Trent took a hard breath. John Jacobs might as well have invaded their space and exploded a bomb inside the studio.

Colin Tomlin declared, "This cannot go unanswered."

"I absolutely agree." Trent turned to Gayle and said, "Make the call."

Edlyn's first words were, "I'm waiting."

Trent heard a mirror image of the woman's terseness in his own response. "We go on the attack. The team will prepare a response using the pastor you have on stand-by."

"I've already placed the call. I'm waiting for him to get back. What else?"

"We get Stone Denning to bring together his cast. Make it look impromptu, but have marketing script a tight, focused response. He's pushing hard to script and film the new scenes, so the cast should be available. You'll need to make that call."

"Done. Anything else?"

There was, as a matter of fact. "Call back your sponsors, the ones that are getting cold feet. Tell them the cost of a minute's air time has just doubled."

There was a silence. Then, "Say again."

"Look, we might as well face it. We've lost them."

"We are talking," Edlyn replied, "of over a hundred million advertising dollars per annum."

Trent swallowed against the rising gorge. "If we run after them, word will get out. We need to hold to what Barry said. There's no such thing as bad publicity. We go on the offensive. We talk about how only life's losers hold on to yesterday. Which is what we're talking about here. Yesterday's lie."

"I like that."

So did he, matter of fact. "Then tell Stone that's the line he should use."

"I want Colin to personally supervise the taping," Edlyn said. "Do I need to make that call?"

"He's here beside me."

"I want this cut and ready to play with our news channel's talk shows. Select two talking heads we should bring on air for support."

"You can count on me, Edlyn."

There was a momentary pause, then she replied, "I'm coming to see that. Now give me Colin."

He accepted the phone and said, "Yes, Edlyn. I agree, we were completely blindsided. Yes. Blood on the street."

He handed the phone back. "She wants a final word."

The phone felt lava hot as Trent pressed it to his ear. "Yes."

"I have a message from my father."

"I'm listening."

"Whatever it takes." Edlyn cut the connection.

Trent took a moment to gather himself. How *dare* that bumbling idiot stand between Trent and his dreams? Edlyn's abrupt message echoed through his head like a cannon shot. *Whatever it takes.* Trent was going to *destroy* that man and everything he stood for. And enjoy every minute.

The people gathered here, his frontline troops, waited in silent readiness. Trent had the distinct impression that many could not understand what had just happened. They'd had everything on their side. The money, the power, one of the greatest empires the entertainment industry had ever seen. Brought low by the assistant manager of a truck depot?

Trent had no idea how to address such a demoralized group. So he did the only thing that came to mind. Which was to pretend he was someone else. For a minute, one brief breath, he forced himself to act as Barry Mundrose might.

He handed Gayle her phone. Then he clapped his hands hard. People jerked involuntarily and turned his way. "Listen up," Trent barked. "Our guns are charged. And now it's our turn."

"Hear, hear," Colin murmured.

"We are going to take the fight to them. On *our* terms. And we are going to *obliterate* the opposition." Trent began pacing slowly, timing his tread to his words. "Colin, we need to split our team into three groups. The first is going to design a script for Stone Denning and one of his stars. The theme is the same. Splice in scenes from the film and the television pilot. We'll pitch it as an advertisement. It goes out tomorrow. It plays all day. Gayle, check and see if Stone and his team are on set."

"Certainly, Mr. Cooper." She turned away.

"The second group is going to feed information about this John Jacobs to every news source we have. People, hear this: their spokesman is a convicted felon. Your job is to spice that dish as hot as you can make it. Are we clear on this?"

"Perfectly," Colin said. "And the third group?"

"That will be my team. We are going to plan the assault to follow this one." Trent clapped his hands a second time. "Who wants to work on strategy?"

To his astonishment, every person in the room responded.

Gayle turned back and said, "I have Stone Denning on the line. He received a call from Barry himself. He has seen the video. Several times, actually. He is on set. He is ready to go."

Colin spoke, his voice crisp and electric. "I will personally supervise that crew. Who is with me?"

Trent smiled at how the assembled group threw their hands in the air a second time. "Colin, could you split us into three teams?"

"With pleasure."

"Gayle, I want you to head the third group."

His words caught them all by surprise. Including himself. Gayle managed, "Excuse me?"

Trent said, "You know the news outlets better than anyone except Colin, and he's going to have his hands full." When she started to object, he added, "It's time. Say yes."

"I—Yes."

Trent then took a step back, and watched the LA manager form his teams. He let the wall take his weight, his legs suddenly weak. He saw that the people were not just reenergized, but maybe even excited, eager to get at it.

Colin moved in close and murmured, "I say, well done."

They worked hard through the night. Sometime after midnight, the film crew returned with enough raw footage to create a bevy of sixty-second bombs. Colin politely enquired if Trent would release some of his own team to assist in the process of editing. Trent could not have cared less. He had accomplished what he intended. They were unified in their desire to bring the opposition down, crush them into the dust.

Toward dawn he reviewed and approved the rough cuts of three ads that would run on the morning news shows. Colin had ordered his other employees in early, and the entire building buzzed with feverish energy. Trent went into the executive kitchen where a buffet had been set up, part breakfast and part all-day meal. He loaded a plate but declined the waiter's offer of fresh coffee. His mouth felt furry from fatigue and an overdose of caffeine.

"Mind some company?"

"Not at all." Trent watched Gayle settle into the chair next to his own. "How do you do it?"

"Do what?"

"You look as fresh as you did last night."

"It's just a shell. On the inside I'm utterly undone."

"I don't believe that for a minute."

She took a bite, then put her fork down. "I don't know why I took all this food. I'm far too exhausted to eat."

"I saw the press release your group put together. It's fabulous, Gayle."

"It's gone out to over fifty newspapers. We'll feed it to the morning shows as we can. Let's hope it does the job."

"The guy is going down," Trent assured her.

She pushed her plate to one side. "You did an excellent job last night, rallying the troops."

"I had no idea what to do," he confessed. "So I pretended I was Barry."

"Well, it worked." She sipped from her mug, sighed, and turned to stare out over the pale wash of another LA dawn.

"What is it?"

"I can't thank you enough for the chance," she said slowly. "It will be hard going back to being Barry's aide."

"Then don't."

She continued to stare out over the Hollywood skyline. Imperial palms rose like inked-in silhouettes against the gathering light. "I found myself thinking back to that earlier trip out here."

"Your screen test," Trent recalled.

She nodded slowly. "There is only one line of work open for an actress with dead eyes. Do you know what I mean?"

"Yes."

"Because I am beautiful and fresh, they offered me a million dollars." She lifted her mug, then set it down untasted. "I was so tempted. I hated myself for how much I wanted something that I would be willing to degrade myself in that fashion. I left LA the next day. I promised myself I would not come back until I could do so on my own terms."

He reached for her hand. "Let's do this together. You and me. Make the dreams real for both of us."

She looked at him, her expression solemn, her eyes holding a grave light. "I was hoping you'd say that."

21

". . . as citizens of heaven . . ."

WASHINGTON DC AND WESTCHESTER COUNTY

They traveled straight from the Kennedy Center to the airport, flying north through a starlit night. Kevin's production crew spent the journey huddled together, working on a concept they aimed to put online before dawn. John heard them field several calls from the Gospel Channel, but did not try to follow the high-octane discussion.

It was after two in the morning when they arrived back at the Barrett Ministries' center. They wished one another a good night and drifted away, all but the production crew. John slept peacefully, a deep and dreamless slumber that held him in a sweet embrace far longer than normal. He was vaguely aware of Heather rising and leaving. He heard birdsong and the sounds of his wife dressing and closing the door behind her, then he slipped off once more. He'd felt a vague desire to join her, there and gone in an instant. When he awoke, the cottage was silent, and the bedside clock read almost noon. He had not slept so late in years.

John dressed and headed toward the main house. The angle where the porch railing met the grove of cherry trees had become their designated prayer corner. As he climbed the stairs, Ruth and Jenny Linn and her parents halted their quiet conversation long enough to greet him. John asked, "Where is everybody?"

"Busy," Ruth replied.

He took that as a polite dismissal, went inside. The two young women were setting up a buffet lunch on the long central table. Well used to maintaining a discreet distance from Ruth and her guests, they greeted John, directed him to the coffee urn, and returned to their work.

John borrowed a Bible from the shelf holding a dozen or so well-thumbed volumes. He took his mug back outside and down to a wooden bench placed between the oaks and the creek. A hummingbird flitted into view, hovering not two paces away so as to drink from a wildflower. He drank his coffee, read a few passages, but mostly he sat and listened to the wind creak the boughs overhead. John sensed a vague rumble of thunder on the horizon, which was absurd, since the sky overhead was clear and milky blue. He thought it probably foreshadowed some great effort that was going to be required of him. But he drained his cup and leaned back in the bench and stretched out his legs. For the moment, it was enough.

He must have dozed off, for the next thing he knew Richard Linn was saying, "John?"

"Eh, yes?"

"The ladies would like to have a word, if you wouldn't mind."

John shifted his bones, stretched, and decided he needed another mug. "Where is everybody?"

"Following your lead."

He rose to his feet and followed Richard back toward the house. "What do you mean?"

Instead of responding directly, Richard said, "What you said last night was truly inspired." There was a certain formality to the way Richard spoke that left John feeling like his words were only a small component of what was going on inside his head. Richard paused at the foot of the stairs. A head shorter than John, stumpy and strong, his dark eyes burned beneath their Oriental fold as he said,

"I felt the hand of God resting upon you while you were with the children."

John had no idea what to say, except, "So did I."

Richard went on, "My wife and I are honored to be a part of this."

John felt the day's ease slip away. He knew without being told that beyond Richard's compliment rose yet another duty. He thanked Richard and followed him up the stairs, then pushed through the kitchen door and recharged his mug. He needed to be more awake than he was for whatever they had waiting for him out there in the prayer corner.

The warm afternoon wind rushed through the trees to his right as he seated himself in the rocker. John knew they were giving him a moment to settle, and appreciated the gesture. When they did not speak, he repeated the question, "What's going on around here?"

It was Jenny who answered. "I woke up this morning with the strong need to follow your lead. I spoke with the others, and they agreed."

"I don't understand."

"We have recorded your message for different audiences," Jenny explained. "We combined your two communications into one."

"My daughter did this," Richard said.

"It is very beautiful," his wife agreed. "Most compelling."

Jenny went on, "Alisha has addressed the African American community. I spoke the words both in Cantonese and Mandarin. Aaron has spoken in Hebrew, Yussuf in Arabic."

"The message is going out to all the world," Richard said, marveling.

"Sounds great," John said, though he couldn't help but think that theirs was a feeble effort compared to the might of the Mundrose empire.

His unspoken thoughts must have showed, for Ruth said, "Tell him what's happening."

In response, Jenny reached for her laptop. She typed for a time, then handed John the computer and said, "Hit 'play.'"

The impact of the video caught him totally off guard. He scarcely recognized himself. The stark power of his words seemed utterly alien. When it was done, Jenny asked, "Do you want to see it again?"

"No." He handed back the laptop. "No."

"GMC is playing the video once an hour. The online site has received over four million hits."

Richard added, "The producer, Kevin, says it's gone viral."

"GMC wants to interview you for a clip they will air with their nightly news program," Jenny said. "I have asked if they could give you the questions in advance, so I can help you with the responses."

John wished he was able to hear such requests without having his gut congeal with fresh fear. "You might as well give me the rest."

Heather reached over and took his hand, the caring wife delivering dreaded news. "Your story is coming out."

He felt nerves rise to his throat.

"Everything, John."

Ruth looked more frail today, her voice a slender thread that still managed to carry great strength. "I want to tell you something. Are you listening to me, John?"

He forced himself to reach beyond the horror of knowing his secrets were now revealed to the world. "Yes."

"The only reason they are attacking us is because we are succeeding. Do you understand?"

"You don't know. You can't . . ." John took a deep breath. Another. John fastened his hands to the rocker arms. Knowing they needed to hear this. Wishing he had said it before they put him on air the first time. "When I was nineteen years old, I was a sophomore at Ohio State and a star of their football team. I was rambunctious and aggressive and full of myself. After we won the regional final, I went out drinking with my buddies. I got into a bar fight, I lost my temper, and I beat a man within an inch of his life . . ." John felt engulfed in the torment of thirty long years. Finally he recovered enough to continue. "The man still suffers from what I did to him. No help I send can ever restore the damaged state I left him in. I was arrested and convicted and did six months in the state farm. I lost my scholarship. I was kicked out of the university. The only person who didn't abandon me was Heather."

He released one hand to clench the flesh over his aching heart. "My entire life headed off in a different direction. My every step, my every job, my every loan application, my every interview—it's all been tainted by that one dark night. My life never recovered."

John slid from his rocker and landed on his knees by the arm of his wife's chair. "I'm sorry, Heather. So sorry."

"Oh, John."

"What I've put you through—"

"My dear, sweet, loving man." She held his face in both of hers. "You have been a wonderful husband and father. You have given me everything you had to give."

"It's not enough. It never has been."

"Have I ever asked you for anything more?"

"No, but you should have. And you should have gotten it."

"I am so glad I'm married to you."

Jenny reached over, gripped John's shoulder, and said, "Lord, as you calm the seas, so calm my brother's spirit."

"I say, amen," Richard said.

"Sit up, John," Heather said.

The others waited as she guided him back into his chair. Though it cost him, John met each gaze in turn, and realized, "You can't still want me to do this."

"No, John," Ruth said. "We think God is going to *use* this."

DAY
TEN

22

". . . at the proper time . . ."

LOS ANGELES

Soon after daybreak Trent sent Gayle to check them out of the Bel Air Hotel. An inexpensive apartment-hotel two blocks from their offices, on the wrong side of Wilshire, would do. Trent knew Gayle was disappointed, but he also knew it was the right decision. His bungalow cost twelve hundred dollars a night and he could better use the drive time either working or sleeping. There wasn't time for anything else, and his ego did not require such elegant stroking. He would leave that for a time when he could truly enjoy it. Once he had survived the current crisis. Because that was what he faced. Either he made this work, or all this was just part of someone else's dream.

Trent left the office building in the bleak light of predawn Los Angeles. The desert to the east felt closest in this vague hour, when the streets were as empty as the sky overhead. The palms lining Wilshire Boulevard were etchings inked into a pale blue-grey wash. Trent stumbled down the side street, checked in to the new digs, and threw himself onto the bed. His weary brain echoed with faint tendrils of worry and stress and fear. His vague nightmares never completely managed to wake him.

Too soon the phone rang with his wake-up call. His body ached with the need for more rest. But he had to get back. He rose from the bed and discovered someone had deposited his suitcase inside his doorway. Trent showered and dressed, left the hotel, and winced at the roar of a city already well into its morning routine.

But as soon as he entered the Wilshire Building, he felt the fatigue and uncertainty slip away. He was back in his element, feeding off the crew's mad energy. A fresh breakfast buffet had been set up in the lobby. Trent made himself a sandwich and poured a mug of coffee. He laughed at a joke he did not need to hear, and climbed the stairs, food in hand, to the fourth floor. He heard chatter echo through the stairway's concrete cavern and knew others felt as he did, that the elevator moved far too slowly for such a time as this.

He passed through the central office area and greeted several of the people on his strategy team. Their clothes were rumpled and their eyes red-rimmed, and some of the hands jerked with the tight spasms of too much caffeine. But Trent saw the pride they were taking in their work and knew the hours they invested, and he thought he had never known a taste quite so sweet as leading this group.

He entered the office Colin had let him have at his request and swiftly became absorbed in the time sheets he had been working on before departing. He turned at a knock on the door.

"My name is Dermott McAllister, Mr. Cooper. Perhaps you've heard of me?"

"No, sorry."

The man was narrow and dressed in a nondescript brown tweed suit. "No matter. Mr. Mundrose suggested you might want my assistance."

"Father or son?"

His smile was as small as the rest of him. Perhaps that was the case with all his motions. Certainly his voice was soft enough to go unnoticed. Then again, Trent reflected, the asp was one of nature's smallest snakes, and also one of the most venomous. Dermott McAllister replied, "I am not certain that Mr. Mundrose Junior is even aware of my existence."

The man appeared oddly put together. At first glance, the face belonged to a man in his thirties. But closer inspection revealed extensive plastic surgery. And Trent was fairly certain the man wore a toupee. Dermott McAllister's face was reworked into a form that might have been handsome, except for how a few angles were not quite symmetric. The chin was a few degrees to the left of center. The nose tilted slightly to the right. One ear appeared a fraction lower than the other. The neck was creased in a couple of places, as though the surgeons had not quite pulled the slack tight enough. But the man's most remarkable quality was his eyes. They were brown and flat and empty as an open grave.

Trent asked, "Help me with what?"

"Whatever you desire, Mr. Cooper. Among the Mundrose Group's upper echelon, 'whatever it takes' carries particular importance."

Trent felt a flutter of fear. "As in, last chance."

"It's so good to know I am dealing with someone who sees life as it is."

"So you are whatever it takes."

"I am nothing, Mr. Cooper. I am no one. Mr. Mundrose sent me to offer what small word of counsel I can, and then vanish into the ether. I do both well, may I say." Dermott McAllister glanced around the windowless cubicle and sniffed. "This is the best space Colin Tomlin had to offer?"

"I asked for it," Trent replied. "I wanted a desk as close to his as possible. You take the one he assigned to me."

"I beg pardon?"

"There's a spare cubicle in the central bullpen. I assume you'll need the privacy more than me."

"Very well, Mr. Cooper, I accept." He gestured to each side of the room. "Now tell me what it is I'm seeing here."

Trent had taped long strips of white paper along both walls. "This first holds what I know about our opposition. I've asked my agency for more complete workups. They should be here any time now."

"And the other?"

Trent turned to the opposite wall. "This is our frontal assault. That's my term. The ads, the online campaign, films, interviews, printed stories, so on."

Dermott McAllister revealed a slight limp as he moved to examine first one and then the other. Trent assumed the man had survived some horrific accident, and for some reason Trent found himself more comfortable as a result. He knew the man was deadly. But their lives were linked now. By far more than what he had scrawled on those paper scrolls.

As if in confirmation, the little man spoke without taking his eye off the sheets. "Now tell me what you really want, Mr. Cooper."

"I—excuse me?"

"These plans of yours, they're all fine as far as they go. But are they enough? That's the question, isn't it. Do they accomplish what is required?"

Trent scanned the two long sheets. When his team had been assembled, he had imagined the events like cannons primed and waiting to be fired. But now doubts rose up and gnawed at him. He confessed, "I never thought we would need any of this. But now—"

A voice spoke from the doorway. "Oh, Mr. McAllister."

"How very nice to see you, Gayle. You look fresh and lovely as ever."

Gayle seemed unwilling to enter his office. She hovered just beyond the entrance, her expression tinted with a fear strong as dread. "I was not aware that you had been . . . summoned."

"And yet here I am."

Trent told her, "I'm expecting new intel from the agency. Could you please go online, download what they've sent, and print out four copies. Keep one for yourself, give one to Colin, and bring us the other two."

"Certainly." She fled.

Trent walked over and shut the door. Gayle's response to the narrow man only heightened his own sense of confronting a monumental event. Dermott McAllister had not merely asked him a question. He was issuing a challenge. How much did Trent want it? How far was Trent willing to take this? He was being offered a choice. He could accept the invitation, and be granted the power to wreak havoc on those who dared oppose him. Or . . .

Trent turned from the door to discover that Dermott McAllister had gone back to studying the strips of paper with the handwritten notes. In a sudden jarring flash, Trent saw himself in ten years' time. Standing in some grand office, staring at a different plan of action but with the same flat gaze. The soft speech. Drawing the same sense of dread from those seated across from him.

Trent walked over to stand beside the man. He could feel the barely disguised energy emanating from McAllister, like the acrid heat that presaged a tornado's arrival. But the force fit the moment. Because the truth was, he had always known it would come to this. Committing himself totally. Claiming the power to wreak havoc on his enemies.

Again he felt that shuddering impact of unwanted insight. He saw what had happened to Dermott McAllister's voice. The acid of old rage had eaten down to where all he could manage was a dry, husky murmur.

Trent gave a mental shrug. Barry Mundrose had said it all. He echoed the words out loud. "Whatever it takes."

"My thoughts exactly, Mr. Cooper."

Trent moved in closer still. "I want them dead and buried. I want everyone who has even shaken their hands to be singed in the process."

"I was hoping you'd say that." Up close the man's surgical scars were much clearer, red tracings along the hairline and forehead and above the right eye. "That is my area of expertise, as it happens."

Trent went on, "I want their campaign destroyed. I want them to rue the moment they decided to take on the Mundrose Group."

The little man faced Trent. "You want to win."

"No, Mr. McAllister. I want the world to know that I am someone to fear. So the next time, they won't even *think* about opposing me. I want them beaten before the next battle starts."

"A man after my own heart." He turned back to the wall. "Give me a few minutes to settle in, and then we'll get to work."

23

". . . whoever belongs to God . . ."

WESTCHESTER COUNTY

Throughout that morning, John watched helplessly as the secrets he had guarded nearly his entire life began to appear on national display. Two of the morning news programs led with his appearance, speaking for a church-led protest movement against the Mundrose empire. The overview of his background was very thorough, and their smirks said it all. Here was a convicted felon, an assistant manager for a truck depot, who dared criticize a renowned entertainment empire for merely another film, another ad campaign.

Over his second cup of coffee, John watched his wife talk on the phone with their two children. They both knew about their father's past because John had told them. Several times, in fact. His son took the current news in stride. He was busy, he had two young ones of his own and a small business to run. John often thought of his son as living the American dream for them both. But he had never said it, because John did not want to add to the pressure that already surrounded the young man. He had not yet heard about the public smear campaign and didn't see what the fuss was about. That particular conversation lasted all of three minutes, which was typical for a call during his son's long workday.

His daughter, though, was a different story. He could see it in the way Heather's answers grew as taut as her face. Sally had come ten years after her brother, when he and Heather thought they would have no more children. Sally was a joy and a trial, both in equal measure. She had made a lifetime commitment to playing the victim, fiercely determined to remain the center of her universe.

Finally John asked, "Would you like me to speak with her?"

Heather covered the receiver. "I'm trying to spare you."

"Maybe you shouldn't. It's my fault."

"No, it's not, John."

"Heather, I'm the one—"

"Don't make me argue with you too." She turned her back to him and returned to the conversation.

John knew exactly what Sally was saying. Why hadn't he known this would come out and stopped it before now. John sighed his way out of the porch rocker and went inside. He felt like he was running away. But Heather was right. He didn't need this. Not now.

Ruth was seated in the kitchen, the cane leaning against the table beside her chair. She thanked the young woman who set down a saucer holding three pills, then told John, "Kevin just called from the studio. They're ready to shoot the next clip."

"Are you all right?"

She revealed an impish smile. "It would be terrible to lie under the circumstances, wouldn't it?"

"Awful," John agreed with mock solemnity.

"Then don't ask." She pointed him down the hall to the study. "Go choose yourself a different suit. Charcoal gray would be nice this time. And don't keep those young folks waiting."

As he knotted the tie that Heather had selected for him, John found himself struck by an idea. He found it oddly remarkable how he could be making plans in the midst of what he had expected to be his most shameful hour. And yet there was no denying the fact that the divine hand was at work. He had come to this realization late in the night, when his sweat had dampened the sheets, and he had wondered if he would have the strength to rise with the dawn. He had no control over the outside world. He could only accept that he was not alone, and he was doing what had been asked of him.

When John emerged from the house, Yussuf and Aaron were standing there with Heather. "I asked them to join us," she told him.

"I'm glad you did." They walked down the lane skirting the low hill toward the main complex. John took his time explaining what had come to him. "It's just the glimmer of an idea. So if you don't want to do this thing—"

Yussuf didn't let him finish. "How can we refuse?"

"It is a good idea," Aaron agreed.

"I think so too," Heather said.

"Though the very thought fills me with dread," Aaron added.

"Join the club," John said.

There was an uncommon hush to the day, with high clouds held aloft by the still air. The heat caused the road ahead to shimmer. John slipped off the suit coat and slung it over one shoulder. To either side of the lane, tiny wildflowers carpeted the meadow with flecks of brilliant color. When the main buildings came into view, he took a long breath and hoped he was doing the right thing.

When the four entered the studio, they were greeted with a silence that mirrored the stillness beyond the portal. John knew they had all seen the disastrous news programs. They probably felt his own shame, doubted his worth. And they were right to do so. He doubted himself.

The young woman with her fishing tackle box of cosmetics patted his face with powder as the technician did a quick check of his microphone. John explained to the producer what he had in mind, and swiftly two more chairs were drawn around and a mock conference table set up on the raised dais. They used portable tables with folding legs and quickly covered the surface with green felt. They miked Yussuf and Aaron and seated them to John's left. Then they were ready, and the producer counted them down, and it was too late to wonder if he was right to do this thing, too late to do anything but speak.

"A lot has been said about me today," John began. "And most of it is true. First I will give you my take on the events that have shaped my life. Then I'll tell you what I really think is going on here."

The tawdry tale of youthful arrogance, too much alcohol, and out-of-control violence tasted like sawdust in his mouth.

"I didn't ever really see the guys who finally took us up on our challenge," John went on. "I was too full of my own power. I was addicted to the red veil of fury that came with the certainty that I was invincible. The next thing I knew, I stood over a man I had reduced to a bloody pulp. Then the cops slammed my face down into a puddle of spilled beer and cuffed me. The steel ratcheted tight, and I knew my life was over. I still have nightmares of that sound, cutting off the future that I had just tossed away."

He felt the perspiration slick his face, and he heard his voice crack. But he knew his decision was right. There was a power that came with the deed, enough to see him through. "My shame was worse than the jail and the trial and the six months in prison. The disgrace and the guilt became a tattoo on my heart. I could never hide from what I had done. My life was reduced to a series of dead-end jobs. For years I humped garbage pans and cleared tables and cooked fries and stocked shelves. I was just one paycheck away from being on the street. I was constantly afraid and utterly helpless. I paid for my mistake. And paid and paid. And the guilt never went away."

He punctuated the end of that sorry tale with a moment's silence. He resisted the urge to swipe at his face. Then he went on, "My only hope came from Jesus as shown through my beloved wife. In Heather's loving gaze I came as close as I possibly could to knowing God's forgiving power. Until that day in church, two Sundays ago, when God spoke to me and started me down the path to this place.

"The question is, why would God choose someone like me? There are a million believers who could do a better job. There is but one answer that makes any sense. God wanted someone who represented the power of hope. Someone whose entire life was a wasted mess, except for this one thing. This one truth. The eternal message of *hope*. And that is what gives me the strength to speak honestly to you today. This isn't about me, no matter what all these other people tell you. This is about the eternal message. Hope is alive. Hope is real. Hope is here and hope is now. Jesus is waiting for you to discover this for yourself."

John turned to the two men seated beside him. "Now I'd like to ask these two friends, my new brothers in faith, to tell you what the eternal message of hope means to them."

Both men gave their own stories of lives reshaped by a hope most people prefer to ignore. John wondered if his own voice had sounded that shaky, and decided that it did not matter.

Then the two men were finished, and the cameras panned back to his face. John realized they wanted him to offer a final word. He said the first thing that came to mind. "When the world of entertainment starts shouting their grim chant that hope is dead, they're nothing more than vultures circling around the dying. But they can't rob you of life unless you want them to. It's still your choice.

"We're asking you to join us in taking a stand. The only thing that matters to these wannabe trendsetters is their bottom line. So to stop them, we have to impact their profit margins. Don't go see a single film released from the Mundrose Group. Don't buy any of their games. Don't purchase anything made by one of their sponsors. On your screen is a website listing their sponsors and products. Turn away from them. Do it now. Your voice will be heard loud and clear."

John was still in the process of unhooking his mic when it happened. The lights simply went out. All of them. The studio was utterly black.

Aaron asked, "What is happening?"

Kevin called out, "Somebody check the mains!"

Then a glimmer appeared from high overhead as the emergency lights came on, just strong enough to show people rushing about, vague shadows cut from the gloom. A young woman said, "The system is fine. Our power has been cut."

"What, to the whole building?"

"Looks that way."

Kevin's voice rose a full octave. "Somebody please tell me we didn't lose the footage!"

A technician called, "Saved and in the can!"

"Okay, boot up your laptops, let's get to editing!"

Aaron looked around and asked, "What just happened?"

Heather replied, "Our opponents have taken this to the next level."

24

". . . though he slay me . . ."

WESTCHESTER COUNTY

Alisha spent most of the day watching John Jacobs lead their team. He was not aware of the impact he was having, which only made his example more inspiring. Time and again she thought of the saying about believers needing to preach all the time, and occasionally needing to use words. Because John spoke very little. But he relayed truth with every breath, every movement.

Alisha observed that the attacks struck like bullets from a gun. First, power was cut to the entire compound, including Ruth's home. Then the phone lines all went down. Then cellphone connections were gone. John's steadiness held them together. He knew about generators, and he knew about using tools. So he pitched in and helped the technical crew restore power. The cellphone tower was visible from the admin building. But when he and technicians tried to drive there, they discovered the front driveway had been sealed off by a bevy of Con Ed trucks, and a four-foot trench was dug where it met the main road.

So John and the techies took off overland and discovered the cable to the cellphone tower had been cut. Once they had that repaired and returned to the admin building, news started coming in. All of it bad.

John received the first phone call, telling him that he was fired. He accepted it with the grim resolve of a man who was not going to let a body blow deflect his focus from the goal. Alisha watched him hold hands with his wife as he explained, "My boss was never one to soften things up. But he didn't try to hide the fact that he hated doing this."

"Especially after the deal you brought in with that New York group," Heather said. She stroked his arm. "Oh John, I'm so sorry," she whispered.

"He said word had come down from the executive board," John went on. "That it was totally out of his hands."

Alisha knew she should probably be worrying about the two of them, but right then all she could think about was the Kennedy Center, and how right John had been. Both about her phoning Tabatha, and her talking to Celeste. And how close she had come to doing neither.

And Alisha realized she had never thanked the man.

Aaron confessed that he and Yussuf had been informed not long before their recording session they were up for administrative review. Alisha had no idea what that meant, but from their expressions, she assumed it was serious. Then came Miss Ruth with the news that all the ministry's accounts had been frozen. The bank manager assured her it was a minor administrative issue, but could not say when funds would be made available.

Which meant they were all gathered there together when John's son called. John listened for a moment, then asked his son if he could put him on speaker so his mother could hear as well. When Alisha started to rise with the others to give the some privacy, John waved them to stay where they were. "Go on, son."

"My company's bank is withdrawing our line of credit, our loan, the works. The branch manager wouldn't tell me why. Just they were reviewing their small-company portfolio, and some aberrations had been revealed in our accounts. I talked with him three days ago—everything was fine."

"When did he call you today?"

"About an hour and a half ago. Does this have anything to do with what you're doing, Dad?"

"I can't say for certain, but I think . . . yes." John looked up as Heather reached over and took his hand. "I'll walk away from this if you ask, son. I can walk away."

"Would it do any good?"

When John hesitated, Heather replied, "Probably not. Your father has confronted a very large group and powerful conglomerate. This is their response."

Alisha waited for the young man on the other end of the phone to bemoan his fate, berate his father. Which was probably how she would have responded. Instead, he simply said, "What should I do?"

John looked at his wife, then asked, "Would you like to pray with us?"

"Sure, Dad. That's probably a good idea."

So they all joined hands, forming a circle with the phone in the middle. Alisha felt a hand settle on her shoulder, and saw that Kevin the producer had joined them. John said the words.

After they hung up, John stared at his big, callused hands and said, "Before I came up here, I'd be swamped by the same awful feelings of guilt and helpless rage. Then I'd do what I've done for thirty-five years. I'd put my head down and focus on the next step."

Heather stroked the point where his collar met his hairline, the simple gesture of a woman in love. "And now, John?"

"It's all so new. I tell you how it seems. I am growing. It probably sounds like a selfish thing to say at a time like this, when my son has come to me for answers I don't have. But that's the only thing that registers in this moment. I'm not blown off course by these events. For the first time in my life."

Alisha was still digesting his words when her phone rang.

She looked at the readout, she saw who it was, and she resisted the urge to go slip away somewhere private. She stepped back a bit, but she kept her gaze on John. There was only one reason why her boss would be calling her just then. And all she could think of was how much she wanted to hold on to what was happening inside that group. With her friends. With their leader.

Celeste pleaded, "Slow down, slow down, Alisha."

But Alisha was too caught up in what had just gone down to apply the brakes. Not to mention what she was doing right then—the first thing that came to her after speaking with her boss. She called the woman who had been her nemesis. Right then, though, all Alisha could think of was how this call was four years in the making. "Like I said, I've just been fired. Eleven years I've worked for them. They wouldn't even tell me why I was let go. Eleven years!"

"I'm so sorry you're going through this, Alisha."

She might have felt God's nudging to make this call. Even so, Alisha felt odd talking so personally with this woman. Four years of issues didn't just fade away. Even so, this discussion felt immensely right. So she left the admin building and walked up and down the little lane where it turned off to the darkened house and her cottage. Now telling Celeste about what had happened to the others. Summing it all up with, "This is pure harassment."

"Of course it is, Alisha. Now tell me you understand what's going on here."

Alisha finally heard Celeste's tone of voice. It might not have been the calm and care Pastor Terry was so famous for. But Celeste was *listening*. What was more, the woman offered Alisha *strength*. Doing all she could to get Alisha back on solid ground.

"Alisha?"

Alisha took the first easy breath since the power had been cut. "They're worried."

"There you go. That's *exactly* what's happening here. One of the world's biggest entertainment groups is so concerned about what you're doing up there, they've taken aim. Now tell me what it is you folks need most of all."

Soon as the one word shaped in her mind, the hand holding her phone steadied. "Prayer."

"There you are. When we're done, you're gonna tell me what else you and your friends need from us. And then you're going to go tell the others that you folks have a lot of us out here, just looking for a way to help out."

John punched in the number that Ruth gave him, hit the speaker button, and set it on the small table between his chair and her rocker. He did not like how Ruth looked, and worried that the strain of being under assault was worsening whatever disorder she refused to discuss.

They were gathered on the admin building's front porch. The building's prefab warehouse structure possessed homey touches in the form of a broad front veranda with wooden railings and flower-clad trellises. Rockers identical to those on Ruth's front patio, right down to one with padding that John suspected no one used except Ruth, furnished seating for the group.

When the pastor came on the line Ruth said, "Good afternoon, Craig."

"The Internet is on fire, Ruth. Tell me what's happening."

"My voice is a bit weak today, Craig. I'm going to hand you over to John Jacobs."

There were six of them clustered around John and Ruth—Jenny and Alisha and Yussuf and Aaron and Kevin and Heather. The others were manning the phones, which had been ringing constantly ever since power and the comm links had been restored. John did a swift recount of what had come down, avoiding mention of his own family's problems. The pastor responded, "It's only the beginning, I'm afraid."

"That's my feeling as well."

John liked hearing the man add himself to their numbers. As he did hearing Craig ask, "What can we do to help?"

"Sir, I actually don't know where to start."

"John—can I call you John? This is no longer about your organization and our church. This is a unifying issue."

Ruth leaned in toward the phone. "There is one thing. John probably won't say it, so I will. His son has a small business. The bank has pulled his line of credit. If he can't find an alternate source of funds by Friday, he will go under."

"Have him call me. I'll make a couple of calls and see if one of my elders in the finance community can arrange a discretionary short-term loan."

"But—" John felt Heather's hand settle upon his shoulder. "I don't know what to say."

"Who else has been affected?"

Ruth said, "All of us."

"You'll need to get your lawyers on this. Do it now. Waiting won't help. Let me know if you need assistance on that side."

She shared a smile with the others gathered around her. "You really are a fighter at heart, Craig."

"Of course I am. All good pastors know when to push back." His strength resonated through the small speaker, lifting the mood of everyone gathered. "I want you to understand that my church is constantly invited to participate in national events. All I can do is share the invitation to visit the web-page list of where to buy products. The rest is up to the congregation and our Lord." Craig Davenport spoke with a natural authority that resonated about the porch. "That is what I did when I first heard of this event."

"Our turning," John said. "That's how I've been thinking of it, ever since I was called to take the first step."

"Your turning. It's as good a word as any. I played the first video before all our services. And I shared it with my network of fellow pastors. Then I left it in the hands of God. What you need to know is this. I've had to assign my newest associate pastor to handle the telephone traffic. We're fielding calls from all over the nation. All over the globe, if I'm understanding him correctly. Because the overture originated here, it's coming back here. And we're getting swamped. I mean, this is unlike anything I've ever witnessed. We are receiving emails and phone calls and offers of help from *thousands* of churches and outreach programs and individuals." He gave that a moment, then went on, "Your call has awakened the church. This can't be ignored by the powers that be. It's too big, and it's growing too fast. Of course they're going to attack."

DAY
ELEVEN

25

" . . . the beauty of the Lord . . ."

WESTCHESTER COUNTY

John awoke twice during the night, reliving aftershocks from the previous day. He lay in the dark, waiting for the sense of helpless dread to overwhelm him. Instead, each time he knew a soft sorrow, an ache deep in his bones. Pain for himself, of course, and even more for his son and the others in his group. The second time, John rose from the bed and entered the cottage's front room. He turned on a light and took the small book from the pocket of his coat. It was the first time he had held it since that Sunday service, and instantly he was flooded with recollections of that hour. The astonishment he had felt, the unconditional recognition that a turning had been made. He opened the book and read a page at random, and knew with utter certainty that this was where he should be. The entire process, all these experiences, all focused upon this very moment. Returning to the discipline of listening and waiting for God to speak. Or not. The important thing was not whether God had something to say. His responsibilities began and ended with making himself ready, available.

The next morning John spent the breakfast hour waiting for any in the group to have a change of mind about him. If just one of the team was having second thoughts, he was ready to step away from the spotlight. Without a moment's hesitation. All it would take was another to say, "The Lord seems to be turning us in another direction. I believe it's time for another up-front person."

They gathered as usual for prayer, which Aaron led. Power had been restored sometime during the night, so they breakfasted in the main house. Afterwards it seemed to John as though they were unified in a need to draw breath. Simply sitting together and absorbing that another day was opening, and they were together. Listening for a new word from God.

Then John saw Ruth try to push herself out of the rocker and fail.

She took a long breath, then said, "John, would you help me, please?" He was already up and moving.

Heather stood too. "What's the matter?"

"Nothing, don't worry," but her voice was very soft, fragile.

John supported the woman's full weight as she rose. Ruth's legs seemed out of kilter, as though she had forgotten how to move them forward. He stayed with her as they made the slow trek down the length of the porch and into the kitchen.

As they appeared in the doorway, the young woman by the counter went on full alert. "Should I get your medicine, Miss Ruth?"

"I'm fine, dear."

"The doctor said that when the symptoms start, you're supposed to take the pills."

"All right, I suppose." The words faded away. Clearly all her energy was required to simply remain upright.

The young woman plucked a container from the kitchen cabinet and hurried over with a pill and a glass of water. Once Ruth took this, she helped support the older woman as they moved slowly toward her bedroom. "Should I call the doctor, Miss Ruth?"

"No. Don't bother him." Her voice trailed off as Ruth pointed to a small settee by three tall bay windows. "Let's go there."

John could hear her breath puff slightly with each step. He asked, "Wouldn't you be more comfortable in bed?"

"Probably. But I want to see my garden." She eased herself down, sighed with release of the strain, and pointed to the chair by the writing desk. "Roll that over and sit with me."

He remained where he was. "What's happening, Ruth?"

"My heart has been weak for a long time. It's grown steadily worse since Bobby passed. I have these spells. Stop hovering and sit, please." She watched him do as he was told, then went on, "Now tell me what I need to hear."

This was clearly no time to argue, though he dreaded even shaping the words. "I think . . . I believe you want me to take over Barrett Ministries."

"I want you to *lead*, John. I want you to grow into the role God has made for you. Now be a dear and open that window."

The breeze filtered in, carrying all the fragrances of spring. "Ruth, I don't—"

"Stop, John. Just stop. I don't have time for this. *We* don't have time."

"I'm an unemployed trucking dispatcher, with no education, a criminal record."

She looked at him with eyes that carried a slightly milky glaze. "How long are you going to hide behind all that?"

"It's the truth. All of it."

"I'll tell you what the truth is, John. I've watched you become a man whose voice touches hearts. I've seen the strength that Heather has loved and nurtured." She patted the back of her hand resting in her lap. "It's time, John. And you know it."

"How on earth can you talk about these things now?" He reached forward to cover her hands with his.

"Heather's told me how you have yearned for a chance to live to your full potential. Here it is. Go out there and lead."

"But I . . ."

His protest was halted by two fingers, soft as petals, coming to rest upon his arm. "None of us can, John. But God wants you to do this."

The fear was as strong as the hunger. "How can you be so sure?"

She met him with the calm directness of a woman who saw far beyond the moment. "Remember this, son." Daylight through windswept branches cast her pallid features in a vague shroud. "God does not call the equipped. He equips the called."

He started to object once again, but Ruth's eyelids fluttered closed. She sighed again, a softly musical breath, and leaned against a pillow. She was soon sleeping.

LOS ANGELES

Every one of the plans Trent came up with was set in motion by the odd little man. Each time he suggested another idea, Dermott gave a thoughtful nod, murmured an approval almost too soft to be heard, then excused himself with the same words. "Let me go make some calls." The remainder of their day was filled with a series of minor successes.

And with each one Trent's dissatisfaction mounted.

It did not help that Gayle remained distant and distressed by Dermott McAllister's presence. Her normal composure was shattered just by glancing in his direction. Trent assumed the strange man had something on her. He needed to find some way to tell her it didn't matter, he didn't care what it was, and in truth didn't want to know. They all carried baggage. It came with the territory.

But that would have to wait, because Gayle's anxiety created an almost visible barrier around her. Her aloofness was a palpable force. She did not let him near.

Then he had his next idea.

This time, when he described what he had in mind, Dermott McAllister showed a spark of very real excitement. Trent saw the flame rise in his eyes, heard him say, "Well, now."

"Is this going too far?"

"On the contrary, Mr. Cooper. I do believe this could prove to be a defining moment."

Trent knew what had to be said then, as clearly as though he read the words in the man's gaze. "I want to be there."

The flame only grew stronger. "I'm not sure that's wise."

But the force Trent felt building in his gut said otherwise. "If it works, people are going to be talking about this for years. Won't they."

"You mean, around the Mundrose boardroom." McAllister nodded slowly. "Yes, they might."

"I don't want to be seen as the guy who hung back and let others take the risks. I want them to know I was in the middle of it too."

"Know it," Dermott added. "And fear you as a result."

"It's a long-term strategy," Trent said. "*If* I make it and actually hang around for a while."

The man had a truly awful smile. The uneven cant to his muscles was on full display, as though one half scowled while the other tried to laugh, and failed. "When Barry Mundrose told me he saw something in you, I had my doubts, Mr. Cooper. For once, I am not sorry to be proven wrong."

He could not help his return smile. "You think it will work?"

"What I think, Mr. Cooper," Dermott replied, "is that this will bury that Barrett Ministries bunch firmly in the ground where they belong."

26

" . . . praise him . . ."

WESTCHESTER COUNTY

When everyone gathered for a buffet lunch, John remained seated in Ruth's rocker on the porch, looking out over the meadow and thinking. He heard several of them talk about Ruth and her strict instructions not to phone the doctor. He heard them list supplies the van driver needed to pick up. He heard them talk about yet more bad news being laid on by the main channels, including what sounded like his very own police booking photo. John listened through the open window behind him, as they described in hushed tones the shock of seeing his bruised and inebriated face as a young man. He wondered momentarily why this news did not bother him in the slightest. Then he went back to his task. Listening. Waiting. Making himself ready.

Heather emerged to bring him a plate. When she kissed his forehead and departed, Yussuf and Aaron took that as their signal and approached him together. "How is Ruth?"

"She calls it a spell."

"A spell," Aaron repeated. "Sounds like a Jewish grandmother."

John asked, "Is it true that your residencies might be under threat?"

"So far they are only rumors," Aaron replied.

"Wouldn't it be better for you to return to the hospital?"

Aaron shrugged. "Better for whom?"

Yussuf asked, "Should we check on Ruth?"

"Ruth said positively no doctors." John had accepted the fact that further prodding would get them nowhere. "Take her a plate, and ask if you can look her over. You know, low key. Since you're already here."

Aaron smiled. "You obviously have some Jewish blood in there too."

"Anybody's guess." John shrugged. "I'm pure American mongrel."

Heather put her head around the door and announced that the chief programmer wanted a word. John found it hard to consider him the chief of anything, as Kevin looked only about seventeen years old. But Kevin Burnes had shown himself to be quietly capable, and spoke with the authority of a young man who knew his business. So John ate and listened as Kevin described a call he had fielded as soon as the phones started working again, from the head of the Gospel Channel. "They want you to do more interviews."

"Tell them yes."

"They want to do a live talk with you on their morning show tomorrow," Kevin went on. He was probably nervous by nature. He twitched in his seat like he could not find a comfortable position, and finally wound himself into a pretzel shape with his left arm linked through the chair back and his legs tucked under him. His glasses were askew, his clothes unironed, and his hair was in desparate need of a trim. Even so, he was a handsome young man whom John was certain would probably clean up fairly well.

"All right," John said. But when Kevin's unease only increased, he demanded, "What aren't you telling me?"

Kevin's swallow was audible. "It's about Jenny."

"A fine young lady."

"I was wondering. Do you think I could ask her out?" He swept the hair from his forehead. "I'm being a little nuts, aren't I."

"Son, you're being human. You don't need my approval for anything, but if you did, I'd say, talk to the lady first, then her old man. And don't hesitate any longer. It doesn't get easier with time." But as Kevin started to unwind from the chair, John asked, "Does the foundation have a lawyer on staff?"

"No, but there's one we use a lot."

"Do me a favor. Think you could hold off on the Jenny thing long enough to get the attorney on the phone?"

"Sure, John. And thanks."

When the young man darted off, Heather drifted over and put her hand on his shoulder. "'The Jenny thing.' Did I really hear you say that?"

The attorney consulting with Barrett Ministries came on with, "Ruth?"

"She's laid up. This is John Jacobs."

"I don't—Oh, wait, you're the man I've seen on television."

"Correct."

"What's the matter with Ruth?"

"She's not well."

The attorney had the self-assured polish of someone who actually believed his time was worth six hundred dollars an hour. "What does that mean, exactly?"

John read from the notes he'd made after Yussuf and Aaron had reported back on their impromptu examination. "She has a history of arrhythmia. Because of other issues, she is not a candidate—"

"I know all that."

"—for a pacemaker. She has experienced negative reactions to every known heart medicine. As a result, from time to time Ruth has what she calls spells. Some are worse than others. This one is severe."

"Is it . . . Will she improve?"

John chose his words carefully. "The doctors are not certain of anything except that she seems to be in no pain."

"Oh, this is not good. Not good at all." The attorney had the decency to appear genuinely upset. "I have a list of instructions in the case of . . . people she wanted me to call, starting of course with her family. Should I begin?"

"Absolutely."

"Oh my, oh my."

"Let me contact her daughter in New York. And the pastor in Austin, is he on the list?"

"Craig Davenport? Right near the top."

"I'll take care of that one too." John let the attorney fumble verbally for a moment longer, then came to the other reason for his call. "Does your firm have a courtroom brawler? Somebody who likes nothing more than a good fight?"

"Does . . . ? Well, of course. Ron Banks. But—"

"Can you see if he's free to talk? Tell him Ruth needs his help."

"Ruth, really?"

"Tell him it's urgent."

The lawyer came back on and announced he was putting them on speakerphone. A second voice said, "Ron Banks here. What's going on?"

John gave a mental sigh of relief. This second lawyer had the bark of a born combatant. Exactly what John thought they were going to require. "My name is John Jacobs. We need your help."

"My associate said this was in regard to Ruth Barrett's affairs."

"That is correct."

"He also told me you have a felony conviction on your record."

Leave it to a courtroom bruiser to go straight for the jugular. "Also correct. Thirty years ago."

"I don't follow."

John sketched out what already had happened. The previous loss of electric power, the continued assaults, and finished with, "My gut tells me this is only the start."

"You're involved in ministry, Mr. Jacobs?"

"Not before last week. I help run the largest trucking depot in the Midwest. Or did. Until I was just fired."

"You have any evidence the firing is linked to the current events?"

"Four days back I was promoted and put in charge of the company's largest new client. Since then I've been on vacation. Working with Ruth."

"In that case, I can definitely go after them for wrongful dismissal. Who's in charge of the opposition?"

"The Mundrose Group."

There was a tense pause, then Ruth's attorney demanded, "You're certain it's Barry Mundrose?"

"We are."

John could almost hear the man rubbing his hands together. Ron Banks's voice carried the hungry anticipation of the fight to come. "I've always wanted a chance to take them on."

The other attorney asked, "You know them?"

"I've seen their operations at work. Barry Mundrose is a bully, and he likes to fight dirty."

But the news left the other attorney palpably nervous. "I'm really not certain this is a good idea."

"I don't care about going after Mundrose," John quickly interrupted him. "That's not why I called. I mentioned Mundrose only so you'll understand they pack a real punch. And I don't care about my job. Well, I do. But that's not . . . There are two issues that can't wait."

"I'm listening, Mr. Jacobs."

"First, they're threatening the survival of my son's business." John related what his son had described. "If he doesn't have his line of credit restored in forty-eight hours, he goes under. The pastor of

Austin's largest church, Craig Davenport, is trying to help. But we won't know anything for certain, and this can't wait."

"I know Reverend Davenport," the polished attorney allowed. "He is solid."

"These tactics sound exactly like Mundrose," Banks declared. "All right. Give me your son's details. I'll get on this immediately. What's the second issue?"

"My gut tells me these attacks are just an opening maneuver. See how we respond. I need you to go after the power company in a way that gets back to the attackers. Ditto for communications. Straight to the boardroom, or maybe the local town council. Strike from a multitude of different angles. And strike fast."

The courtroom lawyer did not actually laugh, but the humor was there in his voice. "That doesn't sound like a ministry approach, Mr. Jacobs."

"I told you, I'm new to this business. But I've been dealing with unions for years."

"All right. Leave this with me."

The first attorney fretted, "Shouldn't we discuss tactics?"

"Absolutely," Ron Banks barked. "Long as it doesn't slow me down."

John smiled at the relish he heard in Banks's voice. "You can reach me at this number," he told them.

27

"How precious are your thoughts . . ."

WESTCHESTER COUNTY

As soon as he finished the phone call, John had a word with the kitchen staff, then went in search of an ally.

Dexter Wise was exactly where the kitchen staff said he'd be found, seated in the grass and leaning against the shed holding the mowing equipment, a sweat-stained hat pulled down low over his brow. High work boots stretched out at the end of long, jean-clad legs. "Mr. Wise?"

"Ain't no mister 'round here, unless you come looking for my daddy, and he's long gone."

"Don't get up. I'm John Jacobs. Can I join you?"

"Shade is free and the grass don't mind. Help yourself."

"Thanks." He already knew the type. Many truckers were the offspring of cowhands, with a wandering gene constantly hungering for the next open road. John had no trouble with their languid nature or the cautious way they dealt with strangers. "I understand you're in charge of security around here."

"There ain't much to speak of. Miss Ruth won't have it any other way."

"Normally I'd agree with her," John said as he lowered himself down. "But these aren't normal times."

"Yeah, I been sniffing that same wind for a day or two."

"How many guards can you count on if things go south?"

"I done what I could. All the men I hired as gardeners and such have experience running toward trouble." He counted silently. "Two are on vacation out of state. That leaves us five. Six plus you, if you're up for it."

"I don't have trouble with trouble. But I think I'm probably going to be busy."

"Yeah, I caught your last spot in front of the cameras. You did good, boss."

"I appreciate that. Look, is there a group you could call on, help us out here?"

"You mean, like, official security? Miss Ruth—"

"She's laid up. I'm in charge. And yes, security personnel would be good, so long as they can start immediately. But I'm thinking about something more, well, informal."

"That word covers a lot of ground."

"It does."

Dexter Wise took his time rising to his feet. "Why don't you and I take us a little drive."

They took Dexter's pickup out through the whitewashed gates. John rolled down his window and sat with his face in the wind as they took the highway south. They skirted Bedford and followed the rough city traffic until the sign came up for White Plains. Dexter spoke for the first time since setting off. "Got me a church down this way."

They skirted the downtown hospital and entered a district Dexter called Mamaroneck. They passed a ratty park and entered a blue-collar district that might have once seen better days, or could possibly have started rough and sunk from there. The church was sandwiched between a homeless shelter and a VFW building. A number of motorcycles were parked on the sidewalk out front.

John followed Dexter into the run-down veterans' building and knew he had asked the right man for help.

They walked a scuffed linoleum-clad corridor and entered a hall about half filled. Most of the attendees wore a combination of denim and leather and body jewelry and fingerless gloves and hard-edged gazes. Dexter bumped fists with several as he approached the empty podium. "I know you haven't started, but that's okay, because I'm not supposed to be here right now. But many of you know Miss Ruth, or you should, since she helps finance this program." Dexter stepped to one side and motioned John forward. "This is a friend."

Only about half the people were seated. The others stood with the stony patience of people who had been fed various lines for years. John met their gazes as he said, "My name is John Jacobs. I'm serving as temporary spokesman for the group that's come together up at the Barrett headquarters."

"You're that guy on TV." The woman was as hard as she was large, with a voice to match. She said to her neighbor. "I listened to him the other night. He's good."

The man next to her asked him, "You done time, right?"

"Some. A long ways back. I've stayed clean for over thirty years. But that's not—"

"What were you in for?"

"Aggravated assault." John put up with it because he had no choice. "I was nineteen and as drunk as I was dumb." He waited through sympathetic laughter. "Let's get back to today. We've become the target of some powerful people. I need roving teams in place to make sure they don't try and bring the trouble home. Ruth's not well, and—"

"What's the trouble with Ruth?"

"Heart." This from Dexter. "Let the man finish."

John went on. "I've got nothing to go on but what they've done so far, which is hide in the shadows and snipe at everybody in reach. But my gut tells me they're going to come in, and when they do, I want to be ready. You in?"

The chuckles and nods told him what he needed to know.

DAY
TWELVE

28

"... how you ought to regard us ..."

LOS ANGELES

Trent and the LA team worked through the evening and into the night. Sometime after ten, Gayle caught wind of what Trent and Dermott were planning. How precisely she became aware of their intentions, Trent had no idea. But by the time they left for the airport just after midnight, she carried herself with a quiet fury. On the drive to the airport, she twice tried to convince him not to do what he intended. When he refused to even discuss the plans he and Dermott had put into motion, she grew frigid with rage. Locking him out. Tightly.

The plane was being refueled, so they settled into the elegant lobby dedicated to private flights. Gayle sat on a sofa and placed her carryall next to her, blocking him out. He seated himself in the chair to her right, where he could study her. Her expression was as cold as marble and as beautiful as a Renaissance statue. Even when she was angry, she remained the loveliest woman he had ever known. He was still trying to find some way of reconnecting when his phone rang. He checked the readout, but the number was blocked. "Trent here."

"It's Edlyn."

It was the first time Mundrose's daughter had ever called him directly. "Just a minute, Edlyn." Speaking her name jolted Gayle, as did his putting the phone on speaker and setting it on the table between them. "All right, go ahead. You're on speaker."

"Can anyone else hear us?"

"Just Gayle. It's after one in the morning. We have the terminal to ourselves."

"Dermott phoned. He felt I should know about your plans. I'm calling to give you the green light."

Gayle went so pale she looked stricken. Trent said to her as much as Edlyn, "I really feel this could be important."

"I agree."

He leaned in, trying to meet Gayle's gaze, but she remained focused on some internal point. "Did you speak with Barry?"

Edlyn took her time responding. "On matters like this, you don't need to ask. Ever."

"Sorry."

"It's okay. You're new. When do you want this to go down?"

"The sooner the better. If Dermott can supply me with the right contacts."

"He's never failed us yet. So tonight, then."

Trent felt the heady flames of danger rise in his gut. "Tonight would be perfect."

Gayle mouthed the word *perfect*. But she did not speak.

Edlyn continued. "Our music division's premier band is launching a new album tomorrow. Barry is throwing a party. I want you to come. It's time you met some people."

For the first time during that long and wearying day, Trent was focused beyond the next task, the next hour, the need to take down his foe. Her words rang through his body like a gong.

"Trent?"

"I'd be honored."

"Good. Their cover art is based on your theme. We've shifted the song we're going to launch as their first single to the one closest to your message."

His theme. *His* message. "Thank you, Edlyn. So much."

Edlyn cut the connection with typical abruptness. He had no idea whether she even heard his final words. Trent studied the woman seated across from him. He wanted to ask Gayle to come with him. But her attention remained focused on what only she could see, her features taut with the argument he refused to have with her. There was nothing to be said. He was not budging. So he remained silent.

WESTCHESTER COUNTY

The next morning John sat in the windowless dressing chamber off the main studio. The room was scarcely larger than a walk-in closet, wooden lockers on one side, and a large mirror with a white shelf littered with brushes and cosmetics and cotton pads and tissues on the other. A stack of well-worn Bibles rested on a narrow corner table. John wore one of Bobby Barrett's suits. He still had the makeup napkin tucked around his collar, and the brilliant lighting showed a point on his cheek where the powder had caked. He sat motionless, staring at his reflection.

He searched for any hint of what he felt going on inside. But all he saw was the same craggy strength, the same determined cut to his jaw. His shoulders still bunched the fabric of his jacket. His eyes were clear and green and held a hint of old pain. His hair was almost all grey now, the color of wet steel. He wanted to ask God for another sign. But there was a hint of dishonesty to the act, as though it should have been enough that Ruth had told him to go and do this thing. Not to mention how the others seemed to accept his new role. So he kept his prayers unspoken, and when the knock on the door announced it was time, he stowed away his fluttering nerves and marched through the door.

Alisha and Heather, the two who had accompanied him over this morning, both embraced him. The black woman smelled slightly spicy, and her hug was powerful enough to insert a new sense of strength to his legs and his resolve. John smiled his thanks, then embraced his wife and walked past the people and entered the lights.

Kevin had stationed a monitor screen to the left of the camera. He waited while the sound technician hooked him up, then— counted him down and pointed to the monitor, which now showed the announcer. The female newscaster was the same woman who had interviewed him before. She might be on the Gospel Channel, but her on-air persona held the same brisk professionalism as the faces on the major networks. "Good morning, John. Thank you for joining us today."

"Appreciate the invite."

"Could we start by asking what developments have occurred recently?"

As John gave a quick recap, he found his words hardening into terse bites, the way he dealt with truckers in a crisis. Snow on the highway, blocked roads, late deliveries, engine failure, whatever. Many truckers liked to chatter when they grew nervous. John's job was to keep them focused, press them to move faster and push harder than they might like. He tried hard not to say such things outright, because the next step was to threaten. And he hated threats of any kind. So he punched with his voice, even when he spoke softly. Like now.

When he finished, the newscaster said, "Do I understand that *all* of you have either lost your jobs or have your positions threatened in some way?"

"Yes."

"And your son's business is faced with bankruptcy?"

"Correct."

"You've had power outages, your access roads blocked, your phone service cut off. Do you blame the Mundrose Group for these attacks?"

"They haven't said. So neither can I. But it's hard to put all this down to coincidence."

"We've been flooded with emails and phone calls all day. Our viewers ask one thing above all else. What can they do to help?"

"They sure can pray."

"I assure you, John, they are already doing that."

"Not for us," John said. "I mean for the Mundrose people."

The newscaster's aplomb slipped. "I'm sorry. What?"

"We are called to pray for our adversaries. I have no idea whether their attacks are over. But the truth is, we're doing our best to follow God's will. How can we expect *not* to be brought into conflict with this world?"

"But—what about your jobs? What about your *son*?"

He felt the burning fury carve its way through his entire being. The helplessness gnawed at him as it had for forty years. But John simply waited it out. When he was certain his words would not be dominated by the old pain and the new worry, he replied, "Of course I'm concerned. But none of this changes what we're called to do. Which is, look beyond where we are and search out God's will. That's why I'm asking your audience to pray for everyone involved in the Mundrose campaign. Pray for a change of heart. For a willingness to make room for God's love and wisdom."

The woman's gaze opened slightly. The careful on-air demeanor, like enamel developed over years, was temporarily erased. "John, I personally commit to doing this on a daily basis." She turned back to the viewers. "I believe you will too."

29

"... for the time will come ..."

LOS ANGELES TO WESTCHESTER COUNTY

The plane began its journey across three time zones, robbing Trent of his morning. He fell asleep and woke to discover Gayle sleeping across the aisle. He glanced at his watch, but he could not make sense of the hour. He couldn't remember whether he had set it forward to East Coast time. He was still exhausted, and yet he felt the same drumbeat of tension and excitement that had filled most waking hours since originally entering the Mundrose boardroom. Trent swung his feet onto the carpet, rubbed his face, then looked down at Gayle.

The jet's seats folded down to form well-padded beds. She had pulled one of the blankets over her, so all he could see was her stockinged feet and her face. Her face was relaxed in a childlike pose, her lower lip slightly extended, as though a dream was causing her to pout. Or perhaps it was their unspoken argument that made her wistful. He watched one hand emerge from the coverlet and stroke away a strand of hair from her face. His heart was filled with a restless hunger. He wanted to reach out, slip his arms around her, tell her . . .

The jet jolted slightly. Trent saw her eyelids flutter, and he jerked his face away, as though he had almost been caught doing something wrong. The shuddering plane forced him to grip the seat backs as he made his way aft. He entered the lavatory, washed his face, tucked in his shirt, combed his hair, and told himself to get a grip.

Gayle rose from her seat as he settled back into his. The turbulence worsened as the plane descended into a gloomy murk. When she returned, her face looked pale enough for him to ask, "Doing all right?"

She seemed uncertain how to respond. The pilot stepped through the cockpit door and announced, "The weather has shifted unexpectedly, folks. Rain's set in. We're getting word of some severe updrafts. You'll need to buckle up for our arrival."

Gayle stammered out, "Is—is everything all right?"

"Oh, sure." But his smile seemed forced to Trent. "Just be ready for a few bumps before we land in Yonkers."

He was gone so swiftly, Gayle directed her question to Trent. "We're landing in Yonkers?"

"I need to—" And a fist gripped their plane.

That was how it seemed to Trent. The motions were unlike anything he had ever known. The plane seemed to fight against some unseen force that wanted to pluck it from the sky and send it hurtling to the earth. They wobbled and they slowed and the jet's engines shrieked in protest. The nose tilted up, then down, then up again. It was similar to the experience Trent had read about from earthquake survivors, when all sense of stability was stripped away, and they were brought face-to-face with death. Because suddenly that was a very real prospect. As the nose shifted down and the shudders became more violent still, Trent knew with utter certainty that they only had a few moments left to live.

Wind shrieked outside the windows as they left the clouds and hurtled toward the ground. From the cockpit came the frantic sound of two pilots shouting against the blare of an alarm buzzer and some robotic voice telling them to level off.

"Trent!"

If he had not been so frightened, he might have laughed with delight at finally hearing her say his name again. But all he could manage just then was to reach across the narrow aisle to clutch her hand.

They were close enough to see the rain-slick roofs when the plane was abruptly released from whatever force pummeled them. One moment they were spiraling toward their doom, the next, and all was calm. They leveled off and descended and landed, the touchdown smooth as silk.

The pilot's expression still held tension when he stepped through the portal and asked, "Everybody all right?"

Only then did Gayle release her vise-grip on his fingers. Trent asked, "What was that?"

As the copilot braked and the engines powered down to a stop, the pilot hit the switch to release the portal stairs. "I have no idea."

Trent walked Gayle toward the waiting limo, holding an umbrella over her. She declared one more time, "This is as senseless as it is dangerous."

"I'm sorry, Gayle, but you're wrong this time," Trent replied. "It is absolutely necessary."

"You're putting your life in danger. For what? You think anyone on the executive floor even cares?"

"I do. Yes."

"You're wrong, Trent! I've worked with them for almost five years. And I'm telling you they only care about one thing. Results."

"Can I say something?"

"It won't change how I feel about this needless risk."

"I don't want to be just another mid-level executive at Mundrose. I want to *be in charge*. I want to be a part of the inner circle. I need to show them I understand Barry's last message, *Whatever it takes*." He swiped angrily at the rain beading on his face. "I can't *tell* them I'll do whatever is necessary to succeed. I have to show them. That's why I'm going."

She stared at him, defeated. "Nothing I say will make any difference, will it."

"No, not this time." Trent knew a bitter disappointment that Gayle wouldn't back his play. Or see how vital this step might someday prove. He pointed to where the driver stood waiting by the limo's open rear door. "I'll see you back at the offices."

Gayle slipped into the limo's rear seat, touched the rain-streaked glass between them, then was gone.

Trent took a taxi into town. Yonkers was not a pretty place to begin with. The heavy rain washed away all remaining color and turned the street scene grim and dismal. The traffic was as snarled and surly as the taxi driver. The cab pulled into an unsightly strip mall and halted before an army surplus store. Trent bought camouflage pants, lace-up black boots, an army-green sweatshirt, and rain slicker, and changed in the rear warehouse. He stowed his suit and tie and shoes in a cheap backpack and returned to his ride.

The taxi deposited Trent in front of a bar whose half-broken sign spit angrily in the rain. A heavy rock bass pounded through the bar's closed door. A long line of Harley hogs warned away all strangers.

Inside, all was shadows and danger. Trent stood by the door, looking for Dermott McAllister, hoping this was indeed the bar where the strange little man had told him to come.

Instead, a dark-haired woman in biker leather walked up and said, "You might as well just hang a sign around your neck that says, Free lunch."

"I'm looking for a guy."

"Yeah, well, the guy isn't here. I'm Della."

"You're Dermott's contact?"

"I'm the one who's gonna keep you alive and get the job done. That's all you need to know." She spoke with the harsh rasp of someone whose voice box had been on the receiving end of severe damage. "I'm still not clear on what you're doing here."

"I'm coming. Like you said, that's all you need to know."

"These guys are my friends. But they're not good at taking orders, especially from someone they don't know. You try to tell them what to do, they'll pound you into a greasy stain in the road."

"I don't need to direct. Matter of fact, I don't need to speak. But I do need to be there."

"Whatever." She plucked a black leather jacket from a chair. "Let's ride."

30

". . . being rooted and grounded . . ."

WESTCHESTER COUNTY

Alisha spent the day working alongside the others in their team. She knew they could sense that something was troubling her. But Alisha did not confide easily. Especially when she felt ashamed of what she was thinking. Like now.

The truth was, Alisha wished she could stop time and just step off. She knew it was wrong. But her thoughts were fashioned on the iron-hot forge of years. And no matter how fine it all might seem to them—following God and doing the right thing for the right reason—she spent all that morning and much of the afternoon feeling like God was distant and silent both. And no matter how hard she worked, or how many calls she fielded, or whose hands she held and prayed with, still she felt a shadow looming on the horizon, felt consumed by the same lancing pain that had been attacking her on and off for two days. *She had lost her job.*

Nobody who hadn't lived through what she'd known throughout her childhood and teen years could understand the impact of those five dreaded words. She had not gone to university because she had been too busy raising her sister. She had none of the special training that the business world valued so highly. She had proven herself the hard way, climbing the corporate ladder rung by desperate rung. She was not just good at her job. She was the best. She had arrived at a position of trust and freedom and responsibility.

She loved her work. She lived for it and for her church choir. They gave her the sense of identity that most women found in a husband and children. These two things were all she'd had in those dark hours when missing her sister had almost consumed her.

And now she had lost them both. The job was gone. The choir was Celeste's in all but name.

She sat in the room filled with ringing telephones, answering calls from churches all over the globe. Surrounded by folks doing their best to be part of God's design. But the dark truth was, her heart was obsessed by the dismal prospect of loss and woe.

Alisha was about ready to take another call and speak words she wished she could feel more fully when her cellphone buzzed. She pulled it from her pocket, checked the readout, and saw it was her church. Alisha moved out of the noisy room, stepped into the admin building's foyer, and hit the connection.

The pastor's wife said in greeting, "This is probably a terrible time."

"Celeste? What is it? Is something the matter?"

"I've been watching that man on the television, and I just had to call." The woman sounded out of breath, like she had run a hard mile, or fought a hard battle with herself. "I didn't want to. But I . . . You know what Terry told me at lunch today?"

Alisha stepped through the building's exit. Beyond the glass doors stretched the broad front veranda, giving the warehouse-styled structure its homey feel. Rain fell in a constant sibilant stream, the air cooled by the damp. "You've been talking with the pastor about me?"

"What do you think, with everything that's going on? Girl, you are being talked about by everybody." Celeste sighed noisily. "Terry says I need to treat you like the sister you are. Even though it might be hard. Which it is."

Alisha liked how the conversation drew her away from her own distress. If only for a moment. "Why is that?"

For a time, the rain was the only sound. Then the Celeste said softly, "I'm so jealous."

"Of me? Are you serious?"

"Do I sound like I'm joking?"

"Just exactly what are you jealous of, woman? Of how I just got fired? Or how I don't have a family to speak of? Or how I'm the one about to lose my choir—"

"You're not about to lose anything."

"Oh, please."

"Can you truly be blind to how much attention you're getting? How you showed up at the Kennedy Center with *Ruth Barrett*, how you saved the day, how it's your face I'm seeing *everywhere*?"

"Sister, I'm hearing you. But your words, they just don't make sense."

"You've got yourself a national forum! You're gonna come out of this a star!"

Alisha opened her mouth and breathed in the damp air. She wanted to correct the lady, remind her that she had to pay the bills, had to find some way of restoring herself professionally. But the pain in Celeste's voice mirrored what Alisha felt in her own heart.

Celeste went on, "You don't have any idea what it's like being a pastor's wife in a big church. Far as I'm concerned, nothing's changed since the day Terry and I walked up to the pulpit four years ago."

Actually, it had been closer to five. Alisha vividly remembered the day. How Celeste had stepped onto the stage in her choir robes and been introduced by her husband. How Celeste had given the congregation a grand old smile, then proceeded to stick her voice out in front of all the others. Alisha had not said anything that day. But she remembered. Oh, my yes, she did.

Celeste said, "I don't have *any* life *outside* the church. And inside the church I'm either lost in Terry's shadow, or I'm drowning in all the expectations people have of me. I spend most of my waking hours feeling completely out of place."

Alisha walked back over to the veranda's edge and stuck her hand out into the curtain of rain spilling off the roof. "I had no idea, Celeste."

"I've spent years wanting to be seen and heard for myself." Celeste's voice cracked. "The problem is, I don't know who that is any more."

Alisha pulled her hand back and examined how her fingers glistened in the porch lights. "Why didn't you say something before now?"

"I think maybe I've forgotten what it's like to talk to somebody about my issues. I've spent years being silent because I didn't want to offend. Didn't want to disappoint. Didn't want to be hurt any more than I already am."

"Does Terry know?"

"He's the only reason I'm still here at all. Terry says I need to love the church, faults and foibles and all."

"Your husband is a saint."

"He is, and sometimes I could shoot him for how all this comes so natural."

"And now he says you need to make me your friend." Alisha liked having a reason to smile. "I suppose that can't be much harder than anything else you've been through."

The rain drummed and sang for a time, then Celeste said, "You know, I feel better already."

The strange thing was, so did Alisha. "Sister, I'm glad you called."

WESTCHESTER COUNTY

The slicker Trent had purchased at the army surplus store helped combat the rain's pelting chill, as did the helmet Della had handed him before he climbed on behind her. As the two dozen bikes thundered down the highway, water worked down the zippered collar and past the wrist-clamps. Trent held the woman's waist and felt the cold trickle down the length of his spine. The ride was endless and the noise fierce. His drenched trouser-legs flapped painfully in the wind, adding to his bone-deep chill.

Trent could not see a thing except the rain-swept taillights of the bikes up ahead. He hurtled down the road behind the woman at a ridiculous speed, the thunderous engine vibrating up his spine and rattling his eyeballs.

It seemed like forever before they peeled off the road and clustered at the back of a defunct gas station, motors revved up and popping once more before shutting down. Trent was not the only one who rose slowly from the saddle. But the woman seemed untouched by the long, cold ride. Della took off her helmet, ran two gloved hands through her hair, and demanded, "Where are the guys with our equipment?"

"Five minutes," someone replied.

Eventually they were joined by two decrepit vans with faded logos half-scraped from their sides. The bikers went about their tasks with offhand brutality. The plan was simple. Chase all the Barrett people outdoors. Fire the buildings. Demolish all transport. Leave Trent's foes isolated and wet and defeated. And afraid. So afraid they'd all slink away and never show their faces again.

Plastic canisters were filled with gasoline and lashed to the back of the saddles. Shotguns were loaded with foam rounds, designed to stun and hurt but not kill. Pistols were checked and stowed. As Della passed out flares and clubs, she repeated the order several times: No live rounds fired unless somebody in the camp fired first, no physical assault unless one or more of them was attacked. Trent could not tell if the bikers objected. They all seemed to be tattooed with permanent surly expressions.

Della waved him over. "You armed?"

"Not even a butter knife."

She reached into a wooden case and handed him a pair of Tasers. "You know how to use these?"

"Point and shoot, right?"

"Close enough. Any last words for the troops?"

Trent turned to the bikers and said, "Smooth, simple, swift. In and out."

"Works for me." Della slammed the van's doors. "Okay, mount up."

Three miles farther on, the bikes turned off the main highway, rumbled past the Barrett Ministries sign, and rattled across a cattle guard. They followed a narrow lane around a bend and entered the rain-swept dark. Trent's heart rate surged in an adrenaline rush. He smelled wet meadows and saw nothing but the small stretch of road illuminated by the headlights. He liked how Della muscled her bike to the front of the pack. This was where he had always wanted to be. This was his destiny. To take control. To lead from the front.

Trent felt the electric thrill of coming battle, and whispered, "Showtime."

31

". . . for the time will come . . ."

WESTCHESTER COUNTY

It was not just the oddest first date Jenny Linn had ever been on. It was the oddest evening altogether.

Kevin Burnes had been around them every day. And she had noticed him, of course. But at the same time, she hadn't. He was friendly and capable and ever so professional. And patient. When she had botched the first seven takes of her appeal in Cantonese, Kevin had even made a joke of her efforts. He had entered the soundstage and seated himself beside her, his eyes alive with what she feared was impatient anger and then realized was humor. He had asked her to promise she wasn't saying anything that would make Ruth upset with him. And then he had praised her for doing what clearly was a difficult trial. So of course she'd noticed him.

But not like *this*. Not *here*, and certainly not *now*.

He had come up after lunch and asked if she'd like to have dinner. And to her surprise, Jenny heard herself say that she would be delighted. Which she was.

"Do you think I should ask your father if it's okay?"

She was about to remind him that she was twenty-seven and had been on her own since university. But somehow there was a sweet logic to his question, a strong sense of rightness. As though he sensed something in the moment and the place, that drew them into a need for harmony that defied the culture or the world beyond the green-clad hills. So Jenny had said, "Why don't we see if they want to come along?"

The evening proved amazingly nice, rain and all. They went for pizza to an Italian restaurant with checkered tablecloths and candles in old Chianti bottles. Their conversation flowed smoothly and was spiced with laughter.

On the drive back, Jenny found it rather natural to reach for Kevin's hand. They sat behind her parents, and she laughed over something she did not actually hear. Then Kevin turned to her and asked, his voice low, "What is the perfume you're wearing?"

Even the way her parents shared a smile over the question seemed just fine to her. "It's called Joy."

Kevin squeezed her hand. "It's really nice."

Jenny did not respond. Because what came to mind was something she was not ready to share, especially with her parents in range. But what she thought was, she would remember this night every time she wore that perfume.

The tires hissed as the van slowed and turned off the road. They trundled across the cattle guard, rose over the first hill, then slowed again to traverse the gravel-filled trench. Then Richard jerked the van to a halt.

"What is it, Daddy?"

"Lights."

Jenny's mother asked, "Are those motorcycles?"

"Big ones."

Kevin released her hand and leaned forward. "They shouldn't be here."

"Why are they blocking the road?" Jenny turned around. "There are more behind us."

"Kevin, call the police." Richard turned around and jerked the van into reverse. "Hold on, everybody."

"What are you going to do?" came from her mother.

He gunned the motor. "Escape while there's still time."

After dinner John joined Dexter Wise, head caretaker, for a walk through the night. The rain fell steadily, as it had all afternoon. John wore a slicker he had found hanging in the admin building's foyer. As they tramped down the silent lane, Dexter tried to phone his contacts at the veterans' hall. He cut the connection and grumbled. "Thought I could count on them."

"That trip into town was probably a waste of time," John said.

Dexter pushed his hood back and ran his fingers through his remaining hair. "Even so, I'd still sleep better . . ."

John caught the man's sudden tension. "What is it?"

"Thought I saw something."

"Where?"

"Out past the first trees."

"You sure?"

"No."

Alisha emerged from the lane joining the house to the admin buildings. "I saw it too." She pointed beyond the veil of water. "Lights farther down the road there."

Dexter squinted into the rain-swept darkness. "You armed?"

"I've never even held a gun," John told him.

Dexter pulled up his slicker to reveal a holster attached to his belt. He popped the catch, but did not pull out the pistol. "Stay close."

"Maybe somebody took a wrong turn," Alisha said doubtfully.

The rain glittered with the flash of lights from around the curve. "That ain't just one car," Dexter said, moving faster now.

As John rushed to keep up with Dexter, he said to Alisha, "How about going back—"

"Why? I'm already wet. Besides, if there's trouble, I want to help."

"It could be . . ." He didn't even want to say the word, dangerous. As though such things had no place here.

"If there's trouble, I want to help," Alisha insisted.

John did not object further. She had as much right to be there as anyone. Headlights lined the top of the hill between them and the main road. They twisted and flashed like disjointed alarms. Then he heard them. What he thought was thunder coalesced into the sound of motorcycles. A lot of them.

When they rounded the bend, John's first thought was, an invasion. A dozen or so bikes swarmed around an SUV, the headlights flashing on the Barrett Ministries logo imprinted on the doors. One biker reached out and hammered the side window with a gloved fist.

"This ain't happening," Dexter growled, and reached for his weapon.

"Hold up there," John said, and gripped the man's arm.

The metallic thunder grew louder still, as another group of bikers rumbled down the lane, halting directly between the first group and the van.

Jenny heard the tremor in Kevin's voice as he warned Richard, "If you go off the lane, we could get stuck."

Richard spun the wheel. "We have to risk that."

But as he started to reverse, a fist hammered at Jenny's window. Richard slammed on the brakes. Jenny could not actually see any of the faces. The helmets formed blank and frightening masks. The rain pelted the van as the bikes rumbled in a tight circle, moving like predators.

Then another biker slipped in close to the van. Where he came from, Jenny had no idea. But there was a difference. He faced outwards. Away toward the others. Jenny had the distinct impression he was guarding them.

The first bikers seemed unsettled by this sudden appearance. They wheeled back a trace. Watching.

The newcomer stopped by Richard's window and swept up his face-guard. His skin was not dark, but he was definitely not Caucasian. The man's features were craven in the manner of an ancient warrior race. The cheekbones were as pronounced as bony fists, the jaw massive, the eyes open and dark and penetrating.

Richard asked nervously, "Do you recognize him?"

"N-No," Kevin stammered out.

The man stood there, waiting. Untouched by the rain or the surrounding danger.

Richard rolled down his window. "Yes?"

"Follow me," the man said. His deep voice carried an accent Jenny did not recognize. "We will keep you safe."

"But—"

The man simply flipped down his visor and maneuvered his bike around to the front of the van. He was joined by two others. The man turned back and motioned to Richard. Then he started forward.

Richard was still hesitating when Kevin said, "There are others now."

And there were. Two to either side of the van. Richard asked, "What should I do?"

"Exactly what he said," Jenny said. "We'll be fine."

Trent was about to break Della's rules and order the bikers nearest the van to break the side window. He could taste the adrenaline's thrill of triumph. Then the rain seemed to condense on Trent's visor, until all he saw was a bleak fog. He could no longer make out the road, or even Della's helmet right in front of him. Della apparently had the same problem, because she jammed on the brakes hard. Another bike rammed Della's rear wheel. Someone shouted. It seemed as though the rain was clogging Trent's ears as well. Then the bike engines went quiet. All of them.

The silence was eerie. All Trent heard was the sound of rain striking his helmet. Trent undid the clasp and lifted off his helmet. And froze.

They were surrounded.

He had no idea how many there were. Twenty. Forty. More. All of them riding nondescript old bikes, all dressed the same way, in slickers and helmets and boots. He tried to see if they were armed. But their hands not holding the controls remained hidden. Which he took as a very bad sign.

Della shouted at the circled men, "Get out of here."

"Now, see, that's kind of funny coming from you." The biker nearest them lifted his visor. He was grey-bearded and narrow-faced, and his gaze was hard as flint. "You're the ones that don't belong."

"Move off, or we'll take you down," Della snarled.

"You can try," the man replied almost casually. "See, my buddies and me, we've been out there in real combat." He scanned the clutch of silent bikes. "We know what it means to face a real enemy."

"You're about to find out just how real we can be." Della lifted the edge of her jacket and started to unholster her gun.

"No," Trent said.

But Della was not made for following orders. She pulled the weapon free and cocked it.

The sound galvanized their opponents. All of them, whoever they were, *moved forward* as one. Menacing in their silent intent.

"Della, put the gun away!"

"I didn't come here to be chased off!"

"No shooting! No deaths! We can't—"

"Can't what?"

Trent could not shape the words, *we can't win*. Shooting even one of them would turn this into a melee. He could see that, even when he couldn't make out any face except for the man directly before them. Della's gun meant nothing to them. "You can't shoot them all."

The van began to move slowly forward, surrounded on all sides by helmeted allies. These bikes rumbled softly as they rolled, the noise muted, an unspoken warning as they passed.

Della glared fiercely at the frightened faces inside the van as it drove by. Rain dripped unnoticed from her hair. "So we're just going to turn and *run?*"

Trent was saved from having to reply by the biker behind them. "We're outnumbered," the man muttered.

The closest biker hit his kick-start. "I'm outta here."

Their bikers thundered into life. The watchers made no move. They simply sat it out as Trent and the others turned around and slowly twisted their way back down the lane. Trent held his helmet in one hand so he could see study the blank visors they passed, trying to catch a glimpse of his unknown enemies. But all he saw was rain-streaked Plexiglas, reflecting the night back at him. Then they were past and rattling across the cattle guard. He jammed on his helmet as Della made the turn and hit the throttle.

Gayle had been right after all. He should not have come.

32

"Let your work appear to your servants . . ."

WESTCHESTER COUNTY

Dexter's friend from the VFW parked his bike and stood between John and the caretaker, watching the last of the would-be attackers rumble away. John was glad his voice remained steady. "I can't thank you enough for coming."

"We weren't going to," the man confessed. "What with the rain and all, we figured there wasn't no need to make the trip. But some of us, well . . ."

"Good to know your danger sense still works," Dexter said.

Alisha stood to John's other side, shivering in the rain. "I was so scared it's embarrassing."

"Ain't no shame in fear," Dexter replied.

"Me, I was quaking in my boots," the vet agreed.

They heard the sound of approaching engines and stepped off the lane. The six bikes that had escorted the van rumbled past. John shouted a thanks, but the bikers gave no sign they had even heard, joining all but three of the others as they rumbled off into the night.

The grey-bearded vet said to Dexter, "Good thing your other buddies showed up when they did."

John and Dexter exchanged perplexed glances. Dexter said, "What're you going on about now?"

"The posse you dragged in for back up."

"Friend, the only people I spoke to were there in the hall with you."

The grey-bearded biker looked from one face to the other. "This a joke?"

"Do I look like I'm joking?"

John said, "You're telling me you didn't know some of those who came to help?"

"I'm saying the only friends I could get to follow me out are the three you see right over there."

Alisha's voice trembled from far more than the cold. "Then who . . . ?"

They stood in silence, studying the darkness through the rain. Finally the biker climbed back on his machine, cranked the starter, and drove away.

Celeste's voice carried the soft lilt of slumber. "Alisha? What time is it?"

"A little after eleven. I woke you, didn't I?"

"No, no, Terry and I just lay down. It's been a long day. Wait just a minute." There was the rustling sound followed by a door closing. "All right. What's the matter?"

"Nothing. Not a single solitary thing." Alisha sat in the padded chair she had drawn over to her cottage's open window. She clutched the blanket tightly around her shoulders. "Except for how I can't stop shaking."

"Girl, are you sick?"

"No. But I should be. I've been standing in the rain for an hour. But I took a long hot shower, and I made some tea. I'm good."

"Why were you out there in the rain?"

"Because."

The pastor's wife huffed softly. "Now you sound like one of my children. The word 'because' don't make a reason. It just starts one. Now tell me what happened."

"I think I just saw . . ."

"What?"

She finally breathed the word she had been thinking for a while now. "A real live miracle."

"Lord, have mercy."

She told Celeste what had happened. Or rather, what she *thought* had just gone down. "And the whole way back to my cottage, I kept thinking one thing. How I had to call my *sister* Celeste, tell her what I've witnessed."

"Now look what you've done. I'm crying. I never cry."

"I believe I've sung that same song myself a time or two lately."

"What do you want us to do here, sister?"

"Pray," Alisha replied. "Pray just as hard as you know how. This is not over yet."

The rain ended while John and Heather prepared for bed. He opened the rear window of the cottage and slipped in beside his wife. Drops cascaded from the roof and pattered upon leaves. It sounded to John like living cymbals. Heather sighed as she nestled in close. John said, "I need to tell you something."

"I'm listening."

"But I don't know if I can."

"Start with one word. See where it takes you."

John described the confrontation with the bikers. By the time he finished, Heather was sitting up, supported by all the pillows except one. She asked, "Where did they all go?"

"They followed the others back out the exit."

"Did anyone think to invite them back to dry off? Or at least thank them for what they did?"

"I tried to thank them. But I don't know . . ." John tried to recall if anyone had spoken the words, but could not. "Tell the truth, I'm not sure of much of anything except they kept us safe."

Heather did not object or argue that he was seeing things. Instead she merely asked, "What are you going to do now?"

John smiled at the unseen ceiling. "Whatever God asks."

She moved closer still. "That's my good man."

DAY
THIRTEEN

33

"What then shall we say . . ."

MANHATTAN

By the time the taxi deposited Trent in Manhattan, he was numb with exhaustion and cold and fear. Della had dumped him off at the Yonkers bus depot and ridden off without a word or backward glance. On the taxi ride into the city he had booked a room at the Millennium Times Square. He checked into the hotel, refused the bellhop's offer of assistance with his backpack, and took the elevator to his room. He dumped his sodden clothes in the trash, hung his rumpled suit in the closet, and ordered a room service meal while he waited for the bath to fill. He groaned his way into the steaming water. But he found no peace. Behind his closed eyelids flashed one rain-swept image after another. How could they have known he was coming? Dermott had assured him the Barrett compound was lightly guarded. Where did they find an army on such short notice?

He dried and dressed in the hotel robe and ate a sumptuous meal, but all he could taste was defeat. They had beaten him.

He wheeled the dinner table outside his door and climbed into bed. His sleep was tormented by the same images and emotions that had chased him into the city.

It was 2:15a.m. on the bedside clock when he rose from the bed and went over to the window to look out from the thirty-ninth floor. The only sign of the departing rain was windswept clouds turned a coppery hue by the city's lights. The air was washed clean, and the surrounding buildings looked etched in wet crystal. The horns sounded softly from far below his post. Trent pounded the glass, wanting it all with a hunger that gnawed at him.

Soon after he returned to bed, the dream rose up and captured him. He was back in his childhood home on the outskirts of Tulsa. The scene was familiar enough, for he often dreamed of being trapped there, never finding a way out or up. In his dream he stood in the center of the kitchen and breathed the same dry acrid air that dominated Oklahoma summers. Only tonight there was a unique difference. Instead of chafing at his prison, Trent felt surrounded by something . . . love?

His mother stood at the battered counter, drying the dinner plates and singing some long-forgotten tune from church. She had done her best to make a home for her only boy, smiling and praying her way through the long empty absences while her trucker husband was out on the road. Church was something Trent had rebelled against at an early age, only in this dream, everything was different. He did not rage against her quiet acceptance. He did not despise their hardscrabble life. Instead, he knotted his tie and he walked with his mother, down the street he remembered so well, and entered the sanctuary at the end of their road. He knelt with her and he sang with her and he prayed. And he felt flooded with the contentment and the joy that he had spent a lifetime declaring was a lie.

The dream sped up then, sweeping him along in a life that had never existed. The church put together a series of donations to cover the cost of his final surgeries, adopted him as a member of almost every family in the congregation. He excelled at university, and he served there with a student ministry. He met a wonderful girl doing pre-law, and they married. He supported her through law school, then she did the same while he completed his doctorate in finance. They moved to Washington. He worked for an investment bank, then a think-tank, then a university. She took time off to raise their three children, then accepted a job with the government. They remained deeply involved in student ministry. They were happy. They loved each other, their children, and God . . .

When Trent finally was released from the dream, he discovered he was sobbing so hard he could hardly draw breath.

Trent fought the sheets for another hour, then dressed in the suit he had last worn on the private jet. He left the hotel and wandered the empty streets. Times Square never looked so tawdry and forlorn than at quarter to five in the morning. He had breakfast at the Broadway Diner, just another bleak face amid the strange predawn company. Trent studied them with idle curiosity, the red-eyed gamblers; the all-night partiers; the corporate types with hard empty gazes; even a pair of weary chorus girls with sparkle across their cheeks. Not a winner among them. The only thing they had in common was brittle desperation, the urge to reach for what they could no longer name. The chase had been so hard for most they had forgotten what they strived for. They just kept running from night to night. Trent finished his breakfast around the bitter knot in his gut.

Memory of the dream still gnawed at him as he returned to the hotel and checked out. He tried to tell himself it was just a typical move for his subconscious to attack him when he was down. But the image of that other Trent Cooper, that happy man and his joy-filled life, chased him from the hotel. As though every decision he had ever made was wrong. As though he had convicted and sentenced himself to a lifetime of angry and futile battle.

Trent arrived at the Mundrose Headquaters at a quarter past six. There was nothing to be gained by waiting. He pushed through the side entrance, greeted the bored guard, and took the elevator upstairs. The knot at the center of his being tightened and swelled at the sight of his suitcase standing beside his temporary desk. He told himself it was only because Gayle had no idea where he had spent the night, so had no alternative but to leave it here. Yet all he could think was that he was one step from taking his final ride down the executive elevator, walking through the power door, and being deposited permanently on the street.

Trent went through the motions for an hour and a half. He answered a few emails, he cleared out his desk drawers, he returned a couple of calls. His voice sounded flat, emotionless. As though the nighttime assault had drained him of the ability to feel anything, even defeat. He found himself thinking about the faces he had seen in the diner. And knowing that was exactly how he looked.

The call came at a quarter past seven. Dermott McAllister spoke in that strangely toneless manner, "Ah, Mr. Cooper. How good to find you available."

Trent searched for some response, but all he could think to say was, "I'm glad it's you."

The little man seemed caught off balance. "Excuse me?"

"That you're the one to wield the knife. No polite emptiness or words neither of us believes."

"You think I'm calling to fire you?"

"Of course. I failed."

"And you're *glad*?"

"Not that it's happening. That it's you. And yes. I am. A clean savage cut. Over and done."

There was a moment's silence, then, "Actually, Mr. Cooper, I am the one who must apologize."

"For what?"

"I'd assured you the Barrett complex held no guards. I was misinformed. I understand from Della that the opposition was quite substantial."

"They had an army on wheels." Trent shivered at the memory, how they seemed to be drawn from the rain, so many he couldn't count. "We were surrounded."

"And yet all Della saw was the fact that they were unarmed."

"They didn't reveal their weapons. That's not the same thing."

"Precisely what I told her. It was your cool head that saved us from a potential calamity."

Now it was Trent's turn to hesitate. A second tremor coursed through him. For the first time, he was willing to accept what he was hearing. "But—we failed."

"You retreated intact. You saved us from a calamity that would have turned public attention against us. You responded wisely to the unexpected." The man gave Trent a chance to respond, then went on, "I confess I thought you were foolish to want to participate personally. A thrill-seeker gone bad, as it were. Now I see I was wrong."

"That's not why I went," Trent said. The shivers assaulted his words, and he didn't care. His entire being resonated to the realization that he had a tomorrow. "I wanted to show Mundrose Group that I understood the words, *whatever it takes*. Understood, agreed, and I would do exactly that."

"The message has been received," Dermott replied.

He knew he should just hang up. Accept the news was good. He had another day to prove himself. But the confusion would not let go. Not yet. "But Barry Mundrose is all about results. And I've been thwarted by them. Again."

"On one level, that is correct. But on another, you have created an enormous success."

"I don't understand."

"I will allow our superiors to explain. Good-bye, Mr. Cooper. I look forward to working with you again very soon."

A half-hour later, Trent was still seated in a motionless daze when others began arriving for work. His mind, however, spun with brilliant speed. Beneath the stunned immobility burned a slowly mounting fury. The dream continued to whisper at him, only now his response was clear. He raged at how he had been assaulted at his weakest moment. He hated how the concepts made a mockery of his ambition and his hunger. He felt the tendrils of invitation and choice become consumed by the fire at the center of his gut. Until finally the whispers and the memories left him alone. But not even that was enough. He wanted revenge. He sat in his shell of rampant isolation. And he planned.

Barry Mundrose's outer office gradually filled with executives seeking passage to the inner sanctum. Trent found himself studying the faces. Their expressions mirrored the hunger and the frustrated rage he felt within himself.

Trent forced himself to focus on the coming meeting with Barry Mundrose. He keyed in his project website and watched the latest advert put together by Colin Tomlin and his team. The stars from the television show and the film and the music videos danced with the ghouls beneath the flaming words, *Hope Is Dead*.

Trent had designed the message as simply a means to an end. He had created the slogan to help him reach his goals. But now he lifted his gaze to the executives clustered at the room's other end. And he knew the logo was in fact branded upon his empty soul. And not just his. He could see it in the frantic aggressiveness shining from every face. Hope was indeed dead. The religious world revolved around a myth. All he'd done was clear away the dross and speak what most people already knew.

Gayle was the last to arrive. She did not look his way, or speak to him. Trent missed her and the closeness they had known in Los Angeles. But he did not know how to breach her carefully erected barriers. She waited until Barry's senior aide was called into the boardroom. Then she drifted over and said, "I didn't know what to do with your suitcase. So I brought it here."

"Thank you."

"I should have asked. But I wasn't thinking clearly, and I—"

"You did right."

"Anyway, I'm sorry."

Only then did Trent realize she was not speaking about his case at all, that her words were for the benefit of the execs clustered in the waiting area. "Gayle, it's fine. Really."

"You're sure?"

He smiled and lowered his voice, filled with an exquisite realization that they had just survived their first fight. "Absolutely. And thanks for saying this."

She let down her guard long enough to reveal her other side, the open longing, the from-the-heart smile. "You were right and I was wrong."

"Actually . . ." Trent went silent as the phone on her desk pinged, the special sound he had come to know as signifying a summons from the inner sanctum. He watched her cross the office and speak too softly to be overheard. All the execs at the room's far end watched, hoping their chance had finally arrived.

Instead, Gayle put down the phone, looked at Trent, and announced clearly, "Mr. Mundrose will see you now."

The strange combination of numbness and secret rage continued to hold Trent as he entered Barry Mundrose's office. The CEO of the Mundrose Empire was seated behind his desk, idly playing with a silver pen as he spoke in undertones with his daughter. As before, Edlyn Mundrose leaned on the ledge by the rear window. Barry greeted Trent with, "Dermott tells me you think you failed."

"I don't know what else to call it," he answered, standing before the enormous desk. "Nothing I threw at them left a mark."

Father and daughter exchanged a long look. Edlyn said, "You don't know, you can't imagine, how refreshing it is not to have the guy in your seat try to gloss over a failure."

"I don't gain anything by hiding the truth. They've bested me at every turn."

"Bested us, you mean." Barry said to Edlyn, "Take a seat, why don't you. Both of you," he added, turning back to Trent.

Edlyn left her perch and walked around to seat herself next to Trent. "On one level, maybe."

"I don't follow."

"You've learned a valuable lesson here," Barry said.

"A lot of them."

"One of special importance. One we've known for years. One we aren't ever to discuss beyond these walls."

Father and daughter waited together, Edlyn swiveling in her chair to face Trent. Their measuring gazes probed deeply. Challenging him to deliver the words they looked for.

A manic glee rose from deep inside, carrying the force of a tsunami wave. He'd never felt anything like this before. Speaking aloud what he had carried with him for years. "The church is our enemy."

Father and daughter had never looked more alike than now, when they smiled. Tight and swift and filled with the same secret anger Trent felt in his gut. "We'd say God is the enemy, except he doesn't exist," Edlyn said.

Barry said, "You understand why we can't speak about this openly."

"It's not about the church," Trent said. "It's about the audience."

"We remain astonished by how gullible people are," Edlyn said. "All this religion garbage should have been left to the Dark Ages."

Because it was a rare moment of divulging secrets, Trent confided, "I was raised in a church family. I still bear the scars."

"Then you know." Barry had gone back to playing with his silver pen. "Our goal is to demolish their power, one brick at a time. So we lost this one battle. The war goes on. We know it, and so do they."

Edlyn added, "Sometimes the best thing we can do is force people to choose sides. So the church is against us. So what? It doesn't matter, when we have this mob of others who flock to our banner."

Trent looked from one to the other. "What about the lost sponsors?"

"Temporary," Barry said.

"We've already filled the slots with others who are only too happy to go after the younger audience," Edlyn said.

"The Millennials are firmly in our camp. That is a victory in and of itself," Barry said.

"Anytime we can guarantee a young audience, we can charge whatever we want for adverts," Edlyn agreed. "We'll clean up."

Barry flicked his pen like a wand, moving on. "We have a new project. Very delicate. We want you to handle this."

But Trent wasn't done. "I want one more go."

It caught both father and daughter by surprise. "You weren't listening," Edlyn said. "Your campaign has delivered the audience."

"It's not enough," Trent said, looking first at Edlyn, then Barry.

"Revenge doesn't work unless it has a positive impact on the bottom line," Barry cautioned.

But Trent had the bit between his teeth. He punched his way through a thirty-second pitch. And waited.

Father and daughter exchanged a long look. Then Barry said, "I like it. A lot."

"It's risky," Edlyn said, then allowed, "but the upside could be huge."

"Another sweep of advertisers," Barry agreed. "Either they are with us, or they're clinging to the myths of history."

"If we succeed, we could crush the opposition," Trent reminded them.

Father and daughter smiled once more. Edlyn said, "I have just the hammer for you."

34

". . . renew a steadfast spirit . . ."

WESTCHESTER COUNTY, MANHATTAN, AND AUSTIN, TEXAS

They gathered in Ruth's bedroom because she had requested it. The invitation from the Mundrose Group had arrived an hour earlier. Ruth lay on her divan and listened as they discussed the request for John to appear on the nation's most-watched news talk show. Craig Davenport was with them via telephone. He declared, "This is a terrible idea."

The group exchanged glances. And they waited. John could see they wanted him to respond. He was not accustomed to opposing a well-known pastor, but in this case he had no choice. "I'm not sure I agree."

"You have no idea, you can't begin to imagine, what they'll have in store." He spoke forcefully enough to rattle the speaker. "Who do they have on anchor?"

Kevin replied, "Katherine Bonner."

"Who happens to be the most aggressively anti-Christian commentator in cable news," the pastor said. "It just keeps getting worse. Look, I've been down this road. You haven't. Let me tell you, they may claim the discussion will be unbiased. They may promise you the moon. But all that flies out the window the instant the lights come on."

Ruth lay beneath a beautifully hand-sewn quilt, staring out the tall windows into the surrounding sunlight and green. Heather was seated on John's other side, nestling his hand in her lap. Across from them, Jenny Linn was seated between her father and Kevin. Craig was saying, "These cable news programs have an agenda, and their audience matches them, believe you me. Who are his other guests, did they tell you that much?"

Kevin replied, "They gave me just one name. Reverend Radley Albright."

The Austin pastor's voice grew even more strained. "Okay, first of all, the man is not a reverend. He was. Before. But he turned away from his faith. It happens. He now teaches philosophy at NYU."

Jenny confirmed, "He's published two national bestsellers on how God does not fit into the national equation."

"They're waving a red flag in front your face," Craig warned. "Challenging you to come out and fight."

"You're probably right," John said. "But I'm still not sure—"

"You still don't get it. Ruth, talk sense to the man."

She replied softly, "I have complete confidence in his judgment."

Time and again John's mind returned to the dream of several nights back. How he had seen himself living a different world. One unsullied by his mistakes. He understood the message. It was what gave him the strength to be here in this place, preparing for a leadership role he had never imagined. God was taking the old life and making it new. For his divine purpose. Nothing else should matter. Not even the enormous misgivings he felt over being used in such a manner.

Craig sighed and declared, "This is nuts."

To their surprise, it was Richard's normally quiet wife who spoke. "Please excuse me for disagreeing, sir. But John is right in this situation."

The quiet voice, the slight accent, the unexpected comment all gave additional power to her words.

Richard said, "My wife is correct in what she says."

"Friends, please, you don't—"

Jenny said, "What if God intends to use this?"

Craig was silent for a moment, then, "The risks are huge. Especially now. This thing is building fast. We haven't seen anything like this in years."

"It's true," Richard agreed. "There has been a tidal wave of support."

Jenny added, "The center is overwhelmed."

Alisha said, "I heard from my pastor's wife this morning. Our church has become a prayer center for the whole region."

"This is true pretty much everywhere," Heather offered. "Churches from as far away as Australia have picked up on what is happening; they want to know how they can help."

Kevin agreed. "Our staff is overwhelmed with responses by email, phone, Twitter accounts—"

"You see?" Craig Davenport almost pleaded. "You really want to risk slowing this down? Even stopping a move of God? And that is what indeed could happen. What *will* happen, unless . . ."

Jenny finished for him, "Unless there's a miracle."

John could tell that Ruth was tiring. "We'll pray about this and get back to you, Pastor. Thank you for your insight. And please continue praying with us and for us." He cut the connection, then asked the group, "Anybody?"

Richard asked, "Is it all right if I say something?"

Jenny replied, "Of course, Daddy."

"I feel we need to do this."

John looked at the lady on the divan. "Ruth, what do you say?"

Ruth replied quietly, "We're surrounded by miracles. God's hand is on us. And this."

Richard said, "I remember something I often thought of while Jenny was growing up, but somehow managed to forget. That this must be how God feels about each of us, his most precious creations. And how here, in this feeling, I have found my greatest moments of hope. For the future, and for the moment."

John looked at the young man holding Jenny's other hand and said, "Call the network. Tell them I'll be their guest tonight."

John stood in front of the main house and watched them load up for the trip to Manhattan. Two old vans so dusty the Barrett Ministry logos were almost impossible to read. John watched his wife set a case in the rear, and it hit him just how absurd the whole deal was. A convicted felon wearing a borrowed suit was going up against the might of the greatest entertainment empire the world had ever seen. His support group was a motley assortment of people drawn from every walk of life, every race, every culture.

Heather chose that moment to walk over. She smiled as she held out the phone. "It's your nephew."

John hesitated. "Now isn't a good time."

"You need to hear this."

He took the phone, turned his back to the others, and said, his voice low, "What is it, Danny?"

"Uncle John, I know it's probably a bad time. But I had to call. I worked the early shift today, and I got home, and I've got a few hours before I head out to the evening service—a church about three blocks from here."

John felt the tension ease from his shoulders. "I'm glad, Danny. Really glad."

"I've been reading my Bible. And I found something. It rocked my world. Can I read it to you?"

"Sure, Danny. Of course."

"It's in—let's see—it's a Psalm numbered 51. I wrote it down. I'm gonna pin it on my wall. I put verse 17 first, then 10 and 12. 'My sacrifice, O God, is a broken spirit; a broken and contrite heart you, God, will not despise. Create in me a pure heart, O God, and renew a steadfast spirit within me. Restore to me the joy of your salvation and grant me a willing spirit, to sustain me.'"

The air seemed to tremble, as if the power John felt was taking shape in the meadow and the sunlight around him. "Those are powerful words, son."

"What I wanted to say is, thank you. I came out of that prison a broken man. You gave me the gift of hope."

The word seemed to take form and shimmer in the air before him. *Hope.*

When he didn't speak, Danny went on. "I'd forgotten what it means to have that. I have so much to thank you for. Meeting me at the prison gates. Getting me this job. The money. The handshake and the words. But right now, all I can say is, thank you for the hope, Uncle John."

John nodded. *I get it—thank you*, he silently said to God. "Danny, will you do something for me?"

"Anything, Uncle John."

"Heather and I, we're involved in something here. This—well, this venture, it's . . . I don't know exactly how to describe it, except that it's big and growing bigger. I'd really appreciate it if you'd pray for us."

"I'll do that, Uncle John." The young man's voice cracked. "Thanks for asking me. Night and day I'll be praying."

The entire drive into Manhattan, John kept waiting for the fear, the dread, to assault him again. Instead, he remained unattached. They were seven in the first van. Richard drove with the same steady smoothness John suspected he applied to everything he did. John asked the group, "Any advice on what I should I say?"

"As little as possible," Kevin replied. "Accept the fact you will not have the upper hand. Whatever you say will be twisted and thrown back in your face."

He shrugged. "I've pretty much lived with that all my life."

"But not in the public eye." Kevin's face was creased in a visual apology. "They will want to shame you."

John surprised himself at how easy it was to smile. "That's all probably true, Kevin. But you know what? This is the first time in years I'm *not* ashamed."

Once across the bridge, traffic slowed to stop-and-go the closer they drew to Times Square. John could see Jenny's forehead crease in concentration. "You have something on your mind?"

"I do, yes. I agree with Kevin, and what he has said is the same as what we heard from Reverend Davenport. On the surface of things, we are headed for failure. But this has been true since the beginning of all these encounters."

Alisha harrumphed a chuckle. "And look how God has turned that one on its head."

"Exactly. I feel this is what we need to prepare for here as well," Jenny went on. "What if God moves in this place? That is the question we need to hold before our minds and hearts. That is why we did not follow Reverend Davenport's urging. On the surface he was absolutely right. We are risking a great deal here."

Richard said, "A very important point. Even if it did come from my daughter." He smiled at her through the rearview mirror.

John realized what this was leading to. "You have something you want me to say."

"If it is what *I* want, then it's all wrong."

"No, no, that's not the way to look at this. Look, we're a team. Why shouldn't the Spirit use you to deliver the words?"

"Because *you're* the spokesman."

"But you've already been helping shape what needs saying, right?"

"After we left Ruth, something came to me. It's very rough, but it's all I had time for."

He held out his hand. "May I see?"

She hesitated so long, Richard said, "Daughter, John is right. Show him."

She drew a folded sheet from her purse, handed it over.

John unfolded the pages and read. Breathed in and out, slowly. Read them again.

She sounded tentative as she asked, "Is it all right?"

"It's better than that," John replied. "It's inspired."

Aaron chose that moment to announce from the backseat, "There is something I wish to say."

Jason Swain sat in his cubicle, one of many in the large room, and pretended to work. Like all the senior programmers of the Austin-based electronic game company, "senior" had nothing to do with age since he was barely twenty. His office walls were only high enough to mask his computer screens from view. The intent was to offer privacy so long as he remained seated. If he wanted to connect with anyone else, all he had to do was stand.

The space was far removed from the office complex where the suits hung out. For one thing, the ceiling here was almost thirty feet overhead. For another, the programmers could decorate their space any way they liked. The young woman directly opposite Jason had a thing for giraffes. Her cubicle held twenty-four of the beasts, the tallest almost nine feet high and grinning down on Jason every time he lifted his head.

The tall, western-facing windows were veiled by diaphanous blinds that automatically descended as the sun began tracking toward the day's end. Beyond the lawns sparkled their very own lake. The programmers had a score of paddleboats they liked to take out at sunset for high jinks and impromptu races. In the far corner was a space the size of ten cubicles that the programmers called the playpen, filled with games and bouncing toys and a pair of unicycles.

When Jason had first entered the chamber, he had thought he never wanted to leave. Today, however, he pulled up the clock on his computer and wished he could just wind forward to the moment he walked out, maybe for good.

His work area held four oversized LED screens, standard for programmers. Two held the code he was supposed to be working on. A third showed the storyboard and script governing the game. A fourth revealed the characters running the various options available to the gamer. As the gamer made choices, the various avenues would either open or close. Jason's current task was to make the action flow smoothly. But right now the figures on his screens were frozen in place. Three ghouls gnashed their teeth at him, holding clubs and swords and other weapons over their heads. Waiting for him to get back to work.

The young woman who appeared in Jason's cubicle evidently knew it did not hold an extra chair—she'd dragged with her a blue ball from the playpen. She straddled the ball, gripping the blue rubber tether, and bounced softly as she said, "What's happening, Jason?"

Abigail belonged to his Young Life group at church. She worked in accounting, was perhaps the smartest person Jason had ever met. She could make her numbers do just about anything except stand up and bark. And Jason figured it was only a matter of time before she mastered that as well.

She was also very attractive. If one managed to look beyond the thick spectacles with their huge pale frames, the muslin clothing with vests layered over everything, the scuffed rubber clogs, and the absence of any makeup whatsoever. Jason had been working up the courage to ask her out. For five months and counting.

Jason glanced at her, then away. "I'm busy."

"No you're not."

"I should be." He glanced at his frozen screens and grimaced at the ghouls. "Maybe I should just quit."

"You said you'd stick it out." She bounced in time to her words. "You were right."

"I'm not doing anything here. Literally."

"That's about to change." She bounced back far enough to glance behind her, scouting the corridor. "You won't believe what I just found."

"Is it good?"

"Maybe." Her bouncing drew her closer, her voice lowered. "Guess which ministry received a half million bucks."

"What are you talking about?"

"Five hundred thou," she repeated. Her grey eyes sparkled with a light remarkably soft, and he thought her voice was musical when she was happy. Like now. "From our own corporate foundation."

"Wait. You're telling me—"

"Yup." Her dark hair floated around her face as she moved up and down. "The newest acquisition of the Mundrose Group celebrates by making a donation to a ministry."

"Which one?"

"Reverend Albright."

Jason could feel his synapses fire for the first time that day. "He's not a real pastor anymore."

"I know that. You know that. But that's not what his website claims."

"He teaches somewhere."

"Pennsylvania."

"And he writes books."

"About God being only a cultural icon that belongs to a bygone age." She was clearly enjoying this.

Jason said, "The donation has got to be tied to, you know, what's happening out there with Barrett."

"Why do you think I'm sitting here?"

"I've got to call Pastor Craig."

"You know how to reach him?"

"He gave me a number to call. Day or night. If, you know, I had something."

"Which you do."

"Thanks to you," Jason agreed.

"You're welcome." She seemed reluctant to rise off the ball. She watched him turn on his cellphone and said, "Guess that's my cue."

Jason was punching the number into his phone when he decided there would never be a better time. "Let's do something, Abigail. You know, go out."

Abigail turned very solemn. "Do you think that's a good idea?"

"Yes," he said, swallowing hard. "I do."

Her smile was glorious to behold. "So do I."

"The Bible contains several different words that we translate as hope," Aaron said. He leaned forward, placing his arms on the space between John and Jenny in the next seat. "The primary words are *tikvah*, which is a noun, and *mekaveh*, the verb. The first time this word appears, though, it is not used for hope directly. That passage is in the first chapter of Genesis, the ninth and tenth verses, where God gathers the waters and creates what will become the Garden of Eden."

Richard slipped the van into a tight parking space, moving the vehicle back and forth twice before turning off the engine. He gripped the wheel and turned about, focused with the others on Aaron.

The young man with his scraggly beard and expressive hands seemed made for jokes. Even when, like now, he was utterly serious. "Why would the author of Genesis, inspired as he was by God, use that particular word in this particular place? Because we are to understand that it is here, in the gathering together, we know hope. God created man from the dust, and sheltered him in this divine haven. As we gather together in divine intent, we reflect the union of all things that existed within the garden. Before sin. Before the fall from grace.

"Here, then, is the *first* meaning of hope. The *highest* meaning. We gather together and seek to understand God's eternal promise. And what is God's fundamental purpose for man? To return the earth to God. When we act in faith and seek to do his will, we become a component, a significant part of the kingdom's return. Here, in this imperfect search, strengthened by many hearts and minds working and praying together, we come closest to God. Through our shared hope in the unseen, through our unified desire to be his holy instruments, we know hope in its purest form."

They sat in silence for a time. John's only comprehensible thought was a yearning to do better. To do *more*.

Then his phone rang. He fished the device from his pocket and told them, "It's Craig."

Jenny's mother asked, "Who?"

"The pastor in Texas," Jenny explained. "The one who didn't want us to do this."

Richard reached back. "Let me take it." He tabbed the connection and said, "Yes, Reverend. No sir, it's always good to hear from you."

Richard listened for a time, and then revealed a smile that transformed his features. "Really? They're certain about this? Excuse me for asking, but we can't get this wrong. No, I understand. Well, this is wonderful. Truly. A gift. Yes, sir, I'll let you know as soon as John is done."

Richard cut the connection, and shared around a smile so great his shining eyes almost vanished. "You won't believe what just happened. Well, actually, you probably will."

35

". . . show them your love . . ."

MANHATTAN

Trent Cooper sat in the dressing room beside Radley Albright. The former pastor glowed with self-importance and stage charm. Trent had skimmed the man's most famous book, which consigned religion to a cultural garbage heap. He had studied the professor's website, which showed clips of him addressing thousands of students, talking about how he had finally seen the *real* light, left the ministry in order to serve the greater good and serve the people of this generation, serve the *truth*. Perhaps it was because the man had said the same words hundreds of times, but to Trent's ears the message carried a calculated tone. As though it had been distilled from the man's observations of society, rather than drawn from some deep personal change. So what the man actually believed, Trent had no idea. Nor did it matter. The longer he had studied the man and his message, the more convinced he had become. Dr. Albright was the perfect implement, a hammer to pound John Jacobs into the earth where he belonged.

The professor's every word carried a pompous weight. "And who are you exactly?"

"My name is Trent Cooper." He spoke around the woman applying makeup. "I've been asked to represent the Mundrose Corporation in the broadcast."

"You're the group's spokesperson."

"Sort of." That had been Barry's idea, have him appear on air. Trent had wanted to object. He was too aware of his physical defects, more past than present, but still—he knew when he grew weary or stressed he still had a slight lisp to his speech. And no amount of makeup could fully hide the shadow-line drawn from upper lip to left nostril. But Edlyn had agreed, in a manner that offered no room for disagreement.

"And the young lady who accompanied you?"

"Gayle is my associate."

"Your associate."

"That is correct." Gayle's presence had made it unnecessary for Trent to explain his exact position to anyone. Being staffed by such an intelligent and beautiful woman who anticipated his every need meant he had to be someone important. By the time Trent had followed Radley Albright into the dressing room, everyone knew with certainty that he was far more than just another corporate mouthpiece.

Albright asked, "So you'll be on the panel with me?"

"No. They are bringing me on after you're done."

"Ah. That is perhaps for the best." Albright leaned in closer to the mirror encircled by lights. "I have a great deal I plan to discuss about this subject. No need to share my limited time on air."

The professor stopped because Trent had slipped from his chair and drawn within inches of the man's face. "I want you to listen to me very carefully."

Albright drew back as far as he could. "I say, there's no need to invade my space."

In reply, Trent grabbed the paper napkin from the professor's collar. He lifted his hand into the tight space between them and crumpled it in his fist. "I am the man who signed your check. I am the man who can make sure you never receive a nickel more from

Mundrose. Or a second of airtime from any of their channels. Ever. Tell me we're clear."

The professor's swallow was audible. "Of—of course."

"You have been given three points we want you to make on air. For this we've paid you half a million dollars. I want you to pound these home with all the strength in your body and mind. These points and nothing else. Clear?"

"I—Yes."

"Your job is not to *discuss* anything. You're being paid to go out there and *bury* this guy."

"Understood."

"Good." Trent rose to full height, snatched his own napkin from under his chin, and turned to the door. "Nice to meet you."

When Trent emerged from the dressing room, Gayle was waiting for him in the hall leading to the studio. Gayle must have seen his ire for she asked with a frown, "Is everything all right?"

"Fine." Trent did not mind the confrontation. The residual anger spiced the moment. "Everything's great."

"Edlyn phoned. She said to tell you good luck."

"Thanks. Anything else?"

"She and Barry want to have a word after the reception." They were going straight from the studio to the music group's launch party in a ballroom overlooking Times Square. It was by invitation only, but crowds of celebrity watchers had been growing all afternoon.

"Do you know what it's about?"

"They have a new project they want you to manage."

Trent tasted the electric punch that came with the realization that it was really happening. He was entering the inner sanctum. The power and the money and even the beautiful woman. All his. "Fantastic."

The control room was beyond a glass wall to his left. The monitors and complex controls and technicians sat or stood at the room's far side. Between them and the production staff were three rows of padded chairs. Gayle asked, "Do you want to go sit down?"

"In a second."

The elevator doors opened and what appeared to be the entire Barrett team spilled out. Trent recognized many of the faces from their video appeals and his own confidential investigations. Which only made the moment finer.

John Jacobs was the last to emerge. Trent stood where he was, glad for the opportunity to study this man up close. The enemy. In person.

Gayle took a step back. Which was good as well. Trent wanted to do this alone. Have the man know him, remember the meeting. One on one. He had never felt more in control. Of himself or his destiny or the moment. It was a heady mix, the power and the friction and the knowledge that this man would soon be crushed. In front of millions of viewers.

"Mr. Jacobs, I'm Trent Cooper." He reached out a hand, standing firmly in place so the man would have to move to him.

John Jacobs was in his late fifties, and bore the features of an aging boxer, strong and battered and wounded and healed. In a manner of speaking. Even his voice carried the mix of defeat and determination. "I'm sorry, should I know you?"

"I am here representing the Mundrose Group."

Jacobs accepted the outstretched hand with a hard grip, his skin rough and yet his grasp surprisingly gentle. Then he said something Trent would never have expected. Not in a million years. "We'll be praying for you."

Trent had the sudden urge to laugh out loud. But he made do with a tight smile, a practiced New York gesture. Over his opponent's head, Trent imagined a giant banner shouting to the world his slogan. *Hope Is Dead.* Trent stepped to one side. "I believe they're expecting you."

He watched one of the studio gophers hurry over to introduce herself and rush Jacobs down to the dressing room. Then he turned to Gayle and said, "Let's get started."

Gayle tapped on the glass door leading to the control room. A middle-aged woman wearing a headset walked over and unlocked the portal. She introduced herself as the executive producer. When the door clicked shut, she remained where she was, staring from the darkened room out to where the people with Jacobs were gathered. The woman asked doubtfully, "Should I invite them inside?"

Trent turned his back on them. "Absolutely not."

36

". . . their day is coming . . ."

MANHATTAN

John Jacobs had never been anywhere near the power core of live television. In any other circumstances, he would have been in awe of the bustle and the glitz, terrified by the prospect of sitting at the conference table beneath the batteries of klieg lights and cameras. As it was, he felt very little. He was led into the dressing room, a fleet of high-octane young people rushing about. He stepped into a small closet and locked the door. He took his time dressing in Bobby Barrett's suit, a slate-grey with chalk stripes. Some lady kept calling through the closed door that there was ten minutes to airtime, eight, six. As though her real job here was to rattle the nerves of anyone daring to enter the national news domain.

When he emerged, a chunky woman with a helmet of brassy hair waited to work on his face. The woman who had been in previously returned and barked that John went on in four. Aaron stepped through the door and asked, "Would you like some company?"

John waved him inside. "That was amazing, what you said in the car."

Aaron had a deferential smile, and a rabbi's way of deflecting praise. A small shrug, a turn of bony hands. "One does what one can."

The makeup lady inspected John and decided, "You'll do."

"Glad you think so," John said, and pulled the paper bib from his neck. "Thank you."

The woman must have found something she liked, because she smiled and said, "Go get 'em, Tiger."

"I intend to," John replied with an answering smile.

He and Aaron walked the hall and joined the others in the studio's antechamber. Directly in front of them was a glass wall overlooking the control room. Three curved rows of theater-style seats rose behind three aisles of computers, sound equipment, and rushing people. The front wall had a long window overlooking the stage and the cameras, while above the glass stretched massive flat-screen monitors. More monitors dotted the rows of controls. John found it encouraging, how the sight of the equipment and the tense voices and the tight clicking of the digital timer did not rattle him. Though his heart was racing, and he could feel the tension in his gut, he was comfortable just the same. This coming interview was just another assignment he had accepted that Sunday morning, seated in church, trying to listen to God.

And whatever came next, John was certain of one thing. He would not be facing this alone.

The bossy young woman rushed over. "You need to move on-stage."

"Just a minute."

She had already started to rush away. "What? No! You have—"

"Back off," John said, using the tone he applied when a bullying trucker got in his space. The woman backed. "Thank you."

John turned to the others and said, "Heather, could you . . . ?"

His wife reached out her hands. "Let's join together."

When they were done, the woman said in the clipped manner of one born to argue, "You are on air in *one minute*."

"Aaron, walk with me." John and the young doctor passed through the control room and pushed through the swinging doors leading to the soundstage. "Any last words?"

"The rabbis had a saying for such times," Aaron replied. "When they gathered with other learned teachers, there would always be disagreements. Heated arguments. Bitter rivalries."

The woman led him around the table and seated him in one of the three seats. The world-famous newscaster was seated at the table's curved end. Between them sat a pastor along with a teacher John recognized from television. The two men started to greet him. John merely nodded and said to Aaron, "Go on."

Aaron leaned in tight by John's ear as the woman fitted him with a lapel mike. "The most powerful arguments are best delivered in the softest voice."

"Let the words speak for themselves." John nodded.

The woman said to Aaron, "Sir, you must leave the soundstage *now*."

The studio's frigid air held an acrid quality, as though the lights gave off an electric odor. John felt perspiration trickle down his back. His heart punched so hard his fingers flicked slightly in time to each rapid beat. He could sense a cloud of dread lurking out in the distance. And yet at the very core of his being, down where it really mattered, he was calm.

He listened as Katherine Bonner introduced her two guests for the show's opening segment. The famous newscaster spoke with the rapid ease of a true professional. She stated her opening position in terse bites. "The world has witnessed a new phenomenon, one that has grown from what can only be described as humble roots into a cause reaching around the globe. And done so in a matter of days. At its head is John Jacobs, a transport executive from Cincinnati. Many of you have seen his video casts, which have now registered over eleven million hits on YouTube. Mr. Jacobs is advocating a remarkable boycott of all products and companies that sponsor the Mundrose Group. Later in the program we will be hearing from a

Mundrose executive. But first, we would like to delve more deeply into what precisely Mr. Jacobs is promoting."

John recognized the anchor's slight smirk as twisting her supposedly straightforward remarks into something else entirely. He also knew there was nothing he could do about it. They all were against him. They had all the world's power on their side.

When John had watched this newscaster from the security of his living room, the woman had displayed a polished charm that ensnared the viewer, drew one over to whatever side she championed. On this side of the camera, everything was different. The perfect hair and the crisp speech and the polished inflection were all part of a mask.

Katherine Bonner then showed the preliminary Mundrose advertisement with the ghouls cavorting through Times Square, all the electronic billboards shouting the same silver message. Hope was a thing of the past. John expected her to then show the response they had developed.

Instead, Bonner turned to Radley Albright, introduced him once again, and asked his opinion of the message, from the church's perspective. John immediately knew the coverage would be biased throughout. But the knowledge did not disturb his calm. The awareness of his shielded state granted him the ability to look at the two, Radley Albright and their host, pretending to be objective in their comments, and plan his response.

The former pastor was a bull of a man who spoke with a remarkably high pitch, a boxer's body holding a tenor's voice. He was reasonable, and he was educated. He spoke in a lilting tone about how any moral system needed to conform to the needs of the present age. Otherwise the culture would dismiss it as irrelevant. He then emphasized how no data supported the claim that entertainment had any impact on individual behavior.

The anchor then turned to John and asked, "Mr. Jacobs, do you wish to comment?"

"I haven't heard a question yet."

Katherine Bonner was at her patronizing best. "We allow our guests to respond once the others have spoken."

But John wasn't having any of it. "I was asked here for an interview. I agreed to that and nothing more. Ask me a question. I will respond."

A trace of red seeped through the woman's makeup. The flush was particularly clear on her neck as she smiled at the person in the middle seat and said, "Dr. Albright?"

"How much theological training have you had, Mr. Jacobs?"

"None. I wish I had."

"What church do you lead?"

"I am not a pastor, sir."

The newscaster said, "In fact, Mr. Jacobs, is it not true that you manage a truck depot?"

"Deputy manager. Correct."

Albright asked, "How large is your congregation?"

"I've already answered that."

"But surely you yourself must see how absurd this appears!" The professor shared Katherine Bonner's slit of a smile. Two highly trained professionals joined in the distasteful task of putting an errant schoolboy in his place. "No training, no background as a church leader, and suddenly you're a self-appointed spokesperson for some ill-fated message that you claim comes from above. This sounds like a throwback to the Dark Ages! Surely you must agree that just because some lunatic claims 'divine guidance,' he can't simply spout off whatever he wants." He turned to Bonner and continued, "This represents the worst face of the digital age, where anyone with a fabricated platform can pass himself off as an authority!"

The anchor punctuated the statement with a slow nod before turning to John. "Mr. Jacobs?"

"Yes?"

"Do you care to respond?"

"Sorry, I didn't hear the man ask a question."

"But surely you must have a response to the Reverend's comments."

"The former reverend is entitled to his opinion."

"Really, Mr. Jacobs. That seems a rather empty reaction to a very telling—"

"May I ask a question of my own?"

The woman thoroughly disliked being interrupted. Her smile was deadly. "Why, of course."

John took his own time now. He took the sheet of paper from his pocket, unfolded it on the empty table before him. Using the silence to strain them both. It was a tactic he had used in numerous negotiations. Transport companies were run on the second hand. They carried this air of constant frenetic tension into every act. Sometimes the best thing he could do was force them to march to an uncomfortable beat.

"Mr. Jacobs?"

"Dr. Albright, is your appearance on the show tonight tied to the half-million-dollar contribution made this morning to your foundation by the Mundrose Group?"

The newscaster and the professor both blanched. Their facial muscles might have been pulled by the same puppet string, their response was so identical. The former pastor sputtered, "That is worse than absurd. It is an outrage!"

John countered, "Recently the Mundrose Group acquired an Austin-based electronic games company. Their trust has now donated five hundred thousand dollars to your organization. Your group's stated aim is to denounce Christianity as a cultural phenomenon that has outlived its importance."

The anchor rasped, "I would ask that you stay on topic."

"I never left it." John met Albright's furious gaze straight on. "Do you wish to comment?"

"The entire issue is absurd, and your allegations are an outrage." John smiled for the first time. "What allegation is that, sir?"

Bonner leaned forward. "Gentlemen, we are out of time. Thank you both for appearing. And now a word from our sponsors."

Trent managed the follow-up interview, but barely. He mouthed the words he had prepared. He spoke with the right amount of indignation. He had spent two hours that afternoon being prepped by one of the group's on-air coaches. He did a good job. But his heart was not in it. He remained dazed by the confrontation that had gone on before. Shell-shocked, really. What's more, he had the impression that the anchor felt the same way. On the surface she treated him with the same crisp professionalism as she had shown Jacobs and Albright. But beneath the surface had lurked a genuine rage over how their prey had escaped. Her ire helped Trent remain on target through the interview. They shared an energy and a determination. When the lights finally went off and the airtime was over, Katherine Bonner muttered quietly, "Next time."

He carried that final note with him down to the waiting limo. Gayle sensed his mood and remained silent throughout the drive. But her perfume and the hold she kept on his hand were enough to soothe him through yet another disappointment. As they entered the traffic and the crowds snarled around Times Square, her phone rang. She answered, then cupped the receiver. "Colin Tomlin wishes to have a word."

He was tempted to put off the head of their LA team. But he accepted the phone and said, "How did they know about Albright?"

"I've been asking myself the very same question. And there's only one answer."

"Austin. Has to be."

"I fear you're correct. We had two of our employees resign today, effective immediately. One was a gamer. The other from our accounting division. Both belong to a church that has been actively supporting this charade."

Trent heard the unspoken apology. More than anything else that night, more than Bonner's determined promise, more even than Gayle's perfumed closeness, the LA chief's remorse helped seal the wound. "There's no way you could have known."

"No. Quite." The marketing director turned brisk. "Where are you now?"

"On Broadway, barely crawling forward."

"I'll meet you at the bar. We really must raise a glass."

As he cut the connection and handed back the phone, their limo passed a cluster of young people cloaked as vampires, carrying a glittering banner echoing his logo. *Hope is dead.* Trent waved at them, wishing he could ignore the dull taste of defeat. These people were his target audience. At least with them he had not failed.

If only it were enough. After all, this was his hour. His time. He was the winner here.

CLEVELAND, TWO MONTHS LATER

John Jacobs drove through the quiet September dawn. The empty streets were bathed in a pearlescent glow. He was not due at the office for another hour, but for years his habit had been to arrive long before he was expected. He spent the time talking with his teams, getting to know them on a personal level. There was little time for such exchanges once the pressures of another day began. Now that he was appointed manager for the entire Midwest, he wanted the staff to know him as someone they could trust.

He and Heather had still been at the Barrett Ministry headquarters when the call had come from headquarters. The same executive who had fired him showed genuine delight as he described how the international produce group had delivered an ultimatum: either the man who had sold them on the company was put in charge of shipments, or they would take their business elsewhere.

John was still growing accustomed to his newfound role when Ruth Barrett had phoned to ask him if he would consider returning to Westchester County. The ministry needed a new leader. She and the board wanted John for the role. They could bring in a pastor or learned seminarian to do whatever preaching was required. But these were new times, and the ministry needed him. Ruth had recovered from her most recent bout of ill health, but everyone was well aware that the current situation would not go on forever. The offer had arrived four weeks ago. John was still praying with Heather over what the Lord wanted them to do. On the surface, he could think of a hundred reasons why naming him to such a position would be a huge mistake. But this wasn't about him. Every time the doubts rose and he was tempted to phone them back and decline, he returned to that simple truth. So he prayed and he waited. And the ministry team was willing to wait with him.

The morning news droned softly in the background, until a new topic arose that captured John's full attention. He turned up the volume and heard, "Stone Denning's latest blockbuster film was released over the Labor Day weekend, and it fell flat on its face. Ticket sales were less than one-fifth what had been anticipated. A Mundrose company spokesman denied the low turnout had anything to do with the recent and highly publicized boycott, and claimed that international ticket sales were reaching new heights. Even so, Hollywood insiders are predicting the group will write down over a hundred million dollars after what can only be described as a disastrous first-week result."

John turned off the radio. He and Heather had been fielding personal calls all week. The ministry had needed to hire new staff in order to manage the tidal wave of support. The tone of most people with whom John had personally spoken had been triumphant. As though they could all join together and claim victory. As though the battle was won.

But John saw a very different situation. This certainty was what kept him waiting on God to respond about the ministry's offer.

The one person who most agreed with him was Alisha. She had accepted a new position as administrative director of Barrett Ministries, and now declared she had been waiting all her life for the chance, only she had not known it until she arrived. Alisha's response to his plea for patience had been unequivocal. Wait for God to speak.

When he pulled up in front of the trucking company offices, a beautiful woman rose from her car and walked over. "Mr. Jacobs, you probably won't remember me . . ."

Hers was a face that any man would easily recall. "You were with the guy from Mundrose at the New York television station."

"Gayle Sayers. I'm sorry, I should have called, but I was afraid if I did, well . . ."

"Won't you come inside, Ms. Sayers?"

"No, no, I—Actually, I really have no idea why I'm here." She spoke with the precise diction of a highly intelligent woman. One who probably did not realize she was twisting her fingers into a nervous knot. "I just wanted to know you were, well, real. No, 'real' isn't quite right. 'Genuine' is what I mean."

"It's not my being real or not real that's been bothering you, though, is it?" John tried to carry as gentle a tone as possible. "You want to know if the One I serve is real, genuine. And the answer is, absolutely."

"Perhaps I should just go." But she remained in place, slowly clenching and unclenching her hands.

"Ms. Sayers, Gayle, could I make a suggestion? Why don't you and I go across the street to that diner, and we'll sit and I'll try and explain to you just how very real all this is."

She remained where she was for quite some time, then spoke in a small voice, "I think I would like that very much."

John excused himself long enough to step inside and tell his office manager he would be a few minutes late. Then he led the young woman into one of the diner's window booths. He asked her how she had come to make this trip, then listened as she described the young man and their relationship, and the changes she had noted in both of them as he continued his climb up the corporate ladder. And how she saw in his own naked ambition a growing resemblance to her own hard-edged lifestyle, something that no amount of luxury or success seemed to ease away. Instead, the gnawing uncertainty only continued to grow. Along with a questioning of all she had considered worth obtaining.

John listened as she revealed far more than she probably either intended or found comfortable. Then, as he began sharing with her the possibility of his own new course ahead, he found himself wondering if such discussions were to become the framework for his future, wherever God directed. And he decided that he would be just fine with such a turning. Whoever took on this role would have their work cut out for them. For John was certain the mission they had been working on was just now getting under way.

This was only the beginning . . . .

TAKE
THE TURNING

GO TO

WWW.THETURNINGBOOK.COM

for accompanying daily devotions,
audio teaching, videos & more.

About the Author

DAVIS BUNN, a native of North Carolina, has lived in Europe for thirty-five years. Davis's academic background includes degrees in psychology and economics from Wake Forest University and a master's degree in finance from the City University of London. Fluent in three languages, he has traveled extensively in Europe, Africa, Asia, and the Middle East.

Davis enjoys a particularly strong following in the inspirational market, often ranking on the Christian Booksellers' Association bestseller lists. He has collaborated with Janette Oke, one of the leading names in Christian publishing, on a series of novels. Davis is a *New York Times* bestselling author and has garnered a number of industry honors, including three Christy Awards for excellence in historical and suspense fiction.

Davis teaches in the Creative Writing Programme at the University of Oxford, where he holds an appointment as a Core Lecturer in the subject of fiction. He splits his time between Oxford and Florida with his wife, Isabella.

IMPACTING LIVES THROUGH THE POWER OF STORY

Thank you! We are honored that you took the time out of your busy schedule to read this book. If you enjoyed what you read, would you consider sharing the message with others?

- Write a review online at amazon.com, bn.com, goodreads.com, cbd.com.

- Recommend this book to friends in your book club, workplace, church, school, classes, or small group.

- Go to facebook.com/RiverNorthFiction, "like" the page, and post a comment as to what you enjoyed the most.

- Mention this book in a Facebook post, Twitter update, Pinterest pin, or a blog post.

- Pick up a copy for someone you know who would be encouraged by this message.

- Subscribe to our newsletter for information on upcoming titles, get inside information on discounts and promotions, and learn more about your favorite authors at RiverNorthFiction.com.

midday connection

Discover a safe place to authentically process life's journey on **Midday Connection**, hosted by Anita Lustrea and Melinda Schmidt. This live radio program is designed to encourage women with a focus on growing the whole person: body, mind, and soul. You'll grow toward spiritual freedom and personal transformation as you learn who God is and who He created us to be.

www.middayconnection.org

MOODYRADIO

Where you turn. For life.

CHRIS FABRY LIVE!

Build up your spiritual immune system as you listen to **Chris Fabry Live!** With a sense of humor and a sense of people, host Chris Fabry discusses the journey of faith, interacts with guests and callers, and offers a few surprises along the way.

www.chrisfabrylive.org

Where you turn. For life.